W9-BQT-118

Acknowledgments

I would like to recognize a couple of people. First Patty. She experienced one of the events written about during her first trip to the dentist many years ago. Dentistry has changed quite a little since then, so forgive me if the story sounds a bit unrealistic. Patty is an avid reader of works of inspirational romance. She pointed me to a rather humorous one a while ago, so I read it. After laughing a lot, I said to myself, "I can write a romance novel that has some humor in it like this," so I did. Also I would like to recognize Robin, who was in the process of editing this book when she unexpectedly passed away.

Chapter 1

WHY DO CAKES FALL?

It was a blazing-hot day. The thermometer registered 107 degrees. Patti needed some flour, so she drove to her favorite grocery store. At the entrance, she paused a few moments. There was some type of misting mechanism spraying vapor into the air. She watched the children as they ran through it, squealing with delight. Their laughter rang out above the traffic in the street. *What a swell thing to do on a hot day like this,* she thought. There was an adorable little girl there having the time of her life. Her dark hair was soaked. Little droplets of water were running down her face. A tiny pink tongue came out from between her ruby-red lips and captured a couple of them. She drew the combination back in, savoring each little fragment of mist. And that smile—it would melt even the toughest heart. What a blessing children were. A far-off memory popped into the cake decorator's mind. This little one was the right age. She looked almost familiar. Patti pondered the thoughts only for a moment before pushing them way back into one of the many crevices in her mind where she kept things like this.

Inside, Patti peered up in dismay at the empty shelf. Safeway was running a special sale on all-purpose flour, but by the looks of things, they had sold out already. She wished she were a bit taller. Was that one bag up on the top shelf? She took a little hop and discovered back in the far corner one ten-pound sack was waiting for her. That was crazy! Why would they place ten-pound sacks of flour that high up? It was an accident waiting to happen. She figured she might just talk to the manager about it. Most people would have no problem lifting ten pounds down to their carts, but there might be an occasional weaker person who could have trouble with it. She needed the all-purpose flour to finish one of her cakes. And not just any cake; it was her special pineapple-carrot cake. Her mind wandered to the kitchen for a moment. She usually used cake flour because it was lighter and allowed her cakes to rise better. But the heavier ingredients of pineapple chunks, shredded carrots, and coconut demanded a heavier flour. Shaking her head a moment, she thought, *Okay, back to the task at hand.* The question was still there. That was how to get the flour down from the top shelf.

Patti was not exactly the basketball type, being only five feet two inches tall. For most of her growing-up years, she hated being short. However, she eventually developed into a contented young woman, learning the importance of accepting her shortness while realizing that whatever God had given her in life could be a blessing. How that could be possible for all aspects of her life, she was not sure, but knowing and trusting in God, she did not worry. Meanwhile, she glanced up and down the aisle. There was no one in sight to assist her, so she bent down and moved aside several ten-pound sacks of whole wheat flour. This enabled her to stand on the edge of the bottom shelf, giving her a significant boost to be just where she needed to be in order to reach the elusive ingredient. In the seconds it took for Patti to perch in this precarious position, a tall dark stranger approached unnoticed. He was dressed in sleek black slacks and a mint-green shirt. She could not help but notice how neat, clean, and well groomed he was. Quickly assessing the situation, he cleared his throat and, almost as if thinking aloud, questioned, "Hmmm … Is there something I could help you with, miss?"

"No, but thank you, sir. I was trying to reach this last bag of flour and did not see anyone around tall enough to help me get it down. I have it now though, so thank you. All I need to do is to step back onto the floor, and I will be fine." At that very moment, her toe slipped off the edge of the shelf, and she began falling. Being the gentleman he was, the stranger stepped forward and caught her midair in one smooth motion. This quick reflex action took her by surprise, and she released the flour. It landed, teetering about halfway on the shelf and halfway off. The gentleman, not standing in a balanced position himself, stumbled backward and fell onto the floor. Patti followed in kind. Instead of hitting the floor though, Patti felt herself land on brawn and muscle. He was built like a rock and very solid. She did not ponder that for long, however. In the blink of an eye, before either had a chance to move, down came the flour, splitting open on the side of the shopping cart. It chose her hero, giving him a dusting of powdery white, all over his clean-shaven face and once shiny shoes.

Patti was horrified at the faux snowy scene and wondered what to do. She was used to working fast in cake decorating. Often, there were only a few short minutes to finish a frosting before it began to set up, so she was very quick in her thinking and actions. She sprang to her feet, all the while silently praying that the strange gentleman was not hurt. Patti spied a roll of paper towels in her shopping cart and in a flash ripped open the plastic. As she began looking around for any type of liquid to moisten the towels, there, sitting in the baby seat of her cart, was a large jar of pickles. With a quick twist of the wrist, the lid opened and the pickle juice was ready to help.

While she positioned the jar beside her so she could get to it quickly, a generous amount of pickle juice sloshed onto one of the stranger's shoes. In a matter of seconds, she was washing the flour off the disheveled face. She uncovered one surprised eye and then the other.

Cal was stunned. First, he was reaching out to catch the lady, and then he was on the floor covered in white. A portion of the flour had hit him square in the eyes, so he was momentarily blinded. He had barely had time to take that in when the flour dust that covered his face and hair seemed to smell strange. As he was sorting it all out, he recognized the peculiar odor was not the flour but pickle juice. Moreover, if there was one thing Cal hated above anything else, especially in sandwiches, it was pickles! Whenever he ate out and a sandwich was part of the menu, he always requested, "No pickles, please." Now someone was washing his nose with this acidic liquid and then his lips. This was just too much to take. With an abrupt jerk, he struggled to his feet, pushing the lady aside. About that time, the store manager and a stock boy came running, the latter with a broom and mop in his hands.

"Is everything all right, sir?" asked the manager. "Are you hurt in any way?"

"No hurts," he retorted, jumping up and down slightly to bounce flour off his shoes. "I'll be just fine. If I can simply remove this flour that is all over me, then I'm sure I'll be as good as new." He shook his head aggressively from side to side several times, and the fine powdery flour flew in every direction. Without another word, he collected himself as best he could and dramatically stomped out of the store, leaving some powdery white tracks in his wake. Patti ran after him, apologizing profusely.

"I'm so sorry, mister. Really I am. I didn't mean to flour you like that. And I am so glad you aren't hurt." She tried desperately to get in front of him, but he was fast!

"It's okay, lady, really. Accidents happen to everyone. Don't worry about it." Cal saw the mist spraying into the air and ducked his head directly in front of it. This caused little white streaks of water and flour to trickle down his face and drip on his mint-green shirt. Though it was spring, one could have mistaken him for someone wearing a Halloween costume.

Shortly thereafter, he was driving his car out of the parking lot. By the time he reached the street, the skin on his face had begun to crawl. The pickle juice started drying, and the combination of it and the flour felt like superglue to his skin. Agony ensued. Cal's face rebelled as the sensation of a thousand pinpricks started attacking him. From the sheer discomfort he experienced, his natural reflex was to push his foot down hard on the gas pedal. He whizzed past several cars, hardly noticing a single one. He just wanted to get home as quickly as possible and get in the shower. The way he was feeling, he just might go in clothes and all! However, one of the cars he passed did notice him. In Cal's rearview mirror, he saw the familiar sign of the law—flashing red and blue lights.

"Oh no!" he groaned. "This is not my day. I shouldn't have skipped my devotions this morning ... maybe even stayed in bed."

Meanwhile, back at the store, Patti returned from the parking lot unaware of the stranger's continued misfortunes. She walked back to the aisle where her cart waited for her. The stock boy finished sweeping up the flour and mopping the floor. The manager was there as well. He turned to her and smiled.

"Are you okay?"

"Yes, I am quite fine. Thank you. I was merely trying to reach the only sack I could find of your all-purpose white flour. And as far as I could tell, the last bag was on the top shelf in the back corner. It is apparent that I'm not very tall. However, as I made my best attempt to reach it, all this happened." She swung her hands in circular motions, pointing out the shelf and floor area that had recently been covered in flour.

The store manager nodded. "Not to worry. We have plenty of extra flour in the back. Would you like me to bring you another bag?"

"Oh yes, please!" she replied. "That would be great.

Thank you. Oh, and I could really use two if you have an extra," Patti added as an afterthought.

"No problem," the manager replied. "We ordered extra for the sale and received several pallets. They are in the back. By the way, would you care for another jar of pickles? A fresh jar will be fuller than the one you have there. It will also lack those little white flour beads floating around inside." The manager's eyes twinkled while he teased his young customer.

"Oh, yes, please. I do need another jar. And thank you, sir. You have been most considerate." As the manager turned to retrieve the goods, Patti whispered a thank-you to her Lord Jesus that no one had been hurt in the mishap.

A minute later, the manager returned with two sacks of flour and a fresh jar of pickles. Patti completed the rest of her shopping without further incident and returned home.

After putting away most of her supplies, Patti turned once again to her baking. It was in her favorite room of the house, her kitchen, of course. When she finished mixing the batter for the pineapple-carrot cake, her movements seemed effortless as she divided the batter into three pans before slipping two cakes into the larger oven and the third into her second and somewhat smaller one. Later, she would bake two more cakes to finish the set. This edible creation was more than just a yummy cake. It held the special title of wedding. In addition to one of Patti's exceptional flavors, the shape was distinctive as well. Each cake was in the shape of a heart, and each heart was a different size. Rather than the standard tiered cakes, like the more popular ones used at weddings, this bride's mother requested four single-layered, heart-shaped cakes arranged around a main larger one. Both the bride and her mother wished for fresh flowers on the cake, yet they wanted something more. There was just one problem; they were unsure exactly what that something was. Patti had just the idea. She would bring natural, fresh flowers and display them with edible ones made out of fondant and gum paste. An abundance of fresh flowers intertwined with handmade ones would be woven throughout the entire frosted area. Patti planned to create the handmade flowers as mirror images of the real ones. This was going to be one gorgeous creation when it was finished, the cake decorator thought. She loved her work. In fact, it was no work at all but a pleasure to accept each customer's order. Secretly, the young lady accepted each new project as a challenge to create and present the absolute best masterpiece possible.

Patti had made plenty of wedding cakes over the past few years. This often led her to think about her own wedding and what she wanted it to be like. While working on the heart cakes this particular day, her mind turned once again to this familiar territory and the questions, always questions. Usually, she probed all of the wedding details, but today her thoughts were mainly about the cake. She wondered if she would have one someday. She would, wouldn't she? Patti hoped so but held specks of doubt. After all, she thought, *What about my social life? Yet no tall, dark, and handsome man has waltzed into my life or even come close to me for that matter. In fact, I have not even gone out on any kind of date for quite some time.*

Continuing on, Patti queried almost audibly if there

was ever going to be a special man for her to love and marry. All the while the cakes were baking in their respective ovens, Patti continued to contemplate her future. She sat down in her favorite kitchen chair near the window. It overlooked her flower garden. Today of all days, she felt most blessed by what she saw in her own backyard. It was simple really, yet as the sun's bright rays filtered through the glass, the entire scene brought a warm glow to her skin and a cozy feeling to her heart. She knew who was with her, and she thanked Him for her life and well-being. She knew it was Jesus who brought the beauty of nature to her attention, and she thanked Him for the appreciation and enjoyment He blessed her with right there at home.

Just then, a hummingbird hovered in the air above a bright grouping of trumpet flowers. As Patti watched the little bird busy sipping the nectar, she began a whispered prayer to her Lord.

"I'm wondering what my husband will be like, Lord. I know that You know me better than I know myself, so You also know I'm very fond of dark hair. And the height thing ... well, You know I would prefer him to be tall. Not really prefer, Lord, I believe I *need* him to be tall. Hopefully, this could make up for my shortness, wouldn't You agree? Think how frustrating it would be to have two short people in the same house. Yes ... Lord, please let him be tall! And one more little thing, please, if You would consider this ... I know You can handle it. Do you think he could be handsome? That really wouldn't be so bad, would it? Lord, I know I sound like I am placing an order, but truly You know my heart, and here is where I must leave things for now. Above all, I pray for Your guidance in all my pathways. Thank You, Jesus, for hearing my prayer ...

Patti thought back over the events earlier that morning in the Safeway store. She had not really gotten a good visual of the face of the stranger who attempted to slow her fall. When she did look at him, she could not really see what he looked like because of the covering of flour, which hid his features. And when he left the store, he appeared ghostly with a thin coating of white still covering him. He almost looked like a mime with those dark eyes peering at her out from the white-like mascara. She remembered the surprised eyes that looked back at her when she removed some of the flour from around them. They were an unusual color for a man's eyes. They were neither green nor blue but something in between. She remembered washing his shapely nose and the funny face he made when the damp towel touched his lips.

As Patti recalled these recent events, it brought a smile to her face and warmth to her heart. Continuing with the mishap memory, she thought about how fast everything had happened. In a few short seconds, they fell and a mess ensued with white flour everywhere, yet the stranger, as quickly as he went down, bounded again to his feet and hustled off. She could still feel where his hands had caught her elbows. They were strong hands. His touch had sparked something within her, something like an electric shock. Who was he anyway?

As her thoughts drifted from baking cakes to her morning adventure and then to her own wedding wishes, Patti heard the church bells ringing for her wedding ceremony. Louder and louder pealed the bells, and then suddenly, she snapped from her dreamlike state, recognizing the sound of her wedding bells was actually the telephone ringing. And it wanted her immediate attention. Patti jumped up and ran to answer it.

"How are the cakes coming along?" a sweet voice inquired.

"Hello!" Patti replied while rebuttoning her sleeve. "The cakes are doing very nicely. At this particular moment, they are baking in the oven and should be ready to come out in a few moments, all except the extra one. They will need a short while to cool, and then I'll have to put them in the freezer for about an hour or so. I can give you a call when they are cool enough to begin the decorating, and then you can bring a sampling of the flowers you want me to copy. How does that sound?"

"About what time will you need them, dear?" The lady on the other end of the phone sounded very confident and totally in control of her schedule.

"I would estimate in about three hours. Yes, that should be sufficient time. I would say about two o'clock this afternoon would be good. Will that be a convenient time for you as well?"

"It'll be perfect" was the answer. "I'll run down to the florist right now and get some sample flowers of each kind and color we are hoping to use. Then I'll see you about two o'clock this afternoon." And with that, the women said good-bye.

Precisely at two o'clock, a light-blue Escalade pulled into the driveway and Mrs. Makaira got out. When she and Patti met at the door, Patti discovered the large box

Mrs. Makaira carried contained all the newly bought fresh flowers for the occasion. At this time, the cakes were just out of the freezer, cooled, and ready, waiting for the next step. Before Mrs. Makaira had arrived, Patti had prepared the cakes with the first layer of frosting so that most of them appeared ready to eat. The decorations lacked only the finishing details: adding onto the cake the fresh, real flowers and their handmade sugary twins and then a trimming of the edges to bring a crisp and detailed final touch. *Yes,* thought Patti, *the floral designs will be the crown on this wedding cake.* As the two women each imagined the entire scene complete with the freshly bought flowers and their handmade replicas, an excitement filled the room. Prewedding planning was always this way. The prospective brides and their mothers were always optimistic. Theirs was going to be the best wedding ever. That was the fun part about doing wedding cakes. Every bride at this stage in her life was happy or at least appeared to be.

"These are beautiful!" exclaimed Mrs. Makaira. "These will be perfect for my daughter's wedding. She's going to be amazed and happily so!"

"Mrs. Makaira, were you able to get any input or ideas from your daughter on the type of theme she wanted for the floral designs?" Patti raised the question because in the past, some brides had wanted complete control over everything.

"No, dear. My daughter told me to surprise her. She and I share many of the same likes and dislikes. Recently, she even confided in me that she believes my taste in interior design is superior to hers. The only concern she had for the wedding was matching the colors. However, I believe that matter has resolved itself. Now the cakes you have made here are stunning. The shades of the frostings alongside the flowers I brought today are a beautiful blend of nature and creativity. Together they will present a perfect color scheme. My daughter should have no worries. I will ease her concern about the cake; that is for certain. Here are the flowers. Have fun with them." She opened the box and pulled out several classically elegant arrangements. Patti saw orchids, calla lilies, roses, and some dainty yellow flowers that she had never seen before.

"What are these tiny yellow flowers called?" she asked, gently lifting a crisp bunch of them from the box. Instinctively she brought them up to her nose to check their scent.

"I really don't know," replied Patti's client. "I spotted them at the florist's and knew upon sight they'd be perfect. I was thinking how beautifully they'd complement the yellow ribbons in the floral arrangements. Don't you agree? During the process, I forgot to ask the florist their name." This comment was followed by a shrugging of the lady's shoulder as if that detail was not all that important to her busy—Patti assumed—schedule.

"Oh yes, I agree! They are petite yet brightly colored and will be simply lovely with the ribbons. I'll need a little time in order to copy them onto the cake, but they appear to be just what I need to fill in between the roses and lilies. I can see the design in my mind already. My only request is I would like several photos of the finished cake, please. This is one of the prettiest cakes I have created to date. You see, I'm redesigning the website for my business. I plan on using this cake for my home page background as well as the cover photo on my portfolio." Patti got a far-off picture of the targeted design in her mind as she spoke.

"You shall surely have them, dear. I will even order the photos in the eight-by-ten size or if you prefer, eight-by-twelve? Would you like that, sweetie?"

"That would be just wonderful!" Patti responded, trying to picture how large an eight-by-twelve-inch photograph would be. She opened her hands a little first for what she thought the width would be and then the length.

Mrs. Makaira continued, "You know, Patti-Cake, I must confess something. Did you know that I went to five different decorators before I found you?"

"No. I had no idea." Patti really looked surprised as that thought penetrated her mind. Five other decorators and this lady chose her?

"Well, I did. And none of them can hold a candle to your talents. You are a real artesian. You really should charge more money for your cakes, lovie. I know I shouldn't be telling you this, but your cakes were the least expensive of all and so superior in quality and beauty. Your work is a full standard above all the others. You could easily charge two or three hundred dollars extra for a cake like this, and no one would bat an eye." The lady spoke in a matter-of-fact way, emphasizing the $200 or $300 as she spoke.

"Do you really think so?" Patti queried timidly as the idea began growing in her mind.

"Most certainly, dear ... I plan to give you an extra

couple hundred for all your trouble and hard work with our order. There, now I have said it."

"Oh! Thank you so much, Mrs. Makaira, but I will not and cannot in good faith charge you more than I originally quoted." Patti was shaking her head back and forth as she spoke. Her eyes were wide and showed a little fire in them. She looked as though it would be wrong if she somehow got a tip for a job well done.

"You don't need to charge me more," the lady answered as a premeditated, deliberate hurt look came into her eyes. "I will just write out your check for two hundred dollars extra, and don't even try to argue with me. Consider it a tip for an excellent job well done and a happy customer who wants to say thank you with more than just words. A young woman like yourself could use some extra money, couldn't she? Have you thought about your own wedding, dearie? If nothing else, you could put it aside for that. I am sure you have thought of your wedding, sweet. I would think a beautiful girl like you would have handsome young men waiting in line to date you."

Patti blushed at the compliment and then continued on the theme of the extra cash.

"Yes, I suppose I could use the extra money, but I would probably spend it on something besides my own wedding and waiting for some tall, dark, and handsome man to sweep me off my feet. There are some nice new cake pans at Nancy's Kitchen Korner. I saw them the other day, and they would be so wonderful to use in my baking. They cost about the same amount as the extra money you want to give me. But really, I can't accept it and that is final," she accented the word *final* with a determined look, and then her eyes softened as a thought popped into her creative mind.

"Actually, back to men, a tall, dark, and I assume handsome man did sweep me off my feet earlier today. Funny that it would come up in our conversation." The pictures of the earlier incident at the store that day came flooding back into Patti's mind. Then a warm, amused smile crossed her face, causing it to shine as if she were standing in a flood of sunlight streaming down on her from a hole in the clouds.

Mrs. Makaira caught the look and had a moment of triumph as she realized that once again her projected generosity had found its mark. *This beautiful young lady could sure use a little education in the finer details of life,* she thought to herself. *When rare, generous opportunities like this come knocking, be sure to snatch them up before they are lost forever.*

Well then, take the extra money and buy those pans, if that's what you need, lovie." The woman added the comment in such a way that it was projected to appear as an afterthought or perhaps Patti's own unique idea.

The two women chatted while Patti worked on the cakes. About an hour passed, and during that time, the young cake decorator put the finishing touches on the frosting and trimmed out the edges. Then she added the delicately designed, gum-paste flowers in mirror images of their fresh counterparts. Each one was positioned exactly in the artistic style Patti was becoming famous for.

Except for the fresh flowers, this wedding cake was complete and ready to go. Minutes prior to the reception, the fresh flowers would be placed in accordance with

Patti's directions in her notes and drawings. She set several different flowers next to the grouping and got an idea of how the colors, designs, ribbons, and flowers would match and complement one another. This truly was becoming a beautiful masterpiece.

Patti helped Mrs. Makaira load each cake into the back of her vehicle. Then they said their good-byes. Patti headed back to the house. She sent up a silent prayer for the cakes to look wonderful but also added prayers for God's blessings on those who partook of the pastry and especially for the bride and groom in their new life together.

Inside the kitchen, she took the check from her apron pocket and was astounded at what she saw. Her mouth dropped open. Mrs. Makaira had not given her $200 extra but $300. *Three!* She checked the numbers once again to make sure. Yes! The mother of the bride had given $300 more than Patti's original quote for the cake! Patti looked out of the window. She noticed Mrs. Makaira had not yet pulled out onto the road but was waiting for the traffic to pass by. The cake decorator thought if she ran quickly enough, she might be able to catch her client. She bounded out the door and down the steps and flew toward the parting vehicle. However, by the time Patti got to the end of her driveway, the Escalade was pulling into the traffic. In an instant, her generous customer was gone. Patti slowly walked back toward the house. Instead of going in the front door, she meandered around to the backyard area in order to gaze at her flower garden once again.

Spring was definitely in the air this afternoon. Fleecy

white clouds frolicked across the sky. A gentle breeze brought the scents of the season, waking her awareness that this was indeed a most beautiful day. Her mind turned again toward the dainty little yellow flowers on her client's cake. She determined right then that she *had* to learn their name. Yes, Patti would go down to the florist and not only find out the name of that pretty little yellow flower but purchase some of the plants as well. She believed they would go well in the flowerbeds with her miniature roses. As far as the check was concerned, she would call Mrs. Makaira as soon as she got home and try to meet up with her somewhere to make things right. She rested in the garden for a long time.

When darkness began to close in around her, she headed for the back door and caught sight of her little hummingbird. It flew past her at nearly Mach speed and then hovered over a pink flower with a deep cup. As if on cue, an idea came to mind, and Patti knew exactly all the details of her wedding cake. A design with fresh flowers and hand-created replicas interwoven with tiny hummingbirds was now her desired plan. She could see it in her mind's eye as clear as crystal. Inside the house, Patti grabbed her sketchbook and quickly began to bring her ideas to life. She wanted to capture the perfect images before the vision was gone. At the top of the first page, a title formed, revealing Patti's wishes for "My Wedding Cake." Needless to say, the ideas required more than one page in order to outline as well as sketch as many details as she could collect. As she drew, her imagination took over. She ended up creating several possibilities for arrangements. Each sketch, however, included her delicate and tiny hummingbird hovering over the deep-cupped pink flowers. Patti sat back and admired her drawings. She had always done well in art class. Several of her teachers over the years had encouraged her to look at a career in art. Patti had thought about that quite a bit, but she liked sculpture and 3-D art projects better than drawing. Cake decorating along with her inherited sweet tooth formed the perfect marriage of all of her combined artistic talents.

"Lord," she prayed, "where were we before the church bells started ringing, er, uh, I mean before the telephone rang? Oh, I remember! We were talking about my future husband. I know You have a wonderful man picked out for me. I have faith that at the right time, You will bring us together. If You wouldn't mind hurrying a bit though, that would be wonderful. Sometimes I'm so lonely I catch myself crying. I don't want just any man. I want one who has a deep love for You, who will be great with kids and has a sense of humor, too. And Lord, if he is handsome, I won't mind a bit. You know my likes and loves, and I know You know I am partial to dark hair and really want him to be tall. If maybe You could arrange for him to be more than six feet tall, well, that would be super! I'm not forgetting how important it is to be a good provider and to have a kind and loving heart. You know how much I dearly love to bake and decorate my cakes, but if Mr. Right is as good at making a living as I am at my cake-making, then with Your blessings, I truly believe I can be a full-time mommy and just love it."

Patti stopped for a breath and contemplated her chosen career. Continuing, she added, "It would be nice though to be able to continue my decorating a little bit on the side. But then again …" And she paused for a moment before continuing. "Oh, Lord," Patti pleaded, "You know how much I'd love to be a full-time mommy … Oh, dear Jesus, I don't mean to ramble on so. Sometimes I just do my best thinking when I talk aloud to You. I do believe You know what is best for me, and I know You have a wonderful plan for my life, which I will follow as You reveal it to me. Still, I dream." As Patti settled back on a comfy chair, she drifted off into a dreamy sleep. A Bible passage, Ephesians 3:20–21 (ESV), popped into her mind as clear as if she were reading the page in front of her.

"Now unto Him who is able to do far more abundantly than all we can ask or think according to the power at work within us, to him be glory in the church and in Christ Jesus throughout all generations, forever and ever. Amen."

Patti gained a bit of consciousness and yawned as the passage registered more clearly. "That would be pretty amazing, Lord, pretty amazing indeed! Right now though, dear Jesus, I surrender to Your will, whatever that may be. I will leave it all in Your capable hands. Thank You with all my heart. Amen." Patti stumbled toward the large, soft queen-sized bed. Little did she know that in exactly fifteen hours, while getting in position to cut the cake, the bride would trip on her wedding dress and to prevent her fall, reach out for the first thing she could grasp.

Chapter 2
IF IT WERE ONLY UP TO MEN

"Jim, are you going to log on to the Internet today?" a woman's voice asked as the young movie star headed out the door. He had been making movies since his childhood and had developed quite a name for himself. True, he didn't get twenty million a picture, but he did quite well. He had just finished a major role in a movie and was between films. He was going to his office to do a little book work. He wanted to buy his own home and needed to see how much money he had.

"Yes," he replied. "I will be on the net. What would you like me to do?"

"Could you look up wedding cakes? If you find any you think look nice, print me out some copies. I want to take them to the cake decorator to see if they can come up with a fresh idea, something stunning, stylish, and extraordinarily unique. Plus, it needs to serve five hundred people."

"I can sure try, but I'm probably not the best person to do research for you on this subject. In the first place, I don't know that much about cakes, wedding or otherwise, and in the second place, how do I know what you are looking for?"

"Don't worry about it, Jim. It's not that big of a deal. If you see anything interesting, just run off some copies. You will probably have the best success if you do an image search first." Jim's sister, Kathy, was getting married in a short time, but for now, they shared Jim's penthouse.

Jim left the home and headed for his office. He went over his books and found that he could come up with two million. In addition, if he took out a mortgage, he could easily have enough money to get into a really decent place. He pondered what it would be like. He was definite; it must have a swimming pool. He loved to swim. He also wanted a dwelling at least three stories high so he could convert the top floor into a private gym. He would live in the middle and entertain his friends at ground level. He logged on to the Internet and searched "houses." He spent a full hour taking virtual tours of fancy homes but didn't find any that came close to the picture he had in mind. Then his thoughts turned to building a home. He really didn't want to build a place because it would take too long. He wanted to get settled and fast. He phoned a friend who was a real-estate agent, and the friend directed Jim onto the trail of his new dream home. He was about to log off when he remembered the wedding cakes his sister wanted him to find. He entered cakes, the plus sign, and the word *wedding* in the search box and waited to see what would come up.

Numerous websites lit up the screen, indicating decorators in every locale, far and near. This could waste a lot of time, so he took his sister's suggestion and did an image search. Three unusual cakes jumped out at him. He scrolled down the list and pressed "next" to bring up a second page. His eyes fell on a delicately designed masterpiece. He clicked on it, and up came a website entitled, Exquisite Cakes. It advertised wedding cakes, birthday cakes, cakes for parties, and cakes, cakes, and more cakes. After pressing the blue-highlighted, underlined title, he watched passively as the parts of the page uploaded and appeared on his screen. And then he saw it again, almost as large as life! It was by far the most beautiful cake he had ever seen. It was a series of five hearts with many fresh flowers all around. The main central cake was different than the ones around it. It was a large, heart-shaped masterpiece, but unlike the others, it had two beautifully crafted, matching hummingbirds facing each other. Their long, slender beaks were slightly touching on the very tip. What a unique idea! The symbolic intent was masterful. What better way to capture the spirit of true, unending love than this? It was simply amazing! The decorator must have taken great care, because all the real, fresh flowers were identical to the edible ones made of very thin layers of what looked like frosting to him.

Jim loved the real flowers that were interspersed among all of the various hearts. It was almost impossible to tell those made of this thin material from the fresh flowers, except for the green stems on the real flowers. A smile crossed his face as he pictured that cake at his own wedding. Then he tried to imagine his bride by his side. She would be beautiful, that he knew. But what color would her hair be? He thought he might like it red. Yes, red hair to go with the dark-red roses that would be on his cake. Then again, what about yellow? These roses were yellow. There were tiny yellow flowers and golden ribbons interwoven in and around both flowers and cakes. So, then shifting thought, Jim pictured a golden-haired beauty. Ah, yes! That's a much better match with the tiny yellow flowers and ribbons. *No …* His thoughts hesitated again. Feeling not completely sure, Jim pondered the color of her hair. It could possibly be something in between. Shaking his head out of this daydream, he clicked on the five-heart cake picture, and it increased in size even more. It was truly beautiful. Not that he had seen many fancy decorated cakes before, but this one stood out, and he believed it was going to be special for his sister as well. He ran the mouse over to file, placed a special type of photo paper in, and clicked to print. In just a little bit, the photo came spewing out.

While the machine was working, he looked at several other cakes this decorator had in her collection. He printed out a number of nice-looking ones and was about to log off when he saw a picture of the cake designer herself. She was stunning! And she appeared to have more than just outside beauty. Jim instinctively knew he was going to meet this little cake decorator and soon. He clicked on the thumbnail, and her picture sprang to life. There, staring back at him from the computer screen, was this gorgeous being with strawberry-blond hair and deep emerald eyes. His mind swirled with questions about her. He wondered how old she was. Was she single or married? Did she have any children? Then his thoughts turned to the unknown number of women who had come into his arms. Their type was all the same—beautiful and shapely on the outside, but inside, there was a commonality as well. They lacked brains but loved his money. Jim longed for a sincere woman with a true heart who didn't revere material things as the number-one priority in life. He wanted someone both beautiful and intelligent who also wasn't motivated to change with a lifestyle brought on by a big bankbook. For just a split second, Jim whispered, almost afraid to say it aloud, "Is it possible to find a woman like that?" Back on the computer, the decorator woman looked intelligent enough, and it just so happened he needed a vacation. He looked up the address and found that she lived in the northern part of the state, Santa Rosa, California. The wedding was only three weeks away. He wanted to bring his sister a sample cake from Exquisite Cakes, and if the cakes tasted anything as wonderful as they appeared on the website, he wouldn't have to convince his sister at all. She'd love them on her own. Jim simply would have to rush this job request as well as bring this decorator here to bake it on location. He took out his cell phone and pulled up his sister's number. Kathy answered.

"Hey, Sis. I went online and found your cake. Some gal over in Santa Rosa is an exceptional, stunning artesian. I looked at several cakes, and there is one that will be splendid for your wedding. I don't want you to worry at all about that part of your wedding. I will take care of it for you. I plan on having this lady come here and make the cake on site. I will pay all of her expenses. Consider it as part of my wedding gift to you and Craig. I guarantee you will be satisfied with the end results. Just give me your wedding colors and consider it done. I have this one handled. It will be one less thing you have to worry about, and God knows you have enough to do between now and the big day for any three brides." His excitement bubbled over into his voice as he spoke.

"Are you sure you can handle this, Jim? I thought you said you probably were not the best one to research cakes, and now you say you have it handled. What happened?" She had a right to question him, since he had at first seemed reluctant. But now here was her little brother bubblier and more enthusiastic than she had seen or heard him in weeks.

"I got hooked, Kathy. This woman is a doll. I have to meet her in person to see if she is married. I am in love, Sister, in love, finally."

"What does a pretty face have to do with wedding cakes? I think you are getting the cart before the horse. I ask you to look up some cakes and you are shopping for your next fling. Are you sure she is as good at making cakes as looking pretty and sweet?" There was a little scorn, along with a note of disbelief, in her voice as she responded.

"Okay, Sis. You found my weak spot, but in answer to your questions, yes! Her cakes are the best I have seen. I looked at no less than fifty different wedding cakes online, and there was one that was so far above the rest, when I saw it, I said to myself, 'This is the one. It cannot possibly be topped.' Go to your Facebook page, and I will send you the photo. I'm transferring it there as we speak. You can decide for yourself, but I'm sure you will be pleased."

"All right, Bro. I will trust you on this one. But if you find out that you cannot do the job or that this pretty face you are so captivated by is just that, a pretty face and nothing more, be sure and give me at least a week's notice to make other arrangements. I want this wedding to be as perfect as can be, and if no cake shows up to the reception, you will have to live with that for the rest of your life, do you understand?" She was getting a bit exasperated now. That was coming loud and clear over the air.

"Have I ever failed you, Kathy?"

"Only about a couple of hundred times, Little Brother, but you have come through for me more than once when I really needed you. This place, for one, where we have had a chance to hang out together. That was a godsend, Jim. I never could have kept up a place like this. It is too expensive for my pocketbook. And it was one of the clinchers that helped me to bag Craig, I think. Yes, thanks to my rich brother, it has been a wonderful retreat for the last several months. I owe you, Bro, so don't blow it."

She was still skeptical, was she? This wasn't going to be an easy sell. He would just have to prove her wrong. If there was one thing Jim loved, it was a challenge. But then, deep down inside, he knew she was a sweetheart. His sister really was a one-in-a-million woman, the kind any man would be foolish to let slip away once he had her in his grasp.

"You don't owe me anything. You are the best, Sis. I only hope I can find a woman half as swell as you. But perhaps this Patti Cake of a woman is the one. I sure hope so. I really will take care of everything this time. You can count on me to come through for you. I am about to order the plane tickets. I will head out to make all the arrangements the first part of the week. As I said earlier, 'Consider it done.' You will be pleasantly surprised with the end results. It will be perfect."

"All right, Jim. You can do this! Your overexcited enthusiasm is convincing me. I'm going to let you handle it all. Go for it and good luck with the woman. Hope it works out for you." With that, she hung up.

The day after the Makaira cakes had been placed in the Escalade, Patti woke up to brilliant sunshine. If there ever was a perfect day in Santa Rosa, it was this one. She had an open schedule. She did a little body pampering. It was nice for a girl to treat herself to some of the finer comforts in life once in a while. After soaking in the hot tub for half an hour, she showered and put on some makeup. She wanted to look very special today, for some reason. She fooled with her hair, moving it this way and that. Finally she placed a portion of it to the left side of her face. It came down and hung beautifully on her shoulder. In the mirror, looking back at her, was a pretty nice-looking woman, if she said so herself. And it was going to be a wonderful day, she just knew it. What to do?

On her way out to the kitchen, she caught sight of her drawings. During the night hours, her subconscious mind had been going over the pictures of her wedding cake. A brand-new design had worked its way to the front of the pack. She grabbed up a pencil and sketched it out. It was perfect! Why not? Yes! She had that extra cake in the freezer even now. She would practice with it. She had never attempted hummingbirds before. After toasting a bagel and spreading a generous portion of cream cheese on it, she dove into the task at hand.

Before long, the lady had a sweet blend of frosting whipped up and ready to go. Patti did not always follow her own recipes. She loved to experiment. This cake had been no exception. She ran out of carrots, so she added more pineapple and coconut to the batter than normal. She had also whipped up the oil until it was charged with thousands of tiny bubbles before folding it into the mix. Why? She didn't know. She wanted to see what whipped oil looked like, she guessed. This cake would not be used for the wedding, so why not experiment? Soon all the basics were done and she started on the hummingbirds. She settled on a final composition of two birds kissing, their dainty beaks just barley touching. In between them, she placed a pearl teardrop-shaped gem. It could represent a morning dewdrop captured by the male from the petal of a dainty flower to present to his beloved— that was, if hummingbirds had beloved mates. Or it could represent a teardrop. There might be some of those in a marriage. It didn't matter. No one but she herself would see it. It took her five hours to complete, but she was lost to the passing of time, chained to her creative endeavor. Creativity completely recharged her physically. There was just something about it that kept calling to come back again and again. Patti loved this cake recipe and could spend a month or a year eating it if need be. That was what freezers were for. She was also very pleased with the end result. There was a bit of deformity to the heart that made it asymmetrical, just a tiny bit. She had taken a little wedge here and another there to make it perfect. Now as she admired the finished work, she snatched up one of the slices and munched away. There was something about it that was fluffier than usual. She recalled the change in proportions and the whipping of the oil, making a note to herself to make a note of it in her notes.

There it was in all of its grandeur. She wished it had a home, for it really looked too pretty to eat. So this would be what her wedding cake looked like, would it? She grabbed her camera and took several pictures from different angles. Glancing at her watch, she noticed it was after twelve. The time had flown by. The strange part of it all was that during the entire process, Patti never messed up her hair or makeup. It would be a good time to change the profile picture on her website. She set the camera on a tripod and took a few selfies. Then she took a few pictures with the cake in front and the decorator in back. *Vanity, vanity,* she thought to herself. But today was her day to celebrate life and her freedom to do whatever she wanted without anyone telling her otherwise. She uploaded the photos to her website and sat down for a few moments of reflection.

At precisely 2:00 p.m., her phone rang. Thinking it was probably a new order for a cake, she answered with a cheery voice. "Hello. This is Patti with Exquisite Cakes. How may I help you?" She was greeted with the most distressed voice she could imagine.

"Oh, Patti Cake!" Mrs. Makaira cried into the phone. "You will never guess what terrible thing happened! The wedding is ruined. I am so embarrassed. If I live to be one hundred, this will be the worst day of my life. All that planning and money and it was supposed to be perfect, but horror of horrors, everything is ruined. Whatever am I supposed to do? I feel like crawling into a hole in the ground and never coming out." The lady was indeed hysterical.

Patti wondered what could possibly have gone wrong.

"Calm down, please! What happened, my friend? It can't be that bad."

"It is the cake, Patti. The cake is ruined, and they never even got to cut it. Oh, what am I going to do? We were taking prewedding pictures, and the Bible boy ran in front of my dear, poor girl. She tripped, Patti. Oh, what am I going to do now?" Patti could almost hear the tears pouring out of the lady's face.

"What happened when she tripped, Mrs. Makaira? What happened to the cake?"

"She grabbed it and oh the mess! You wouldn't believe it. Your beautiful cake landed upside down on the floor. I am so embarrassed. The wedding is due to start in half an hour. Can you work miracles on your cakes?" Patti could tell by her voice that this little mother was about to have a nervous breakdown if something wasn't done to better the situation.

"What was the damage to the cake, Mom?" She didn't know why that name seemed appropriate, but somehow, it just came out.

"Oh, it is a grand mess. It broke in half, and all the flowers and trimmings are smashed. It was the center cake too. Oh, dear me!" She was literally crying now, and the cake decorator was very sad for her, very sad indeed.

"Where is the church? Perhaps there is something we can do. How long do you think it would take me to get there? I will bring my patch kit and see if anything can be salvaged." Patti had to say something reassuring to try to calm the poor, distressed soul. She might have a heart attack if she didn't get control. That would really make for a memorable wedding.

"The reception is in the basement of the Catholic church on Elm Street. You could probably be here in ten minutes if the traffic is not bad."

"I am heading out the door now. If you can hold the cake cutting event off a little, I think we can work something out. Try not to worry."

"Oh thank you, lovie. You are a real sweetheart. If you can fix this cake, I will forever be in your debt." With that, she hung up. Patti ran to the cupboard and grabbed her kit. She also went to the freezer and pulled out several frozen, premade flowers and placed them in a box. She was heading out the door when she chanced to see the hummingbird cake. It was heart-shaped. It had the right colors. That was it! In a matter of five minutes, it was loaded into the vehicle and she was pulling out of her driveway. But Lady Luck was not with the Makaira wedding this day. Murphy's law was working overtime.

The guests were arriving and being seated. The band was set up. The mother of the bride was busy examining her daughter's dress. Some of the frosting had gotten on the sleeve. Fortunately it was white on white. Then it happened—one more unfortunate incident. As the bridesmaids were lining up, one of them fainted. She toppled to the floor, hitting facedown. Her knight in shining armor failed to catch her. If Mrs. Makaira was hysterical before, she just about blew a blood vessel when that happened. There was a lot of scrambling and a couple of screams. A medical doctor in the group was petitioned to take a look. The girl opened her eyes, but blood was coming from her mouth. The doctor immediately called 911. This was one wedding that would be delayed. About that time, Patti arrived on the scene, asking where the cake was. Seeing all of the commotion, however, she wondered how this new problem could be solved. To make a long story shorter, the strawberry-blond cake decorator ended up taking the place of the unfortunate maid. It all happened rather quickly, as if a dream were being acted out. Once Patti assured the distressed mother she had a replacement cake and that problem would be solved, she felt so much empathy for the family that she was surprised at what came out of her mouth. She would remember it as long as she lived. She went up and placed her arm around the weeping mother and said, "Don't worry about the bridesmaid, Mom; she is about my size. I will fill in for her. Let's get this couple married. Okay?"

In less than twenty minutes, she was marching up the aisle with the others. Most of the people in the congregation never knew about the replacement bridesmaid and that a dear, sweet mother, on the second most important day of her life, was spared more embarrassment. Everything after that went off without a hitch. One might have wondered why a bridesmaid was adding freshly cut flowers to the most beautiful cake imaginable before the reception got underway, but it was a secret Patti would cherish and keep close to her heart. She sent a small prayer heavenward after it was over.

"Jesus? Even though I did not have plans for myself on this beautiful, sunny day, You did. You knew we would need that cake. You also knew a bridesmaid, overcome by exhaustion and perhaps emotion, would take a tumble and not be able to do her part as planned. You even prompted me to look my best today. I did not know why, but You did. It was to ease the distress of a dear mother and daughter on their very special day. I think that was just swell of You, Jesus. You really did have it all planned out. Thank You for allowing me to serve you today and show a little of Your love to others. I would like to make a resolution to trust You more for You surely can be trusted. Please forgive me where in the past I have not trusted. And again, Jesus, be especially near that bride and groom. Make their life pleasant, and may they establish their home on the one true foundation, Jesus Christ. If they do that, together they will be able to weather any storm or trial the old devil may throw at them. Oh, please bless that marriage with Your special blessing. In Your name, Jesus, I ask. Amen."

Chapter 3
THE LAST SHOE TO DROP

Several days had passed since Patti encountered the dark-haired stranger in the Safeway store. She hardly gave him a thought anymore. She was busy with baking cakes and spent some of her time visiting her friends. After being an unexpected player in the Makaira wedding, it seemed as though all the ladies her age were getting married. Patti was twenty-four and still had no prospects in the marriage department. Glancing at her schedule, she noticed that for the next three days, she was free. A thought crossed her mind, and Patti decided to go to her parents' house to spend a minivacation with them. It would be good to get away and take a small break from her routine. She packed lightly and got into her SUV. The trip to her parents' home was only an hour away, what she referred to as a "quick jaunt." The timing was great, and she silently thanked Jesus for His continuous watch over her. A little time away was what she really needed, and He always knew what was best. As her trust in Him grew, she was learning that more and more. Moving along smoothly in minimal traffic, Patti was making great headway. Barely had she reached the outskirts of the city when all of a sudden she heard a pop and then a flopping sound. At the same time, she felt the car pull strongly to one side. Patti pulled over onto the shoulder of the road and got out. Oh no! This couldn't be happening. What she knew but didn't want to believe was that her tire was flat. *Ugh! Oh well,* she thought, *I better get busy before it gets dark. And, Lord, keep me safe while I do this, please.* With prayers said, she went to the back of her rig and popped open the hatch door. Patti retrieved the tire arm and jack.

She was just placing it under the axle when a deep voice boomed out, "May I help you?"

Patti, startled, not having heard anyone approach, turned in the direction of the voice and looked up. *Hmmm,* she thought. This man seemed familiar, but she was not sure. And yet, there was something about those eyes.

"Oh, it's you," remarked a dull, monotonic voice. "What seems to be the problem this time?" he queried with disinterest.

"I have a flat tire. How do you know me?"

"At Safeway, a few days ago, I tried to catch you as you fell but caught a sack full of flour instead. Washing my face with pickle juice was quite creative. You must be a quick thinker."

Patti's face started to get hot as she realized just who had stopped to help her. She quickly took her eyes off the man and glanced down at her feet, not wanting him to see the crimson color that was starting to creep up her neck.

"I bake and decorate cakes and needed a special flour that day. I'm very sorry about the unfortunate mishap. When the flour fell like snow and covered you, I didn't know what to do at first, but then without thinking, I automatically began to take action in order to remedy the situation. When I saw the flour all over your face, I wondered what I could do to help you. I knew the flour needed washing off right away. Pickle juice was probably not the best choice, but it was right in front of me ready to use. You seem to have survived though. Were there any problems after you left?"

"Nothing that a little time didn't heal. Aside from my face feeling like pinpricks for a couple of days and getting a ticket for speeding, I survived decently enough."

"Well, I am so sorry. Please forgive me." Patti looked up again into those blue-green eyes.

He looked back for only a moment and then with his hand moved her gently to the side so he could get to the tire. Perhaps he was a little shy she thought. At least this time he was not dressed in shiny black pants. He finished placing the jack under the axle and then proceeded to crank the handle. Soon the flat tire was off and the little temporary spare on. Cal finished tightening the bolts on the wheel and told Patti where to find the nearest Les Schwab tire store.

"You should not drive on that wheel any farther than is necessary. It's not good for the transmission. By the way, where are you headed?"

"I have a couple of free days in my schedule, so I decided to visit my parents. I'm almost there, and I remember there is a Les Schwab Tire Center not more than a couple of blocks from their house. I'm sure it's the same one you mentioned."

Cal held out his hand to Patti. "We were never formally introduced. My name is Cal Ripland. What is your name?"

Patti returned the greeting, holding out her hand as

well. "I'm Patti Murray, but my friends all call me Patti Cake. The nickname grew from the fact that I am a cake baker and decorator. I'm able to create all kinds of designs or styles and flavors to match anyone's whim or desire. Anything one is able to imagine, I can duplicate. I am so pleased to make your acquaintance. I'm certainly glad this meeting turned out better than our last. Thank you for stopping to help me. I really appreciate it, and I'm very sorry about the incident in the store."

Just then, Cal's cell phone rang. He mechanically reached for it while Patti bent down to pick up the jack.

"Yes, this is Dr. Ripland. How may I be of service?"

A doctor, Patti mused silently. So, Cal was a physician. *How interesting,* she thought. Meanwhile, the few seconds from when Patti picked up the jack to what happened next were humbling to say the least. A little bit of oil from the jackscrew slid onto the side of the mechanism, making for a very slippery jack unbeknownst to Patti. At her attempt to return it to its place in the back of her rig, it slipped right out of her hands and dropped with a heavy and audible thud. The air was immediately filled with a painfully loud "Eeeyowwwwww! Ouch! That was dead-on horrible!" Cal agonized, while he jumped to get out of the way. Then trying to regain his composure, he quickly disconnected his phone call and maneuvered over to the edge of the trunk of Patti's rig where he sat down. Continuing, Cal complained, "Did you need to make such a direct hit on my toe? And my toenail, too!" His question pleaded for an explanation. His tone and words of pain preceded and motivated Patti's next action. Although the entire episode had happened within a matter of a minute or two, for Cal and Patti, time seemed to stand still. The next instant, Patti flew into motion. She had his shoe untied and off as well as his sock and was massaging his foot by the time he looked down at her. Already, the blood in his big toe gave the nail a dark crimson color—just about the same shade as the color in Patti's cheeks. She was so embarrassed. Cal closed his eyes, trying to will the pain away. No sooner had he done so than they flew right back open in shock and disbelief! Patti had grabbed some ice for the pain from a cooler she kept in the back of her SUV. The icy reception to his foot and big toe sent chills shooting through his entire body. He started to shake and shiver vigorously. Patti, feeling mortified from experiencing another mishap with this stranger, continued apologizing and giving herself a lecture on being so careless, all the while ministering to Cal's hurt foot.

"Now, Patti M., just look what you have done to this poor man. You need to be more careful!"

Then Cal added his own comment, "Yes, Miss Murray, I agree with you wholeheartedly. First, you smash my toe, and then you freeze it. Now how could that jack have landed so perfectly on the big toenail of my foot? Are you positive that wasn't a calculated skill of yours? You're an accident waiting to happen, miss, and when I show up, it happens!"

"Oh! Dear me, no! There was a bit of grease on the jack, and it just slipped right out of my hand when I went to pick it up. Look! You can still see it." She held up her small hand, expecting him to examine it and agree with her. "And the ice, well, I got that to numb your pain."

"It's numb all right, and you're saying the jack just

slipped like your foot slipped off the shelf in the store? Isn't it curious that both accidents happened exactly at the right moment?"

Patti blushed again and fumbled another apology. She really didn't know what had come over her. She spent hours in the kitchen and seldom had any mishaps. However, whenever this man appeared, Patti became all thumbs—or in this case, numb thumbs, because her thumb couldn't hold the grip she had tried to maintain on the slippery jack.

Cal grimaced at his toe again and then looked around for his shoe. He spotted it out in the road. He thought he better get it before it was run over and ruined. He stood up and looked both ways before heading toward it, but he was too late. A muddy four-by-four came barreling down the road and passed them at high speed. Smack! Right over the shoe ran the truck, and not just any part of the shoe but right over the toe! It flipped up, sailing into the air, and when it finally landed with a splat, it was directly in front of him. He stared at it with disdain. Just a few days ago, Cal had spent almost a day's wages for those shoes, after a similar pair had been floured and pickled. Now these were in ruins too—smashed and flattened just like his toe. He picked up the shoe without incident and limped to his car, leaving his sock hanging on Patti's bumper. Without warning, another anguished howl was emitted into the air when Cal stepped on a sharp stone. Needless to say, his entire foot was very tender. He wiggled into his car with as little pain as possible and then slammed the door shut. How it happened he could never understand, but the closing door also caught the little finger on his left hand. Another howl of anguish erupted, hardly muffled by the closed car window. Had she been a betting woman, she would probably have felt that what he had just gone through was enough to make a preacher swear. But no unruly words of that kind escaped his lips. Was he a Christian? He had to be married. Only a married man would exercise such control over his tongue.

Patti watched in dismay as he roared off. Now she had really done it. "Lord? Whatever was the matter with me? I feel so bad, and if I could, I would just disappear never to come back to be more trouble to anyone. I know that won't help anything, Lord, but I don't know why I have run into this man with such bad luck." Abruptly her focus changed, for at that moment, she spied Cal's missing sock. She would make a point to return it to him. She knew his name now, so his address should not be that hard to find. She tossed the sock into the back of the SUV, walked slowly around to the front, and climbed in, looking forlorn and emotionally worn out. Patti drove slowly and cautiously all the way to the tire center. How could she ever make it up to this Cal guy? And to think that he was a doctor too! She couldn't let this go on much longer. Patti had a bright idea. What about making him a cake? She could make one of her specialty cakes and bring it with her when she returned the sock.

Back at the center, the tire guy told her that her flat could not be repaired and that the one on the other side needed replacing also or the same thing might happen. She would need to buy a new one. That was not good news! How could she pay for it? Then she remembered the extra

$300 Mrs. Makaira had given her. No new pans with that money. It would go for tires.

The weekend at her parents' was a quiet one. They talked about the good old days when Patti was in high school and college. They tried to recall the names of the boys whom she had dated. Patti had her favorites, but she wondered where they were now. None of them became very successful, as far as she knew. Patti had never been very close to her parents. They adopted her at the age of six. Her real dad had died while on a tour of duty in the armed forces. Then, when her mother became ill and was diagnosed with cancer, she didn't live long enough to see Christmas that year. And to lose both parents so closely together was devastating to the child. There were no other family members with whom Patti could live, so she lived with a family in a foster home. But that was a short stay of six months before a couple adopted her. "Mother," as she learned to call her adopted parent over time, wanted to have children more than anything in the world but was unable. Patti always believed that life would have been different if her adopted mother had given birth to her. As a result of seeing her mom's pain and sometimes visible sadness, Patti had done quite a bit of soul-searching regarding the challenge of being a mother. She wondered if her mother's life view would find root in her own confidence to be able to love and accept any children she might have or if she should even have any in the first place. She prayed and prayed with tears and questions. She believed she had no divine answers regarding motherhood, so she came to the decision that she'd consider being a single parent if she did not marry. Poor Mother! Nowadays, it would be possible for her to give birth, given the advances of science and medicine, but years ago, it wasn't always possible or if possible very demanding financially.

Patti fingered a small, heart-shaped gold locket that now hung on a special chain around her neck. She didn't wear it often but decided to bring it and wear it this weekend while she was at home. If she dwelled on the circumstances surrounding the locket for too long, she became sad to the point of depression. While the family reminisced about her past loves, there was one of her boyfriends who was never mentioned. This weekend was no exception. His name did not even come up. Her mother wanted her to marry and was obsessed with it. She also made clear her desires that Patti not only marry but have lots of children. Mother couldn't wait until grandchildren filled her home. A silver tear ran down Patti's left cheek. She wiped it away and with it the thoughts running through her mind. Life was too short to dwell on misfortunes for any length of time.

"God, You know all things," she prayed. "I have made a real mess of my life. I've often made wrong choices. You have given assurance that all things work together for good to those who love You. I believe I love You. I don't really know how strong my love is. Your kind of love is different than human love. You love the unlovely. You love unconditionally. You love me for whatever reason, and I don't always love people that way … or even myself. Help me not only to be worthy of Your love but to love others as You do. Amen." From somewhere in the back of her mind, a Bible passage came shining through her thoughts. *"And this is the reason that we love Him, because He first loved us" (John 4:19).*

The weekend continued uneventfully, and soon it was time to return home. When Patti arrived at her house, she unloaded the things from the back of her SUV and took Cal's sock in to wash it. When she looked at her phone, she noticed her message light was blinking. She pressed the play button and heard a man talking back to her.

"Hello. I am looking for Exquisite Cakes. I want you to bake me one of your cakes. I saw your web page. Could you please return my call?" Patti took down the number and dialed. She saw that he had called from a cell phone. The voice on the end of the line was pleasant. She guessed he was fairly young.

"I found your website on the Internet and am interested in a heart-shaped cake I saw there. My sister is getting married in three weeks, and I will be in town tomorrow. Could I please meet with you to discuss the design?"

Patti agreed and gave him her address, and then she set up an appointment for four o'clock in the afternoon on the following day.

Jim's flight to Santa Rosa was short and sweet. Alaska Airlines delivered him to his destination in record time, and the flight attendant who waited on him was a beauty. Her number even now was tucked inside his sports coat pocket. He rented a car and found the directions to Patti's place. He pulled into her drive about ten minutes early.

Patti heard the car and looked at her watch. If this was her client, he was early. She quickly ran a comb through her hair and touched up her mouth with lip gloss. The doorbell rang, and she hurried to open it. There, standing before her, was Jim. She recognized him immediately, or at least she thought she did. She could picture him in a recent movie she had seen.

"Pardon me, but are you Jim, from the movies? You look so much like him."

Jim grinned before lying, "Not really, ma'am. I just look like him. A lot of people mix us up. I have signed a few autographs for him, but he never thanked me personally. No, this is another guy. If I had his money, do you think I would be here looking at cakes?"

"No, I don't suppose you would, especially not at my place," replied Patti. "Hollywood is a long way away. I don't suppose any movie star would come all the way to Santa Rosa to buy a cake from me. I am not really that well known." Patti sighed a little bit as she spoke. She really was not.

"Would you like to be?" Patti was startled at his inquiry. For the first time, she looked at him, studying his features and mannerisms. He was around six feet tall and had long blond hair and blue eyes. He appeared easygoing, and by the way he dressed, she could tell he had money. Perhaps he did know some influential people, but cakes were a little out of the average man's concern. Cakes usually were talked about in women's circles. She opened the door and invited him in. They sat down and began to discuss what he requested.

"What cake did you have in mind?" she asked.

"On your website, there was a pretty heart-shaped cake that was all decorated in many different kinds of flowers with ribbons, birds, and roses. I want one like it."

Patti opened her book to the picture of the Makaira cake.

"Is this the one you had in mind?"

"Yes, I think my sister would like this one. Can you make it large enough to feed five hundred people?" He got the question off quickly, like it was the most important thing about the cake, the size.

Patti looked at him again with a bit of surprise. And this time, a quizzical expression appeared on her face. She wasn't sure if this character was believable or not.

"You said this was for your sister? How come you are taking care of the wedding cake for your sister? I have never had a bride not want to be a part of designing and the putting together all parts of her wedding, even the cake. Did she send you here to order it?"

"Uh … n-n-noooo," he stammered. "I, er, wanted to give this to her. She did tell me to look up wedding cakes on the net, and when I saw you … or I mean the cake, I came to see what you … I mean, what your cakes were like. I know her theme and color scheme so I can make the right calls in this order. Besides, I did spend a couple of hours and this cake beat everything else I saw. I actually told my sister I would handle it."

"Well, while you're here, you can look at several pictures of different cakes. I'm sure I can come up with one your sister will like." Patti had complete confidence in her ability, and it showed in her features.

"I want this one," he replied. "Will it feed five hundred people?"

"If you cut it into small enough pieces it will, but everyone then would only have a couple of bites. I could make the middle heart with an extra layer. That would add one hundred people to its capacity. All you need is a couple more side cakes to make up the difference. So we could make the middle cake with an extra layer and two extra hearts. What flavor would you like them to be?"

"My favorite is chocolate, but my sister would prefer lemon. She is really fond of that flavor. I think you could probably make three or four different flavors since there are individual cakes." Jim, enjoying this part of their conversation about cakes, wanted to take this beautiful decorator to the next level. And so he began.

"Are you married?" he inquired, hoping she'd say no.

"No, I'm not. Why do you ask?"

"Are you seeing anyone?"

"No, but I'm confused. Why does my marital status have anything to do with baking and decorating cakes, if you please?"

"I thought maybe we could go get a little something to eat at a restaurant and there discuss this cake thing further. I am hungry; it's no ruse. They only gave out a small bag of snacks on the plane. Here is why I asked about your social life, while we were in a restaurant, I didn't want your boyfriend or husband to come in and surprise us while we were eating. There is not a lot more to discuss except the arrangements. I really do want that heart-shaped cake for my sister, but it needs to feed five hundred people. Perhaps we can figure out how to do that over dinner. Do you know of any swanky restaurants in the area? I'm from out of town, you know!"

"We have quite a selection of restaurants here in town, depending. What kind of food do you like? Did you have a certain taste in mind?" The young lady tried to remember the locations of the different places as she responded.

"I like all types, but this evening, I'm craving seafood, so hop in my car and show me the way to a good seafood restaurant. I'm taking you out to dinner."

"My mother warned me never get into cars with strange men. I'm afraid I need to drive myself. It will be better that way anyway. I have another appointment with a customer at seven this evening to discuss their cake order. We could still grab dinner, though, if you want, then if necessary meet again later to finish the details for your sister's cake. How does that sound?"

Jim made a clever quip but extended his hand to the decorator. "I know your name is Patti Murray. I saw it on your website, but I never gave you mine. It's John Stratton," he lied again. "I'm from LA and am feeling a bit out of my comfort zone. I took a room at the Garden Inn; it's supposed to be a five-star hotel. I flew all the way out here and rented this beautiful new car, and now you say you won't even give me the courtesy of chauffeuring you out for a while? Oh, Miss Murray, you cut me to the quick. Straight to the heart!" he teased. "I'm hurt, and I'll survive, but think of all the effort I went through just to meet with you."

"You are absolutely right, Jim—I mean *John*, if that's

your *real* name. You give me even more reason why I should not ride with you, especially at this time. We have only just met and do not know one another. My mother always told me never to ride with strangers from out of town. So, if we are to get going, you can follow me in my car to the restaurant."

"What else did your mother tell you about men and dating?"

"She said I was never to trust anyone I do not know and then sometimes not even after you know someone. I think that's good advice, don't you?"

Moments later, the two cars sped off with Patti in the lead. She headed for the Brasserie Restaurant on Railroad Street. When they arrived and were seated at their table, the waiter brought them menus and took their drink orders. Patti fascinated Jim. He loved her wit and realized she was quite different from the stream of empty-headed playthings he was usually entertaining. All the other women knew he was a wealthy movie star; therefore, he did not trust any of them and their ulterior motives. There were hundreds of good-looking women running around wanting to marry money. He was sick of it. This girl, oh, this girl … she was different, really different! If he could keep up the charade, he might win her over. And he would know she'd like him for who he was inside and not the money thing. He also did not want any other people questioning him about his identity and hinting that he was the actor Jim from the movies so he took out and put on a pair of sunglasses.

"Now, how can we get that cake to feed five hundred people?" he persisted.

"If you want it to feed five hundred people, I will have to either make the side hearts as large as the center heart, or I can make extra side cakes in heart shapes to match the theme. Or one other idea is to make a second-layer smaller heart on top of the center cake. I simply need you or your sister to choose what you'd like best. And I suppose if you wanted it as is, only larger ... hmmm," Patti continued, her voice becoming lower and lower as she thought through the different plans. "I could make a larger flat cake and cut out a heart shape." Patti was whispering now. "There is only one problem in doing that. The second and third layer would need to be exact replicas. Now if I only had those pans I saw at Nancy's Kitchen Korner, I wouldn't have to take a chance of imperfect cake shapes."

"How much are they?" asked Jim, straining to hear her every word.

"About eighty dollars," she replied, surprised anyone heard her last few thoughts. Patti was not one to take favors.

Jim, in a flash, laid two crisp one-hundred-dollar bills on the table from out of his wallet, while asking, "Will that cover it?"

"That's wayyyy too much," she replied, handing one of the bills back. As she made the gesture, she noticed that Ben Franklin had a sly smile on his face.

Jim waved the bill away and replied, "Consider it a

down payment on the cake then. By the way, how much will this cake order cost?"

"Do you want it with or without the real flowers?"

"I want it with the works, and I will need it delivered to Los Angeles. You do deliver in person, don't you?"

"Well, for that distance, it will cost quite a bit extra for the delivery alone. However, the best way to get your cake there, perfectly set up with 'the works,' as you say, would be for me to come to the location. Do you know anyone who has a large oven or perhaps two of them in the same kitchen? If so, I could make the cake there and do this thing right with all the trimmings. Also being in the area would allow me to be close by if any last-minute adjustments need to be made. So, the bottom line really is an expensive proposition, but 'if you have the money, honey, I have the time.'"

Jim grinned, and his adoration grew for this beautiful, witty decorator with each passing minute. Still smiling from ear to ear, he invited Patti to come to LA.

"I would love to have you come and make the cake on site. I'll pay all of your expenses, so don't worry about that. And if you want, I'll even set you up in a hotel unless you would consider staying at my place. I am sure you'd enjoy yourself a lot more in a penthouse than in a stuffy old hotel room and having to run back and forth each day. A hassle, wouldn't you think? Besides, I do have a large oven. In my penthouse with not two but three baking racks. I sometimes bake thirty-six-inch pizzas in it."

"I'd like to meet your sister. As for you offer, I don't think so. For now, I'll accept the hotel room. I just remembered another saying of Mother's: never sleep over at a strange man's house, especially if he's from out of town." Then Patti hid her smile behind her napkin as she teased this Jim-John character, who was declaring himself not to be who he really was. Patti knew he was the movie actor. Well, he was the spittin' image of the actor with his voice and mannerisms. Plus, and this was most important, she had a gut feeling about the guy.

"It sounds as though your mother was very protective of you. How did you ever manage to get out of the house at all? And on your own, too, or does your Mother live with you in your house at the present time?"

"No, she doesn't," Patti answered, picturing the recent weekend she had spent away. "I've been gone from home and out on my own for years now. But just last weekend, I was home for a visit, and we had a nice long talk about my finding a suitable husband. We went through the list of all the guys I dated in high school and college, and Mother decided none of them are good enough for me."

Jim paused and pondered her comments for a long time before he responded. Then he continued the conversation. "Patti—may I call you that, or would you prefer Miss Murray?"

"Oh please, by all means, you can call me Patti if I can call you Jim," she tested.

"Like I said, it happens all the time. People get me mixed up with that guy, but he runs around in a limo and has his own driver. Did I mention that I met him once?"

"No. It might be very entertaining. How did it happen and where? I want to hear the whole story."

"Before I tell you the story, I want to ask you a question. How would you like to bake cakes that run into the thousands of dollars?" At this point Jim removed his shades and plunked both of his elbows down on the table. Patti's protective mother might object but he had snared more than one woman doing this. He now deliberately violated all of the social distance rules and leaned forward, moving his head to within a few inches of her face, then proceeded to stare directly into her eyes. Patty could not help but stare back. His blue eyes had little gold flecks in them. As she watched the flecks appeared to move in circles, heightening the deep, sky-blue color. She was hypnotized and could not help herself. Whatever he was doing, it was working. Jim now gave her a silent, mental command. "You are mine!"

"That would be very interesting," Patti tore herself away but he drew her back ever so gently. The young decorator was not able to grasp completely the concept of that much money, thousands of dollars per cake. Again her mind began wandering into this new subject, again just as quickly he drew her back. Jim wasn't finished speaking. Knowing she was snared he deliberately gave the thought command again. "You are mine," he winked his right eye then in a serious tone, continued, "I have several influential friends. And there are no cake decorators in our vicinity that even come close to your talents. I researched a number of them, and so did my sister, Kathy, and none of them hold a candle to your works. If you would like to expand your income, client list, and really get your name out there, you need me. Just say the word, and I will put lots of people in contact with you. Whatever cakes you can imagine, you'll be able to create just like you told me earlier. Let me give you one example. My friend

Dave came into a little money when his old man died. He wanted to throw a party but not sound like the old man was gone, if you know what I mean. Dave's dad loved Jack Daniels. So for the party, Dave had a cake decorator make a four-foot-tall cake that was a replica of Old Number Seven in memory of Dad. This guy made a killing. He walked away with more than ten thousand dollars for making that cake. There were hardly any expenses for the cake guy, 'cuz he made it on site, bein's it was so tall and all. So, yeah, he made a fortune in profit!"

Patti wondered at this story. She also wondered why this man in front of her had suddenly changed his accent and the tone of his voice. If this wasn't evidence enough of his acting ability, nothing would be. She was also intrigued. She had never come close to getting $10,000 for a cake, but then she had never made a four-foot cake either.

"This may be a stupid question, Jim, but did your friend Dave enjoy any of the liquid Jack Daniels at that party," she mused.

"He certainly did. We all did—got drunk, that is. I had a bad hangover the next day and missed work. Was my boss ever mad! She would have fired me if she could have."

"Your boss is a woman, Jim?"

"Well kind of. You probably have watched *Malcolm in the Middle* a time or two. You know the theme Song, 'You're Not the Boss of Me Now,' by the group They Might Be Giants? That is kind of the way it is with my boss. She would like to be my boss and control all the decisions for sure, but I won't let her."

Their meal arrived, and as they began to eat the

delicious seafood, Jim wove the tale of how he and the actor met. Patti had the privilege of hearing how the two men met in a restaurant while both were eating, of all things, seafood! One would have thought Jim was repeating a memory as his words and details flowed as smoothly as practiced lies are able to unfold.

"He even hinted at the fact that we could double in one of his movies if the need arose. He has my telephone number, but unfortunately I have never received a call from him."

Patti was amused at Jim's story but was a little glad it began to wind down because when she glanced up at the wall to see the time, the hands on the clock indicated it was time to leave right away. Patti always made a point to be punctual, either to be ready on time or even a bit early for her appointments. She bid Jim good-bye as she handed him one of her business cards. She suggested he call as soon as he was able to work out the details for this wedding order, the dates, times, travel, and any other necessary arrangements that Patti needed to make in order to prepare and schedule time for his sister's wedding, and then she was gone.

Jim remained seated at their table in the restaurant for nearly half an hour before leaving. He really missed the young lady companion who had graced his life the past few hours. Lucky for him, his flight was leaving early the next morning. He could be back in LA by early afternoon and get on with his house hunting. Perhaps he could find a place and purchase it before this Patti Cake woman arrived. With new neighbors, he might just be able to keep their prying eyes out of his private life for a while before they realized who he was. He did indeed enjoy a good rest during this brief getaway. It was great to be away from the daily grind and experience a little freedom of choice as well. He might just do it again if a continued friendship with this mysterious strawberry was possible. Perhaps he would even find an upscale place to rent for a few months if he could not convince her to move quickly. Deep inside Jim knew this was one of those one-in-a-million woman like his sister. She had everything he wanted and needed plus so much more. Santa Rosa, who would have believed his one and only could have been just a few cities to the north? The alcoholic beverages he had consumed were taking effect. He should probably get back to his room and grab a little rest. With the flight and everything else he had planned, tomorrow could be a very busy day. All and all he considered this first pitch to be a hit of great success. He had gotten to first base only but … next time he saw her, he knew he would score a home run.

Chapter 4
CAN A HOUSE BUY LOVE?

Jim went directly from the airport to his office where he happily discovered a message awaiting him from his realtor friend, Karl. In the message, Karl explained he had found two homes that closely matched the description Jim had given. Immediately, the returned vacationer picked up the phone and called him. They made an appointment to visit the homes that very afternoon. These mansions included extensively large interiors, as well as elaborate outdoor living areas. They had more than one outdoor patio and pool with lounging areas. The landscaping in and around the grounds was meticulous and grand. Located farther outside the city and into the suburbs, even the driveways were more secluded than his current dwelling. Just the main building alone dwarfed his entire penthouse altogether. As the realtor pulled into the drive of the first home, Jim grew more than hopeful—he was elated in fact. This home appeared to be exactly what he was looking for. The first thing he noticed was that it had three stories. He put on his shades and walked up to the front door with Karl. It was a privilege just to be able to actually step inside, and Jim was excited to begin. First, Karl pulled out the standard key and unlocked the box. Then he pulled out a small remote control and deactivated the security system. Finally, a small brown envelope produced one more key from inside the box. The door was unlocked and opened. At last, they were inside.

There were three stories just as Jim had requested. The ground level was very spacious. The house had many windows, and a large fence surrounded the property for secure privacy. With each step, Jim grew more and more enthusiastic. As he looked out the window, he noticed the landscaping. It was luxurious—lush and balanced with earth, water, and plants. Looking out the various windows, to his delight, he discovered the yard was perfect from all angles. The kitchen looked out over a small waterfall flowing at the backside of an herb garden. Jim wondered if Patti could cook as well as she could bake and decorate cakes—not that she would need to if things worked out well between them. He barely knew the woman yet he knew enough to realize that Patti could certainly spice up his rather dull lifelike existence. So far, he had refrained from marrying because he hadn't felt the need to tie himself down to one woman for a life sentence. Women were plentiful, and he never had to worry about going anywhere alone unless he chose to. Yet for some reason, after seeing Patti's picture on the website, followed by meeting her in person, he began to have feelings for something more in life than just shallow experiences and acquaintances. At long last, his desire to share his life with someone was taking a small hold somewhere inside. There was this longing growing stronger with each passing day. Jim did not want to share his life with just any woman. He wanted a special one-in-a-million woman. Was there a woman out there somewhere who was unspoiled with wealth, had some semblance of intelligence, and had a good heart? He thought for a moment and then realized none but Patti fit that picture ... so far.

Upon hearing his name, Jim snapped out of his daydream and continued his tour. Off the master bedroom on the first floor was the main swimming pool. French doors opened out onto a large patio where a modern-styled, rather grand-looking, sunken spa sat within flagstone. Except for the location of the master bedroom on the first floor, everything Jim saw appeared to be perfect. They approached the stairs; however, as Jim began the ascent, Karl interrupted.

"There's an elevator if you care to use it." Karl led Jim over to the elevator door and pushed the call button. It opened instantly. Within seconds, they arrived on level 2. This floor was where Jim wanted to live if he purchased this home. The first room they entered was a huge and spacious bedroom. The carpet was soft and plush, and as one stepped onto it, there was a deep thickness that cradled one's foot. The full bathroom, complete with another large spa, had two shower heads emptying into it. This swayed Jim into another daydream or thought that both he and his wife would not only be able to shower at the same time but also control the temperature of the water on their own side. Jim had been frustrated with his former experiences. Some of the women he had dated had ventured into the shower with him, and the water temperature he wanted was always too hot or too cold for the girlfriend. He liked to finish off with a cold shower. *Believe it or not,* Jim thought to himself, *that water temperature issue really had interfered with my relationships.* A couple of girlfriends decided it was not such a little problem, and they broke up with him over this water thing. Now that would never need happen again.

Snapping back to the reality at hand, Jim noticed a huge center room large enough for every entertainment gadget imaginable. An area for a giant three-D television was ready and wired with large speakers mounted in the walls. Although no television was present, the wall was prepped with mounts and ready for installation. Doors closed over the area, so if he wanted to cover the tube, he would be able to do so. The other assortment of rooms fit in quite nicely with what he had imagined. He made up his mind before he ever entered the elevator to continue touring the third and final floor. This level would accommodate his office and gym. He loved working out and as he contemplated this fact while at the same time looking around the room, Jim realized to convert this space as he wanted would be a quick and easy job. They entered the elevator and were at ground floor before he could count to five.

"This elevator is fast, Karl. It's a lot quicker than running up and down all those stairs."

"You're right about that," responded the older man as he pulled the keys out of his pocket. "Do you like what you see so far?"

"It's perfect. I don't even need to see the other place, or any others for that matter. I've made up my mind. How much are they asking?"

"Right around six million" came the reply.

"Good," responded Jim. "That's well within the price

range I'm looking for. Call the owners right now and offer them five million, cash. I'll be calling my bank and arranging for financing just as soon as I get home."

"Aren't you getting in a hurry, Jim? You haven't seen the second place yet; I think you'd better take a look at it before you make a decision."

"I don't need to. I like this one." Jim gave a final, matter-of-fact emphasis on "I don't need to."

"Okay, it's your call, but you might really like the other place. Of the two, I'd choose the latter. It's only a little farther out of town, if you have time … or would you rather not? I mean, if you are in a hurry …" Karl's voice drifted off into the silence as a picture of the occupants and their looks of anticipation crept back into his mind.

Jim looked at his Rolex. Well, he thought, he did have plenty of time, so why not? But he could not even imagine anything better than this dream home here.

"Okay," he replied to his friend. "Let's take a look at it then, but it'll have to be really exceptional to beat this one." The realtor sent a quick text message to the expectant party. Then he and Jim hopped into the car. In a few short moments, they were pulling off the road onto the driveway of a large, spacious estate. It sprawled out over the top of a rolling hill. It was not three stories but a trilevel with an open Spanish design. There was a lot more square footage to this house, too. The gate opened automatically as they pulled up, and a gatekeeper looked into the car, addressing the realtor by name.

"It's good to see you, Karl. The owners are waiting for you in the house. Please, drive on in." The car crept forward over the spotless driveway. There was an immediate sense of warmth about the place. Now that Jim felt this homeyness around him, he realized the last house was void of any feeling whatsoever—no warmth, nothing along the lines of a home but rather a structure with techy gadgets and gizmos strewn about, yet strangely empty of life. This place, however, gave Jim a solid, positive appeal, drawing him in as he viewed the grounds. As far as upkeep and landscaping, this home included a much larger lawn and everywhere his gaze fell, it was tidy—no, it was *immaculate*! Jim thought the price tag on this one had to be a lot higher. Karl stopped in front of the five-car garage and got out. At the same time, a small, pretty lady opened the front door and invited the men to come in.

"We have been expecting you, Jim, and you too, Karl," she said softly. "We have seen all of your movies, Jim. I think they should nominate you for best actor in that last role you played. That was a great movie! Oh, please, come on in."

Jim thought he recognized this woman. There was something very familiar about her, too familiar.

As the young actor entered the door, he was immediately impressed. The place was warm and lovely. The furniture was in perfect order. Everything went together like pieces in a puzzle. The kitchen, well stocked, was equipped with an abundance of cupboard and counter space. The warm scent of home-cooked food drifted out from the oven, and suddenly, Jim was very hungry. An elderly man with silvery gray hair appeared in the doorway, and Jim recognized him instantly. This man was Jim's very first manager. He had retired about five years earlier and now looked older than Jim ever remembered him. He went up to Ken and grabbed his hand with a warm, firm grip. As the two men shook hands, Jim began to speak.

"It is so good to see you again, Ken. This home of yours is more than beautiful, you know? Do you really plan to sell it? Are you able to leave this splendor?"

"Yes, Jim. The upkeep alone is too much for Mother and me. And it seems to grow into a bigger and bigger burden all the time. Our son wants us to settle down into a charming little place located in the Palm Springs area. And we are looking forward with excitement to this new chapter in our lives. And too it'll be good to be closer to our family. You know, our grandchildren are at that age when we could really enjoy them. So we plan to move as soon as you purchase our place." The elderly gentleman still had a spark of humor. He winked at Jim after finishing the last sentence.

They continued their tour of this vast residence. Jim was more and more impressed with each step he took. Every room was spotless, and there it was again, that homespun feeling of warmth and coziness. There was one other thing, but he could not put his finger on it yet. A thought popped into his mind, and he wanted to buy everything in the house, not just the outer shell. He wondered if it were possible. Jim could buy everything, furniture and all. If he could afford this, it would be the best place possible for his life. It was more than perfect, and it would be so wonderful to settle down into such a comfortable environment. All he believed he needed was a true-love wife. Then he'd be ready to raise a family with four or five rowdy kids. After all, there was life built right into this place. The kids could safely romp and play in the yard to their hearts' content and be secure doing so with the gate and wall surrounding it. However currently, Jim had no wife nor kids with whom to settle. He figured this home would be great in about three years. That would give him plenty of time to woo this Patti Cake girl or any other lovely woman into his waiting arms for forever. He was so preoccupied by his thoughts on how he was going to accomplish this feat, he completely missed a part of the tour, including one of the swimming pools, until the party was ready to leave the grounds and at the patio doors.

"This is the pool I was telling you about, Karl." Ken opened the door and went out onto the deck. Jim followed, trying to stay focused. The backyard was even better than the front. Though not as spacious, it was large enough for a couple romping boys, and there was a full-sized basketball court. The outdoor court flooring had a spongy feel and was much easier on the feet than hard, cold cement. Jim had never seen anything quite like it before. He picked up a basketball from the rack and dribbled up to the hoop. As he landed a hook shot, he heard applause and looked over to see the husband and his sweet little lady sitting side by side, holding hands like newlywed lovers. Jim thought about how nice these people were. Earlier, in his youth and beginning career, he believed they were so difficult and hard on him, always demanding his best performance. However, through the years, he grew to love them fiercely. In a moment of impulse and youthful inexperience, he just up and left them when a producer wooed him to come over to his company for a big-budget movie offer. Or rather, in a flash decision with only thoughts of big money and stardom, he ran and never looked back. Deep down was a residue of great regret and guilt. So Jim hadn't planned on seeing the couple ever again. He believed he was gutless not to face them but had tried to leave that in the past—until now. He had known about their plans for trying to secure a new contract. They had been planning that for quite some time. What he didn't know was they had worked very hard and managed to get Jim not just any movie contract but one for Disney. All the papers were drawn up and ready to present to the lad; they had planned to surprise him. When he up and left, they took quite a loss. He decided to apologize right then, since they were both there in front of him. He returned the ball back to the rack and ambled toward the waiting couple. Looking deep into the eyes of the little lady first and then her husband, he confessed a heartfelt apology and explained he had no excuse but foolhardiness for his leaving without so much as a word. He truly was sorry for the lack of compassion and judgment he exercised in his sudden departure. He realized in doing so what an inconvenience he had caused these dear people to endure in their hearts as well as their wallets. His words were elaborate, but he wanted to express how deeply sorry he was for what he had done so he knelt in front of them and took both their wrinkled hands in his own.

"It was foolish of me to leave you folks. At the time, I was much younger and mainly focused on two things: bigger and bigger than that. I wanted a fat wallet and bigger roles, even main characters. And at the time, these desires consumed me. However, if I had a chance to redo everything again, I would have stayed with you. Could you please consider forgiving me?"

Without any hesitation, the little lady stood up, placing her small, free, wrinkled arm around his neck while giving him a warm, motherly hug.

"Of course I forgive you, sweetie," she whispered in Jim's ear.

Ken also leaned in closer, but he was not as affectionate.

"You were my favorite actor, Jim. You always have been. The first time I saw you, I fell in love with you. You were a son to me and will always be so in my heart. We have followed your career and silently cheered you on all the way. You have worked hard and have finally made it to the big league. I'm not so sure if we could have kept up with you. Of course, there were those few edgy films in which you weren't the star character, yet all in all, they paid off. We really want you to have this home of ours if you'd like it. There's no one else in the world we'd rather sell it to than you, Jim. We know we could easily get a high-end selling price for our home here, but Karl mentioned that your range was a bit lower than that. You see, we are far more interested in having an owner who loves it here and will enjoy it for their family as we have, more than monetary gain. So that's the reason we are willing to bring our price down."

Jim looked around at his former employers and gave the elderly sweetheart a gentle hug.

"I wish I would have known you better when I was in your employ, but what I learned to know about you, I have always loved. You were like a second mom to me, only you made more of an effort to spend time with me than my real mother did. I guess that nature's maternal instinct is a lot stronger than I ever knew. I am so thankful for all the love you gave me. In a way, I believe your love helped me be strong on my own and believe in myself to keep going. I really appreciate all you did for me, especially your guidance and support in helping me begin my movie career. I could say that you were there with me all the time. I don't know if I'm responsible enough to fill this house though. I have no wife, and I certainly would hate to see that luxurious kitchen go to waste. However, it is possible I may have found a prospective partner." Jim paused for a moment, thinking about recent events. Everything was happening so fast! Continuing on, Jim explained, "It was only yesterday I met her, yet already I'm in love. By the end of our short three hours together, I sensed a kindred spirit about her, like I had known her all my life. She's intelligent and beautiful, creative and witty, and bakes and decorates cakes for a living. I just placed an order for my sister's wedding cake. It is one I chose from her portfolio, and it is a beauty! Here is a picture of it." He pulled out his cell phone, opened his photos, and scrolled down to the bottom. Then he leaned over and showed it to the couple. They were genuinely impressed. Then he showed them her picture. There looking back at them was this movie-star-like creature of beauty. There was something about her eyes that showed her intelligence and wit.

"I intend to remove this sweetheart from her regular element and see if the lifestyle of the rich and famous will spoil her as it has all the others. Right now, as I see her, she is perfect. It is sad though, because often if one adds a little money on a woman, there's a turn from sweet to sour and a bit of prickly, too, I might add."

Now it was Ken's turn, and he spoke up.

"I know what you mean, Jim. I looked for years for just the right woman, and then God sent this love to me. She settled me down, bringing peace and order to my life. Don't settle for second rate, Jim. If you look long enough and far enough, you'll find the love of your life. They say women are like apples. The best ones are at the top of the tree, but few men will take the time and make an effort to climb up and pick one. Instead, they settle for the ones on the lower branches or even scoop some off the ground. A woman scooped up off the ground is rarely, if ever, a good idea, Jim. The ground is where all of the rotten ones lay. Reach for the best, Jim. Reach for the top. Don't settle for less than the best."

The four reentered the home and finished the tour. The cook called them to dinner. The noon meal was lavish with course following course, all served on a delicate yellow rose-patterned bone china. The four friends chattered and laughed during each course. Ken's little missus stopped to share some of the chef's culinary secrets of success. Fresh herbs, fruits, and veggies from their own estate grounds were the main secret everyone enjoyed. The afternoon passed quickly following their meal, and in everyone's mind, it was over too soon and time to say good-bye. Karl and Jim bid adieu, and as the two men parted, Jim looked back and surveyed the scenic estate. All that it lacked was the sweet little face of a strawberry blonde somewhere a plane flight away in Santa Rosa.

"How much do they want for this place, Karl?" asked Jim, hoping the price would not floor him.

"They are asking $13.5 million. However, for you and only you, they are willing to lower the price to $11 million. Their reasons as they explained to you were to see you there and happy in the home they loved so much. To them, your happiness will make up for any monetary difference. They also had a request if maybe you wouldn't mind. From time to time, they'd very much like to bring their grandchildren over for an occasional swim in the pool. You know how much kids love water, and this was home to the entire family. They all love the place! And there's one other thing you need to know. They want to sell it to you furnished, just as you saw it with all the same furniture and decorations. That alone must be worth more than $2 million. They said they'd only be taking their personal belongings to their new home in Palm Springs. You know, Jim, I've been showing this property for more than a month now, but when I called and mentioned that you were interested in buying a house and I was planning on bringing you over, they were ecstatic. They both insisted in meeting with me privately in order to fill me in on all the details. You really should take it. I'm guessing you'll never find a better place for the value. And that's a fact. This couple must really care a lot about you to make that kind of an offer."

Jim paused to contemplate the events that had occurred over of the past couple of days. In his mind's eye, he was able to visualize Patti Cake baking her cakes in that spacious kitchen and sitting right beside her in the plush, cushioned chair; the sweet, little missus, who really was the only mother he'd ever known, and there too, the father he had come to love. His real mother was always off away from home, traveling the world with some boyfriend or another. And Dad, he was long gone. He dropped out of sight years ago when Jim was just a lad. That was before his talent and good looks were discovered and quite accidentally by this very couple.

Finally, after thinking everything through, Jim decided, "I will do it under one condition, Karl. I found a cake decorator for my sister's wedding reception, and she is coming to town in a few weeks to make the cake here on location. If Mrs. Sears will grant us the use of her kitchen, *and* I can persuade Patti Cake, this cute decorator, that I will buy this house for her and myself if she will make the best cake of her entire career, then I'll take it."

Karl chuckled at the latter part of the comment, surprising Jim. Karl seldom cracked a smile. In fact, he was usually very serious and all business, so it was good to see that this affluent friend of his could relax a minute and smile. He made a sly remark. "I do not expect you will have any trouble at all persuading Miss Patti Cake to marry you. If I were a gambling man, I would bet you could persuade any girl you wanted to marry you. I think you have yourself a house."

The two pulled up to Jim's penthouse, and he hopped out of his friend's car. There was a crowd of fans and tourists waiting. As he made his way to the door, cameras began flashing and blinding him, and one tourist even jumped out smack in front of the popular actor, trying to block the way so all had an opportunity to get his photograph. This stranger began taking photos at a close-up range, forcing

Jim to cover his face and run. The door opened quickly as his sister saw the predicament and ushered him into their home and out of sight from prying eyes. Jim thought about the new home and what an advantage it would be with the gate and tall walls. *Oh,* he thought fervently, *to keep the paparazzi out of his life! Wouldn't that be just wonderful!* He confirmed in his mind that the next day, he'd take his sister over to get her opinion of the place. He thought how much he'd miss her after the wedding. She was really the only family he had, with the exception of his chef and a part-time housekeeper who came in three times a week. But they were not *real* family; still he was glad to have them in his life.

Back in Santa Rosa, Patti had just put the finishing touches on another beautiful cake. This one, she had contracted with delivery included. It was for this reason she had purchased a small van. She kept her new little van in the garage where she could easily load her delicious treats conveniently from the kitchen. She took three cakes out, one at a time, and carefully placed them in the rig. She returned to the kitchen door to lock it securely and then got in the van and closed the garage door with her remote as she drove away. It took less than half an hour to arrive at her destination. She carefully carried the cakes into the reception area of the church and finished the touch-ups with her frosting kit before and after stacking the layers. This was her classic white wedding cake. The wedding was very economic, and costs had to be kept to a minimum.

Patti noticed the decorations were elegant yet inexpensive. As she placed the miniature bride and groom on the top layer, she spotted a teeny speck of frosting on her index finger. She quickly placed her finger in her mouth and was surprised to feel a sharp point on one of her teeth. Patti wondered if perhaps part of a filling had chipped off and fallen out. It had been more than a year since she had seen her dentist. Was it possible that her teeth had developed some problems? She'd call and make an appointment the very next day to see her dentist as soon as he had an opening. The countless tastings of frosting had finally taken their toll, branding her with a sweet tooth as well as giving her a nice cavity.

Patti picked up the payment from the bride's mother and drove home. She decided to look up her dentist's phone number right away and not wait. After all, it was only three o'clock in the afternoon. Certainly, the office would be open. She dialed the number and waited.

A scratchy voice answered. "Dr. Ripland's office. How may I help you?"

"Yes, I'd like to make an appointment with my dentist. His name is Smith something. Dr. Joel Smith, I believe. Does he have any current openings?"

"I am sorry, ma'am, but Dr. Smith retired a few months ago," explained the scratchy voice. "He sold his practice to Dr. Ripland. We have transferred all Dr. Smith's regular patients, who wished to stay, and we would be happy to have you come in for your checkup to get acquainted with Dr. Ripland at that time. Our soonest opening though is 1:00 p.m. two weeks from today. Would you like to take that appointment?"

"Let me look at my schedule, and I will get back to you in a second." Patti returned with her appointment book and checked the date. There were no orders due or any baking scheduled for that day.

"One o'clock would be fine. I have that time open, so yes, I'm available and would like that time please." After she hung up the phone, Patti sat down in her favorite chair, intending to read more of her current novel. She was over halfway finished with it. She had read only a few pages when she jumped up from her chair with a startled revelation. Dr. Ripland? Why did that name seem so familiar? Then she remembered, and as quick as she could, she returned to the phone and hit the redial button. She'd ask if the new dentist was Dr. Cal Ripland. The office phone rang and rang, but there was no answer. His office must have already closed. She would call first thing in the morning. Somehow, she had to know. If this was *the* Dr. Cal Ripland she had met in the store and once again along the side of the road, she'd just die of embarrassment. Ripland was not that common a name, and her intuition suggested that he was the very person she felt she had so unintentionally abused.

Suddenly, Patti grew very tired. It had been a long day. She thought she'd wash the flour dust and frosting from off her tired muscles, catch a quick meal of fresh fruit, and then settle into bed for the evening. Passing by her floor-length mirror on the way to the shower, she caught a glimpse of herself and realized it was time for a leg wax and mani-pedi the next time she went to town. Turning the shower on, she waited for the water to warm before entering.

Patti stayed in the shower for a full half hour. She seldom had the time to afford such a luxury, and when she did, she cherished every moment. She emerged with deep, wrinkled skin and rubbed herself dry with a soft towel. Then she groomed her hair. Then, slipping on a silk nightgown, she retired to the kitchen. First, she peeled an orange and then a banana. She was finishing up with a small apple when the phone rang. It was her closest friend, Kit. She was bored and wanted to get out of the house. She offered to bring over a movie and popcorn. Patti was really not in the mood for company, but after the food entered her stomach, she suddenly felt less tired. Perhaps a movie was just the diversion she needed.

"Okay, Kit. Come on over and bring a good movie with you. Remember last time it was really awful, a real dud."

"You'll like this movie, girl" came the reply.

That was the only thing that bugged Patti about her friend. She insisted on calling her "girl." Patti hung up the phone and dressed quickly. Fifteen minutes later, the doorbell rang and in walked Kit, all bubbly and excited. She nearly ran to the entertainment center and popped in the movie. She grabbed up the remote, and within seconds, large letters began to scrawl across the screen.

"This film has been modified from its original format to fit your television screen." The music started, and the introduction came whirling in from a background of white clouds and blue sky. A golden unicorn appeared, and soon the title exploded onto the screen—*Forever Jinxed*, starring Jim Callahan and Julie Petersen. Jim's picture appeared in several stills from various angles followed by Julie's, and then the names of the other actors appeared.

As the film progressed and the main characters graced the screen, Jim began to look very familiar to Patti. She could have sworn that she had been out to lunch that very week with this hunk. He walked the walk and talked the talk of the very man who had entered her doorway just days ago. It was the man who had handed her two crisp one-hundred-dollar bills in the restaurant. It was he and no other she had entertained. There was only one difference that she could see. The man who came to her house called himself John Stratton.

She grabbed the remote from the arm of the chair where her friend was sitting and stopped the movie. Kit was quite upset at this sudden turn of events, but when she saw the bright eyes and broad smile of Patti Cake, she knew her friend had something very important to say.

"He was here, Kit, earlier this week." Patti was jumping up and down in her excitement, and Kit was wondering if her friend had just flipped her lid.

"Who was here, Patti?"

"He was, the movie star, Jim Callahan. He was in this very house ordering a cake for his sister's wedding not less than seventy-two hours ago. He took me out to lunch."

"No way, girl. You are loonier than a baboon. There is no way you could have entertained Jim Callahan here." The look on her face was one of accusation. Her friend was lying.

"Yes way! I'd swear on my mother's grave except my mother is still living. At least my adoptive mother is living, I mean. Anyway, he told me he saw my web page and liked the cake so much, he flew all the way from Los Angeles to order it in person. He's sending me tickets in the mail and paying all my expenses to bake the cake on site. I mean it. I really do."

"I don't believe it. Someone was putting you on. Didn't this so-called look-alike call himself John, you said?"

"Yes, and he said he was often asked for pictures and autographs as if he were Jim, the movie star. All the time, he was questioned if he were the actor. When asked if I thought in my wildest dreams the movie actor, Jim Callahan, would order a cake from me, I promptly suggested the star probably wouldn't have the time to be perusing the Internet for cakes, let alone flying across the state to see or taste one. But the guy who was here and the actor on the screen is one and the same person … or they're identical twins. And I don't recall Jim Callahan being a twin. There was only one movie where he doubled as a twin, and Jim played both roles."

Patti and Kit sat down in their chairs and continued watching the movie. The story was funny. It was a recipe of comedy and romance, well seasoned with the occult. Julie was the jinxed one. She discovered that there were latent powers within her that made her do crazy things. She was perfectly fine most of the time, but whenever Jim came around, a disaster always happened. As the film progressed further, Julie learned to control her powers and used them on the man who pursued her love. In the end, the two never did get together, much to the dismay of Pat and Kit. Instead, Julie used her newly controlled powers to land a young millionaire tycoon. It was another sad saga of a beautiful woman forsaking true love for power, prestige, and money. Women had and have been doing that for centuries, and most likely will continue as long as civilization exists. The girls concluded the film must have been directed by a feminist. Kit backed up a few tracks and stole one last glance at the golden-haired man in the scene where he was dressed only in his briefs. "If you land that hunk, girl, you'll be the most coveted woman in all of California, maybe the whole world!" Kit then bid her friend good night. "I want to know all about it," she declared. "You have to call me the instant those tickets arrive. I won't believe it until I see it with my own two eyes. And then, I still might not believe it." With that, she was out the door.

Patti was really tired now. She undressed and crawled into bed. She dreamed about walking around in a spacious yard with Jim by her side and baking large four-foot cakes in a huge, open kitchen. And who was that sweet little lady with the silver hair beside her, handing her the ingredients? She awoke to the phone ringing. She rolled over and groaned before looking at her clock. It was nine in the morning already. Had she really slept that late?

Chapter 5
IS THERE SUCH A THING AS A SOUR TOOTH?

Mrs. Sanford, Cal Ripland's nosy neighbor, watched from her window and was just in time to see Cal hobbling, barefoot, up to his door. She craned her neck but couldn't see what he was carrying. Why did he have only one shoe on? Wasn't it just a few days ago when he got out of his car with his face covered in what looked ever so much like the white makeup of a pantomime actor? There were even circles around his eyes where the makeup artist painted something special, though what it was she was unable to decipher. Now he was hobbling around with one shoe on and one shoe off. She called Reata, her neighbor across the street. Perhaps Reata could get a better view of things, but Reata could not see either so she scurried to the cupboard and grabbed her binoculars.

"It's his shoe. He is carrying it in his hand," Reata answered. "I wonder what happened to him this time."

Cal had been quite the topic of gossip around this community lately. There was a young lady who had come over to see him three or four times. They figured she was his girlfriend. Then one weekend, an elderly couple had dropped off a tiny, dark-haired child, who appeared to be a miniature model of perfection and cute as could be. She had jumped out of the car and run up to this man, calling him "Daddy." He scooped her up in his arms and carried her inside, closely followed by the elderly couple. So even though he appeared to be single now, these two neighbors deduced he must have had a wife at one time; otherwise, how could he have a daughter? After he had moved into his apartment, it took them about a month to discover he was a dentist. When he arrived home one day with flour covering his face and clothes, they wondered what he was up to. Now, in his limping state of arrival, their curiosity was really aroused.

"What do you suppose happens during his patients' visits at his office, Reata? To come home in such conditions, one really wonders what goes on. I know this sounds crazy, but do you think he gets in fights with his patients?"

"I don't know," Reata replied. "Personally, I hate going to the dentist. That needle they poke in my mouth hurts like the dickens. I have a rather high tolerance for pain too, but if some man with a tender jaw came to have a tooth pulled, he might just stomp on the dentist's foot if he got mad enough."

"Or if he got hurt enough," chimed in the other.

"We need to spread the word that he just might not be the best dentist to patronize in town."

"Yes, you are quite right. If he is that dangerous—and it appears that he is by the looks of things—it's really our duty to warn people in this community that there may be trouble if they go to him to have their teeth worked on. They might live to regret it."

"Then again they might not live to regret it," added the other. "It's guys like this that give dentistry its bad name."

Oblivious to his neighbors' concerns, Cal limped into his home and jumped in the shower as quickly as he could. On the way out, he surveyed his body in the foggy mirror. He was getting a little flabby. It was probably time he went down to the gym and signed up. A few years earlier, there had been bumps and bulges in all of the right places. Granted, he was no Arnold, but his wife had thought him quite the man. He sat down on his bed and looked at his toenail. Right then, he remembered that three years earlier, he had smashed his thumb and purchased a battery-powered "Sizzler." That was the name he had given it. It had two prongs touching each other. When a person pushed the button, the tip of the sizzler got red hot. It would burn through a toenail or fingernail without the pain one would experience if a pin were used to poke a hole through in order to relieve the pain and pressure.

He looked around and remembered where the gadget was. He found it in the medicine cabinet and tested it. The batteries were dead. After rummaging around, he found a couple of AA Energizer batteries and replaced the old ones. He was rewarded with a strong buzzing sound, and in a couple seconds the tip was red hot. He carefully pressed the sizzler to the bottom of his injured toenail. He knew he'd feel a lot better if the pressure of the blood building up was released. As soon as the hole was burned through, a spurt of blood shot out and splattered all over the bedspread. Cal murmured under his breath some unpleasant thoughts that tumbled out into words he rarely used. He usually controlled his speech, but under the circumstances, a cuss word might be okay. Anyway, if that woman had not dropped the jack on his toe, none of this would have happened. Now he would have to throw the bedspread away.

As soon as he said the words though, he felt guilty.

"Oh, Lord," he cried. "I am sorry for losing my temper. I should be more patient. I know that You wouldn't swear. Please forgive me. But that Patti Cake woman got under my skin. Who is she, Lord? She looks so familiar. I have seen the color of her eyes somewhere. Her face looks like someone I know, but I can't place her. Why did You allow her to do it? You could have made the jack miss my toe. You are all powerful. I'm as mad as a hornet. Please help me to control myself. I haven't had these feelings for such a long time. What has gotten into me?"

He looked at the bottom of his foot where he had stepped on the rock. It still hurt but was not punctured. He lay back on his bed and pondered this strange little woman who was thrown in his path on these two unfortunate occasions. She was very pretty. Her face was symmetrical and well defined. Her strawberry-blond hair was just a little wavy and fell softly on her shoulders. She seemed very intelligent, and her personality was quite pleasant too, but the question was this—was she really accident prone? It certainly appeared to be true. What were the odds of two incidents like this happening so close together? One in a million? Or were the odds spread out further? Either fate was playing a nasty trick on him, or she was indeed an accident waiting for him to come by. Another thought entered his mind. In spite of the two unfortunate experiences, he wanted to know her better.

He decided he might even risk taking her out for lunch someday. Surely something bad couldn't happen a third time in a row. Right?

His mind quickly turned to Carissa. She needed a mommy. Grandma and Grandpa had taken her in shortly after Cal's wife had died in a car accident. Grandma was the only mother Carissa knew, and Grandpa was fast becoming her father figure. She needed to come home, but he could not care for her properly while still single and alone. Cal needed a wife and wanted a wife who would not be afraid to raise another woman's child. Patti probably was not the right one for Carissa even though the resemblance between them was uncanny. But neither was the shapely dental assistant who had just recently thrown herself on him at work. Where could a guy go to find a decent woman these days? And not only a decent wife but a loving mother as well?

"You know, God. You know. But please! I need a little help here. Time is flying by so quickly, and my little girl is growing up. Oh, God, please help."

Cal ate a light supper, watched the news, and turned in early. His toe was feeling much better. He went to the trash and looked at the first pair of new shoes he had thrown away just a few days ago. They were the same shoe design as his second pair. After examining them, he discovered the one that was pickled and floured matched the one with the smashed toe. If he polished up the other one, it would serve as a mate for the remaining shoe from the second new pair. That would save him a little money and allow his budget to replace the bedspread. He tossed the pickled shoe and the smashed one back into the trash and then placed the others neatly under his bed before pulling back the covers. In a few minutes, he was sound asleep.

A few days passed. One morning, Cal dragged himself out of bed and decided to take a jog around the block. He put on his sweats and slipped on his running shoes. He only took two steps before remembering the toe. It had been feeling quite good, but this shoe bent right where it hurt, so running was out of the picture, probably for at least a week more. He made a quick breakfast, and before he knew it, the hands on the clock told him he had better get to work.

At the office, Sherry was already getting things ready for his patients. She was an efficient worker and a great asset to his new business. As the day progressed, he went from one room to the other and everyone seemed to be comfortable when they left. He was good at making his patients feel relaxed and comfortable. He prided himself on being as painless a dentist as any out there. Some of his patients wanted to use gas or take a pill to help them relax if they were nervous about going to the dentist; however, Cal was able to work without those additives so to speak. Now, as the day was drawing to a close, he was glad to know there was only one more patient to see. Sherry pulled him into the office.

"This last patient is a replacement. We had a cancellation so I bumped up an appointment from another of the people transferring from Dr. Smith. We are at 72 percent now, and that's excellent for the few months you've been here. I expect we will convert a full 90 percent of the transfers by year's end."

"Do you have this patient's digitals ready?" asked Cal.

"Yes." She smiled and lightly scratched herself a little in one of her more private areas. She was quite pleased that he noticed. He quickly turned his head in the other direction, trying to avoid getting any more embarrassed.

"What are we looking at here?" he asked as he focused on the monitor.

"She has two cavities right next to each other. You can fill them both at the same time. Also a portion of one of her fillings has fallen out. By the way, Cal, how did you come to know her? She said she has met with you a couple of times, and she even brought a cake for you today?"

"I have no idea, Sherry. What did you say her name was?"

"I didn't say her name, but she said you know her by Patti Cake and that she made a cake for you. You haven't been hiding anything from me, have you, dear?"

Cal dropped the papers he was holding and moved quickly over to his office chair. He sat down and then promptly broke out into a cold sweat. There was a roll of paper towels on the bookshelf, so he ripped one off and wiped his forehead. After that, he gazed out the window for a few minutes. Out of habit, he reached into his pocket and took out a couple of breath fresheners. His mind suddenly went numb. Sherry brought him back to reality with a concerned tone in her voice.

"Dr. Ripland! Is there something wrong?"

Startled, Cal turned around to his assistant. She was especially pretty now with that look of concern imprinted on her features. Her face was just inches from his. He couldn't resist. He gave her a quick kiss on the cheek and then sprang up out of his chair.

"Nothing at all, Sherry. I am just glad this day is nearly over! I think I'll go out this evening and stuff myself at the King Buffet. Perhaps I will even get drunk. Oh, but then I would not be able to drive home. And besides I don't drink. Maybe I should start."

"Mind if I tag along?" she asked, tilting her head a bit and intentionally leaning in for another kiss. She didn't get one.

"Not tonight, but I will hold you to it sometime in the future, okay?"

"Okay, Doc. Then we have a date, don't we?" she asked.

He never responded. He simply left the office, heading toward his last patient.

Sherry followed Cal into the room where Patti sat waiting in the chair. Neither she nor the dentist was prepared for what happened next. Patti smiled sweetly up at the doctor.

"I brought this back to you. You left it in my car." She held out her hand with his sock in it. She had washed it, and now it lay neatly folded in her hand. Cal was not usually given to embarrassment, but this was twice it had happened in less than an hour. At the sight of the sock, his face turned three shades of red. Sherry noticed it right away and started to turn red also, only her red was from anger.

"How on earth would one of Cal's socks end up in this lady's car?" she grumbled.

"It was quite by accident, miss. Cal happened to stop and help me with a flat tire and I ended up with his sock."

Cal regained his composure and put a brave smile on his face.

"Thank you, Miss Murray. The other one in my drawer will certainly be glad to be reunited with its mate. Now about your teeth, you have two cavities right next to each other. I have time to fill them today, or if you need, we can set up an appointment to fill them next week. What would you prefer?" He responded with all the professionalism one would expect under the circumstances.

"If you have the time now, then we had better do it" was her reply. She looked up to him with those rare-colored, trusting eyes. Perfect confidence written on her every expression.

"My schedule gets all mixed up at times. I never know when someone will call for an emergency cake. I had to deliver one just last week. I hope you like strawberries. The cake I brought you has fresh ones in it. I made a special trip to the farmer's market to purchase some home-grown ones that were vine ripe. Those commercial strawberries are not very sweet, but these, these will melt in your mouth. You will need to use the cake up quite quickly though, or they will spoil. Your wife and kids should love it." Patti watched closely as she made that last remark. He turned and looked her square in the face.

"I do not have a wife. She passed away a few years ago. So it will be only me. Is there a way to eat the fresh strawberries out of the cake and put the rest in the freezer? I do like strawberries, and I will remember to eat it up quickly." He walked out of the room before she could respond to any of his questions. He was gone for a long time—at least it seemed that way to Patti. She started to get nervous when he didn't come right back. After all, it really had been too long since she had seen the dentist. The assistant came in though.

Sherry propped open Patti's mouth and placed the bracket that held the jaw in an open position. She had done this hundreds of times before, but this time, she deliberately placed the device a little lower than was allowed. It really stretched the back of this client's jaws in a most uncomfortable position. Patti started to gag and then let out a muffled screech, coming right up out of the chair. Cal caught sight of her through the window and hurried to her side. In his haste to get there though, he stepped on the pedal. The chair came up toward him at full speed. Patti was thrown forward with the motion, and one of her knees struck him between the legs. With that unexpected jolt, his foot slipped off the pedal and one knee struck a lever at the side of the chair. The whole thing dropped with incredible speed. There was a thump as it hit bottom, and Patti was thrown back against the chair, giving her neck a little whiplash. She was still howling about the pain in her jaws when the dentist recovered. He took her chin in his hands and gently moved the prop to a more comfortable position. He saw exactly what Sherry had done and became quite upset. He believed she probably did it intentionally from spite. He gave her a stern look of warning. Sherry hadn't even taken the time to swab the area where the needle would penetrate with the numbing solution. He levered the chair back up and looked into Patti's eyes.

"It will be all right, Miss Murray. I am known in my circle as a painless dentist."

Patti could not respond because of the thing in her mouth but managed to get out a few sounds. "Aaaaaaaaaaaaaakaaaya." Her eyes were wide with fear.

This painless dentist knew he'd have a lot of work to do to calm this one down. In order to stay ahead, he might need to bring out the nitrous oxide, better known as laughing gas. He applied the numbing solution to the side of her jaw and left the room for a bit. It would take a few minutes for the tissue to become numb. When he returned, there was a needle in his hand. He asked Patti if the side of her jaw was numb, and she said it was. He poked the needle in the area and started to move it around. Suddenly a horrid taste filled the poor lady's mouth. The needle had come out of its socket, and the Novocain poured all over inside. Patti nearly came up out of her chair again, gagging for the second time. She managed to collect the nasty-tasting stuff in an area at the edge of her tongue. She had to get rid of it, or she would choke. She turned her head and let fly. The liquid, with a generous portion of saliva, came propelling out of her mouth at great speed, along with the end of the needle. It landed squarely on the unsuspecting foot of the assistant. Sherry jumped back as if struck with acid. There sticking out of her loafers was the needle that had just moments ago been in the mouth of the patient in front of her.

She stomped out of the room, muttering something under her breath that neither Patti nor Cal could hear and probably wouldn't have wanted to.

In a few minutes, Cal had Patti reseated comfortably.

Everything was ready to go again. He had to reshoot the jaw, and this time Patti couldn't feel a thing. The whole inside of her head was numb. The rest of the process went along fairly smoothly and, fortunately for Patti, completely painlessly except for a toxic headache. Before long, the cake decorator was out of the chair and moving toward the office. Just before she left the room, however, she ran her numbed tongue over the area that had just been filled. Some blood came out of her partly opened mouth and dropped on the floor.

"Ooooeeeeeeeeeeee." At the sound, Dr. Cal came running back into the room.

"Docca?" questioned Patti as best she could with a thick tongue. "Shoaud thaar ve ah jaggaudd edge on my ooth?"

"No, everything should be fine. Sit down, and we'll have a look." Patti took the chair again, and soon it was adjusted properly. Cal pulled out his mirror and looked at the area. There was fresh blood from a cut on her tongue, but that was not all. There, looking back at him, was the hole where her filling had fallen out. He had filled two teeth but had overlooked the tooth that had the missing filling. After drilling out the old stuff, he had forgotten to fill it. How could that have happened? Never, even in practice, had he done such a stupid thing. And the hole he drilled was very large. Why? He looked at his tray of tools and spotted the magnifying mirror. It was the one with the greatest magnification possible. He started to turn red all over again. In his haste to get this over with, he had made still another mistake.

"I am sorry, Miss Murray, but we seem to have a problem."

"Aah frovlum?" she questioned. "Whah kine of a frovlum?"

"Really, you have to believe me. I have never done this in my entire career. I never filled the tooth with the broken filling. There is still one to go. I am so sorry. I was in such a hurry to"—he paused a moment before continuing—"to do a good job I completely forgot this tooth."

In such a hurry to get rid of me is probably closer to the truth, Patti thought.

Sherry was waiting in the office for longer than the usual wait. It usually did not take long for the patient and doctor to walk to the office; however, when neither appeared, she slowly walked back to see what was taking so long. She half expected to see them kissing, but Patti was back in the chair and Cal had placed the larger, softer apparatus in her mouth.

"Sherry! Will you bring the bib back? I still have more work to do on this last tooth."

Sherry stalked into the room. She looked all over for the bib but could not find it. Finally she spotted it on the counter. She placed it back under Patti's chin and looked around for the pin to hold it there. It was nowhere to be seen. She went through all of the drawers but could not find it. Then she wondered if she had accidentally thrown it in the trash. She opened the lid and started rummaging through the can, but there was no pin. She banged around in the cupboard above the trash, but it wasn't there either. Several sterile pads fell out and landed on the floor.

Patti took all this in with a look of dismay and wonder. What was happening to her? Was this payback for all the pain she had caused Cal?

"Sherry!" scolded the dentist. "What is all that banging about?"

The assistant looked at her boss. He was filling the tooth now. The bib was neatly pinned around Patti's neck. *Where in the blank*, she thought, *did he find it?* This was just too much for her, and now she was very, very angry. First this pretty woman came waltzing into the office, claiming to know the dentist whom she, Sherry, had claimed as her own. Then this same woman appeared to be on very intimate terms with Cal by producing one of his socks. And if that wasn't enough, this horrible, awful lady had deliberately bribed Cal with the most beautiful cake the assistant had ever seen. Not only were there real strawberries inside, but this, this thing had made some out of frosting that looked even more real than the real ones. Aside from showering all this attention on Cal, Patti Cake, as she referred to herself, had also spited his closest associate, the very woman he was supposed to be dating, by spitting all over her shoe. But that was not all. This horrid woman also had stabbed her with a needle. It was just too much in one day for poor Sherry to handle. Now Dr. Cal, obviously taken by this woman, had joined together to simply humiliate her, and she would not tolerate this treatment another minute.

Sherry slowly went over to the tray where the tools were kept. There, just in the reach of her jealous hand was the instrument that he used to rinse the teeth. She picked it up and sweetly asked, "Calvin, dear, do you want this to rinse her teeth now? It looks like there is a bit of filling there by her tongue that needs to be rinsed and sucked up in the tube."

"Yes, Sherry. I am ready for it."

"Then you can have it!" She spoke angrily and turned the device directly toward his ear before letting it fly. The water came out full force all over the side of Cal's unsuspecting face. He winced, slowly got up, took a towel, wiped himself, and then turned to his assistant.

"You may be excused now, Sherry. I will not be needing your assistance anymore. And I want to see you in my office first thing in the morning. *Do you understand?*" He lowered his voice as he enunciated the last sentence.

"But, Dr. Ripland, I didn't mean to—"

He cut her off midsentence and lowered his voice with an emphatic order. "I said you may be excused now!"

Sherry ran out of the room crying, and Patti wanted to shrink down in the chair and disappear. This would be a dental experience she would never forget.

After the assistant left the building, Cal pulled up his chair and sat down next to his trembling patient. She looked like a frightened little child in the big dental chair. The filling was finished, and he gently removed the rubber support. He let his strong hands linger on her cheeks for a moment, feeling the softness of her skin. She could feel nothing, however, but as he looked into her eyes, something happened to Patti. All the tension and fear she had experienced drained away. There was something about this man that moved her deeply. His eyes were filled with compassion and sadness. She saw instantly that he realized this appointment had not gone well and was very, very sorry for what had happened. He looked like a little puppy who had just chewed up the shoe and got caught.

"I am so very sorry, Miss Murray, for all the trouble

you've had to endure here today. None of this should have happened. It never has before. This has been the worst set of events I have encountered, bar none, and of all the people in the world to have it happen to, it had to be you. Truly, Patti, you can never know how sorry I am and how I really wanted this to go smoothly for both of our sakes." He lowered his head and shook it from side to side with great distress. Patti tried to respond sympathetically, but her tongue would not obey her desire to move it and speak properly.

"Augggg," she managed to sound out. "Eatt cawed ah haa-uned ta aanyoune. Eatts no vigg deeal. Jusss forget eatt eva haa-undd."

Cal wanted to take this sweet, little thing in his arms right then and there and hold her close forever, never letting her be hurt again, but that probably was never going to happen, especially now with this disastrous afternoon appointment. He had nearly injured her very seriously. And to think that just a few hours earlier, he had, in fact, decided to risk asking her to accompany him to dinner some evening, but now that was impossible. What would he say? Imagining a scenario where he went ahead and asked her, he thought of saying, "Well, Patti, since we seem so good at beating each other up each time we meet, why don't we take the battle to the next level? We can go down to a nice restaurant, have a smashing good food fight, and then retire to my place for dessert where we'll eat some of that delicious, fresh strawberry cake you baked!" He smiled a little to himself as he tried to imagine what her response would have been to that. Then again, he remembered the words of his father the last time he had seen him.

"Calvin, no woman worth having was ever won by timidity. You won the heart of Linda, and it will happen again. It is just a little bit more complicated this time. If you ever find another woman you think you might be interested in, don't let anything get in the way of becoming acquainted with her. You need to leave the past behind and get on with your life. You need to raise your daughter, and she needs a mother. We are becoming way too fond of her. It is going to rip our hearts out to let her go, we love her so much, but it needs to happen and soon, because I think if we have her for even one more month, Mother and I will have to move into your house with her."

He didn't know if the anything his father had mentioned would cover the everything that had happened between him and Patti Cake, but perhaps good old Dad was right. The least he could do now though was accompany her to her car. They were the last ones in the building. He held the cake in one hand and opened the door for her with the other. He locked up, and they walked quietly to her van. Then he heard his voice talking.

"Miss Murray, I wanted to ask you to dinner tomorrow evening, but I am afraid what happened in the office today will scare you away from me so bad that you would never consider it. Could that possibly be what you would do if I asked you out? Perhaps if we had an appointment to meet somewhere and didn't just bump into each other unexpectedly, we could avoid the trouble we seem to have had at our last three meetings."

Patti was quietly looking at the ground. She opened

her purse and took out her keys before looking up at him. When she did, he noticed that she had a lopsided smile on her face.

"I oooud love to go to dinna with oou tomorrow evening." She was getting a little better mastery of her tongue. "Call some-ime in the moan-ing to fill me in on aw the details." With that, she was inside and driving away. Cal stood there holding his cake. Yes! Good old Dad! He really knew what he was talking about.

Chapter 6
HEADS OR TAILS: JIM'S OR CAL'S?

Jim looked at his schedule. He had three places to go that day. His first stop was at the studio. He was not looking forward to this meeting. His director wanted to go over the scripts for their upcoming movie, and she was a regular slave driver. On top of that, the movie location was in Ireland, and they'd be leaving two days following the wedding. The security guard recognized him and opened the gate. Katrina had been working with Jim for about eight years. She had taken him from a minor role in a weekly TV show to a couple of big-time box office hits. Her specialty was romance. She had chosen Jim more for his looks than his acting abilities. Her romances demanded good-looking men, though she did not like them to be macho. On the contrary, Katrina wanted her men to be ever-so-slightly feminine with good muscle tone. Jim had semilong blond hair and was more beautiful than handsome. In this movie, he was supposed to have a full beard though, and it had to be real. So the razor had been put up, and after only three days, the whiskers were driving him crazy. He glanced at the full-length mirror in the hall before entering her office. His face looked like a pile of bristles.

Katrina's actresses dominated their men. And likewise, she dominated Jim. He did not like being pushed around by this woman, but he could not complain about the money. Women had come out in droves to see his last two flicks. He heard rumors around that he was one of Hollywood's sexiest men, but Jim wasn't sure if he believed them. Katrina was a feminist and wanted to see women in everything. She wanted to create a generation of women who ruled the world. Her movies were making a difference. If she kept pounding away, it just might happen. After all, wasn't a woman now running for president? This was her hope, her dream, and what drove her to drive him beyond his limits sometimes.

"What took you so long, Jim? I have been waiting more than half an hour! Now that you don't have to spend forty minutes every morning pampering your face, a normal person might think you could get to work at least five minutes early. I've had time to go through the whole script, and we have a lot of changes to make."

"Sorry about being late," Jim replied with a pasted-on look of consternation on his face. "My sister wanted me to get a few things for her at the store. The wedding's coming up in less than two weeks, you know. Everything has to be just right."

"You are fortunate that it is a wedding of one of your family. If it was anything else, you could forget it. We would be off for Ireland early," she threatened. "The delay in filming has already cost me close to a half a million dollars. So don't go asking me for any more favors because I will not hear of them. Do I make myself clear?"

"Yes, Katrina, I mean Miss Dunstan. People only get married once, and this wedding is very important to my sister and me."

"People don't get married just once," she retorted. "I just met a man yesterday who is not ten years older than you, Jim, and he is on his seventh wife. This day and age, you can pick up a spouse as quickly as you can a pet. And you can get rid of them just as fast, too."

"Well, Sis said once would be enough for her. This man is the man."

"I have heard that story a hundred times before and nearly every broad I heard it from is with a different man now. Some of them have had two or three. But why are we arguing? We need to get to work. Look at these changes. I'm going out of character a little here … and I have revamped five of the scenes. The dude who wrote this story wasn't too bright. He needs to go back to grade school. The plot's okay, but it just doesn't offer enough character development for our theme to surface. You have a lot of fans. You're every woman's dream man. I've created a puppet, a beauty boy who is great in bed and easy to rule. He is the perfect partner. He does whatever his woman wants him to do. When she says jump, he jumps. When she says it's time to get in the shower, he hops in the shower. When she wants him to look good to impress her rivals, he looks smashingly good. When she wants to get even with her enemies, she sends him to do the job and her enemies think he is their friend the entire time he is taking them out. So don't go thinking on your own, honey.

I have you right where they want you. You will stay there like a good dog till we run out of these kinds of women and that will take forever because we are growing stronger every day. I'm creating thousands more of these women with every movie. And we shall overcome!"

"You may be right about that," Jim responded as he let his mind drift to the strawberry-blonde. She was not that kind of woman. He knew it; he had a gut feeling about it. Then he continued talking. "Go easy on me. The last movie I got dumped and hit the ground hard. Give me a little break this time. You can at least let me end up with the woman I love and not have her chasing off after some rich, fuddy-duddy."

"You know you like the money, guy," she added. "I took you from peanuts to gold in just a few short months. So count your blessings. There were a dozen others I had lined up ready to take your place if you didn't cut the mustard, but you came through for me. And you have done well. Now that we're on a roll, I intend for us to ride the wave all the way to the top. And I hope that takes forever. That's good job security for me, so let's get to work. By the way, did you hire a bodyguard for yourself yet like we talked about last week?"

"Nope," replied Jim. "I haven't been threatened yet. Frankly, I don't see the need. What are they going to do? Jump out of some dark alley and mug me? People love me. I don't have any enemies."

"Don't be too cocky about it, dude," Katrina responded with a prophetic tone in her voice. "If you don't get a bodyguard soon, it'll be just my luck to be in the middle of my biggest hit and you'll get bumped off. Then I'll have to somehow make you die in the movie and come back to life. That is why we'll shoot some of the first scenes first and then shoot most of the last act and ending. That way, I can have you acting after you're dead."

"That's real comforting," Jim replied sarcastically with a bit of scorn thrown in. But I am not planning to die in near future. In fact, I'm considering buying a nice house and settling down with a pretty little woman I met in Santa Rosa. I want to marry her just as soon as I get back from Ireland."

"You're not serious, Jim. Please tell me you're not going to do something stupid like marriage." The movie producer came right up out of her chair and placed her face about three inches from his.

"I am serious, Katrina. I really like the house, but it won't be a home unless this little lady is there as my wife. I want to keep her in bed until she gets very pregnant, hopefully with triplets and follows them with twins. I want kids and a family. I am tired of being alone." He had quickly backed away from her threatening, in-his-face gesture.

"You? Alone? Not a chance. I have seen the string of babes that come to you. Why would you want to settle on one woman? You have got to be crazy. There are hundreds of big-breasted sweethearts waiting to lay you in every city of the USA, and that's not the only country either. You can pick out the prettiest princesses and have them all eating out of your hand. You belong to the world, Jim, not to any one woman. You are beginning to scare me now. Just about the time you make it, you are about to blow it. All your work will be wasted and mine too. Your career won't mean a thing if you marry. Where do you and your sister get off on that kick? Marriage is for the weak, and I want you to be strong. Please don't go off and do anything stupid, Jim! It's dumb, dumb, dumb." She stomped off a few paces and pounded her fist on the desk, scattering several of the papers she had been presenting. They fluttered to the floor; some even went into the trash can.

"Now look what you made me do, you idiot. What do you have rattling around up there in your brain anyway, marbles or peas or something else like rat turds? It isn't common sense; that is for certain. Stupid. That is what it is."

The rest of the day went a little better after she cooled down from her raving. After going over the script, Jim went to his travel agent and purchased the tickets for Patti Cake. He had them sent electronically and requested that they be delivered in person to her house with a poem he had written. From there, he planned to pick up his sister and take her to see the home he was buying. He also wanted to talk to the owners again and make sure they would open the kitchen to his new friend. She would love this woman, and that would bond her to him. He knew exactly how to pull it all off. After all, wasn't he an actor? Patti Cake would never know what hit her. In just a few weeks, she would be madly in love with him and he would pop the question just before Ireland. If she said yes, and he knew she would, he planned to take her on a prewedding trip. She probably had never been out of the United States. She would love Ireland. He was whistling as he started for home. There would be one stop first though before he met Sis. He would get a six-pack for the evening and find some sweet thing to warm him up. He knew just the person. She had been a frequent visitor to his place.

At the party store, he picked up the beer. He got on the cell phone and called ReAnna. She answered with a voice so sweet he started to get excited just thinking about the evening to come.

"I'll be by to pick you up just before six tonight, okay? We'll go out to eat somewhere, then plan our evening together."

"You've got yourself a date, Jimmy. Do I get to pick the restaurant tonight?"

"Yes, sweet. Anywhere you want. After dinner, we will go out for dessert."

"Don't you mean go in for a dessert, dear?" she questioned. "Ooo! I can hardly wait. Last time dessert lasted a very long time. I love very long, sweet, tasty desserts, don't you? I cherish every minute of it. Can we put chocolate syrup and whip cream on top of it tonight? Come and get me now and take me with you and your sister to see your new house."

Jim thought it over. No, that would not do. He wanted to impress his former employers. ReAnna was just too brazen and too wild for any civilized impressions, at least the kind he wanted to make.

"No, I have to take Sis there alone. They loved her when she was little, even had her star with me in a movie, and, well, it's family. You know how that goes." He put her off and was about ready to hang up when he heard her scream. He asked if she was okay, but there was no answer. He heard the phone drop to the floor with a thud. In the background, he heard some men talking and ReAnna's muffled cries. He did a quick U-turn and went roaring off toward her apartment. If he hurried fast enough and did not get stopped by the police, he could reach her place in five minutes flat. The time flew by fast. She did not call him back! He called her cell phone. The automated voice mail message came on. That was not good. When he arrived at her apartment, he quickly drove into her driveway. There was a dark van there. Two strange men were just taking off. As the rig backed past him, he saw a white hand reach up and scratch frantically at the window. She was in there all right. He backed out and followed, tailing them all the way. They headed for the bad part of town.

Jim had a gun with him. He had started carrying one several months ago. He was a good shot. That was one advantage the movies had given him. He took it out of the glove box now and aimed at the rear tire of the van. The first bullet missed, but the second one found its mark and the vehicle went out of control. It swerved and veered off the road onto the median. The driver vacated the wheel and started running away. Jim let him go. When he got to the sliding van door, it was locked so he shot it with his pistol. He nearly ripped it off its hinges. There being pinned down to the carpet was ReAnna. This big, ugly dude, obviously drunk, was all over her. Jim stuck his pistol in the guy's ribs and ordered him to get out. He obeyed without resistance. Jim's main concern was the girl.

"Are you okay, ReAnna?" he cried with great distress while keeping the gun trained on her captor.

"Yes, I'm all right, Jim. I am so glad you were on the phone when these idiots came. I met them at the bar a couple of days ago, and we got drunk together. I was supposed to go back the next day for another date, but something came up. I guess Jumbo here didn't like to be stood up."

"You're right, lady. Nobody stands me up. You tell me you're going to do something, and you will do it or pay the consequences."

"Look who's talking, big guy. You want to argue? You talk to my gun," Jim threatened.

"Hey, I was just joking wid you, man. Didn't mean no harm to you nor this pratty thang. She owes me that date. I came to take what was rightfully mine. It was just a friendly visit. No harm done."

"You don't think rape is a big deal? Well, you can tell that to the police." Jim took out his cell phone and dialed 911, all the time keeping the gun trained on the big guy. He gave the address where they were and had just hung up when he sensed a movement. The first guy had acted like he was running off, but he had really gone only far enough to circle back. He was creeping up from the rear of the van. He had a piece of someone's tailpipe in his hand. Jim didn't know how to keep the gun on one guy while keeping from getting hit with the pipe by the other. He was an actor, wasn't he? He made a daring but very quick move. Just as the pipe came down, he dodged but made it sound like he got hit. It was such a sickening, convincing sound that ReAnna screamed. At the same time, he shot the pistol putting a hole in the van just inches from the second guy's hand. He dropped the pipe and jumped back. Jim now started to slowly sink down while staggering backward. He moved fast and far enough so he could keep his eyes on both men. He intentionally swayed from side to side. The effect was magical. The gun pointed first at one of the thugs and then the other. They each in turn held up their hands in caution, motioning for him to quit pointing his pistol at them. He appeared not to notice. At the same time, he started rolling his eyes around in his head while shaking it back and forth like a crazy man. Foamy stuff came drooling out of his mouth. Then he went into convulsions while continuing to point the pistol first at one and then at the other. Another shot came out of the gun and took out the little heart-shaped window in the side of the vehicle. The guys each jumped back about three feet with that one. He had played this role in a movie once as an epileptic boy. It looked terrible and was very convincing.

ReAnna had recovered enough to peer out at him again and cried, "Oh, my no! He's having a seizure. Back off and give him some air!" she commanded.

The guys didn't move. They just continued staring at the convulsing movie star with a look of horror on their faces.

"I said *back off*, ya jerks! He could die if we don't get help."

Just then the sound of a siren was heard in the distance, and the two came out of their stupors, hopped in the three-wheeled vehicle, and roared off. They turned into an alley not far away, abandoning the rig.

Jim sat up and quietly asked, "Where did they go?"

"You scared the life out of me, Jim. How did you do that? You really looked like you were dying."

"It was all an act of self-preservation. I wanted to get their minds off of hurting you or me without shooting them. Your words were absolutely convincing. You were wonderful. Are you okay, sweetheart?"

"Yes, I'm fine now, but I hate to think of what would have happened if you hadn't come and rescued me. Thank you! I owe you my sanity, maybe even my life. But next time you try to do anything foolish like acting as if you're dying or something, let me know ahead of time so I can be prepared."

"You did just fine, ReAnna; in fact, you were perfect. It looks like you need a ride?" Just then, two police cars came around the corner and stopped when they saw Jim and ReAnna. The two motioned toward the abandoned van and pointed out the direction the guys had run. One patrolman started after them on foot while the other made out a report and took down the description of the suspects. ReAnna knew one of the guys and gave his name.

"They couldn't have gotten far," the first officer told them. Then turning to the couple, he continued, "You are Jim from the movies, aren't you? You two had better get out of here. This is no place for a person of your caliber. We will call and let you know if we come up with anything. We'll probably need you to come down to the station and identify these guys when we bring 'em in."

With that, the police were gone.

Jim called his sister and told her he would not be going to the house. He began to think very seriously about hiring a bodyguard. He hated to let his freedom go, but if he were dead, freedom wouldn't do him any good, so why not take the proper precautions before that happened? He took ReAnna directly to his place, quieted her down a little, and held her close as a sliver of a moon rose over the smog-cast skies of LA. This would be a long and wonderful evening. He would order pizza and have it delivered. Then have a little *dessert*!

Patti woke up in the morning with a splitting headache. She ran her tongue all around her mouth. She could feel again. The jaw where the needle had penetrated was a little sore, but all in all, there was not much pain. She dragged herself out of bed and took some Tylenol. Luckily she had a light day of work ahead of her. She decided to fire up her hot tub and continue reading her book for a while until this headache was gone. Then she would think about breakfast. Her hot tub was completely secluded. When it was the right temperature, she slipped into the foamy swirls. The warm water massaged her entire body and made it feel warm and rubbery all over. When she got out, she was so clean her toes squeaked on the floor. Ten o'clock came, and she put a bagel in the microwave and then got out the Philadelphia Cream Cheese. She poured a glass of orange juice, and she felt fine. What would she do today? Cal would call sometime, but he could reach her on her cell phone. Why not go and purchase the cake pans?

Patti took her time looking around Nancy's. She got some cake flour and a ten-pound bag of confectioner's sugar. Two gallons of buttery shortening also found their way into her cart. She checked the eggs. Some of them were cracked. These she traded for good ones from another carton. Then it was back home again.

About the time she pulled into the driveway, a parcel truck pulled up and signaled for her to come. The man gave her a large envelope. A dozen red roses were placed in a symmetrical arrangement. They were beautiful. So this was how Cal treated his ladies? He must have had others. Nobody that handsome could have gotten as far in life as he was without running into at least a couple of good-looking women. She thanked the driver and headed into the house. She selected one of her best crystal vases, and placing the stems of the roses underwater, she cut the ends off at an angle. Then she added the little packet of powder to the water and placed them into the vase. They filled the room with a mild fragrance. Maybe Cal would not call. Perhaps the card held a "Dear John" letter, or in this case, a "Dear Patti" letter. That was probably it. He didn't have the guts to face her on the phone so sent roses to soften her up. She was about to rip open the envelope when the phone rang.

She picked up the receiver and answered. "Hello, Exquisite Cakes from Patti Cake. May I help you?"

"I surely hope so" came Cal's pleasing voice from the other end. "How is your mouth feeling this morning after yesterday's fiasco?"

"It is quite all right, thanks. This morning, there was just a little soreness where the needles went into my jaw, but other than that, everything is just Jim dandy, except for a splitting headache. How is your leg where I landed that kick?"

"No problems there. I was just calling to apologize again for yesterday's unfortunate accidents and see if six would be a good time for me to pick you up?"

"Six? Great! I'll be waiting, and by the way, Cal, the roses you sent me are absolutely lovely. I have them in a vase on the table this very minute. The whole kitchen smells like a fragrant garden now. Thank you so very much."

"Roses?" Cal questioned with a surprise in his voice that carried over the phone wires. "I didn't …" He stopped in midsentence and hemmed and hawed around a little before continuing. "The roses. Okay, whatever you say." He grew silent again and then added, "See you at six. Good-bye, Patti."

Patti thought it strange the way he cut her off so fast, but then perhaps another of his patients was having a bad tooth day and he had to run. She took the envelope to a recliner in the dining room and sat down. When she opened it up, she saw a beautiful poem laid out on the page. Most poems were not arranged prettily, but this one was. The sweet scent of cologne came wafting up to her nose. It smelled ever so much like the beautiful red roses on the table.

Patti Cake

Patti Cake, Patti Cake, bakers' woman.
  Ah, can you bake me a cake as fast as you can?
    Take it and make it and frost it and gloss it.
      Then throw it on the airplane for Sister and
      I
Can't wait until I see you getting off the plane.
  And I'm counting the minutes until we meet again.
    Kathy is excited to meet you when you come.
      Enjoy these lovely roses. This little poem is done.

Love, Jim

Patti looked at the word *love*, and then saw the name *Jim*. So he was a poet, and he was Jim.

"I knew it was him. He either forgot he called himself

John or is playing a trick on me since I called him Jim. I wonder which," she muttered to herself as she once again looked at the roses. Then she remembered thanking Cal for them. No wonder he acted surprised. What would he think? He had mustered up the courage to ask her out to dinner after all the trouble they had undergone only to find out that another guy was in her life and quite a womanizer at that, sending her roses and all. Poor Cal. He had every reason to give up on her now. She tried to picture herself setting across the table from the blond man. Then she tried to put the dark-haired one in his place. Jim beat Cal hands down. He was really a gorgeous man, like one of her cakes. That would be very nice to wake up to every morning for the next fifty years or so. Were these men really interested in her? It had been such a long time since she had had any suitors, she hardly knew what to do with one, let alone two.

Patti looked in the envelope again and pulled out her plane tickets. The stinker had booked her four days early. What was he trying to do, ruin her business? She remembered a couple of cake-decorating classes she had taught. There were about three women of promise. She decided to give them each a call and have them fill her orders while she was gone. She would forward her home phone number to Nancy, and if the orders got too heavy, Nancy could call the others. Patti decided she really needed a vacation, and Pam, a college roommate of hers, resided in Palm Desert. Perhaps while in the area she could spend some time with her. That would be great, just like old times!

The afternoon flew by. Precisely at 6:00 p.m., Cal drove

up. He got out and came to her door. She was dressed and ready but did not invite him in. Just a few days ago, Jim had driven up the same driveway and invited her to ride with him. She had refused. "Oh, Lord, why was it different with Cal? I honestly don't know him, not really … yet why do I believe Cal is less threatening? There's just something about him, Lord, and besides, You know I don't really trust myself with that good-looking man from Southern California. Oh, Lord, I need help with this. I do! I have had trouble enough controlling my thoughts when he is near, let alone my actions. And if I let myself be off guard for a moment … well, let's not go there." As Cal opened the door for her and smiled, she came back to the present moment.

"You look very lovely this evening, Patti." The young lady noticed he looked her all over, up and down and all around before making that complement.

"Thank you, Cal. You don't look half bad yourself. Did you have a good day at the office?" She had to look up at him. He was so very tall. It made her feel small and vulnerable, but she liked it. It was comforting. He looked as if he could take care of himself and her too if the need ever arose.

"It was fine except for one thing; my assistant quit. She was just trained and had everything organized, but the incident yesterday upset her so, she told me she never would feel comfortable in my office again."

"I am sorry to hear that, Cal. I didn't mean to cause any trouble between you two. It is hard to find dependable, knowledgeable help these days. Do you have any prospects for another assistant?"

"I placed an ad in the paper today. Last time I did that, I was flooded with calls, so I don't think it will take long. I want to check out the market first, but if I don't see anyone of promise, there was another hygienist I almost hired. She is still looking for work, so I will probably hire her."

The car was driving out of the yard now. Cal was very quiet. He was thinking deeply, and it seemed to Patti he wanted to say something but just didn't know how. She ventured a guess that perhaps he was thinking about the roses and her prior conversation with him on the phone. She decided to ease his mind over the issue.

"About the roses, Cal, I hadn't opened the card yet, and I just supposed they were from you since your call came just after they arrived. They are from a client of mine in Los Angeles. I am making a special-order cake for them. It is a big wedding. They found me from my website. There was a cake I made for a lady a couple of weeks ago. They want the same cake. They are flying me out there to do the baking and decorating on site. The roses came with my plane tickets. It was just a nice gesture on their part. I understand the wedding will be very large. The cake has to feed five hundred people. They even gave me money to purchase larger pans and will have a special oven there for me to use. I leave in a little over a week."

Cal looked very relieved at the news. *At least the roses weren't from some man,* he thought. After that, he lightened up a bit and even cracked a few jokes. They went to the newest restaurant in the area. There was every kind of food imaginable. They were directed to a section where the lights were dimmed. Off in the distance, live music played while the couple dined. Patti had to admit that it was quite romantic. As she looked out the window, she could see the lights of the city as they painted their exquisite patterns up and down the avenue. A light drizzle was falling, causing the lamps to mirror themselves on the street.

"This is really beautiful, isn't it, Cal?" she asked, looking deep into his eyes for his response.

"Yes, it is very nice. I came by last evening and checked it out before bringing you here. I wanted to be sure you would enjoy yourself." He was looking back at her. A little twinkle in his eyes mingled with a somewhat serious expression. There were just the slightest hints of a couple of indentations on his cheeks. With the light reflecting off his shiny dark hair, he was strikingly handsome.

"Why, thank you, Cal," she responded with a smile of gratitude lighting up her face. "That was thoughtful of you. I appreciate it, really, and it is very lovely."

They finished their meal and looked around. The band was playing a soft love song. Some of the couples were dancing.

"Would you care to dance with me, Cal?" she asked and then added, "That is if your toe has healed up." There was just the slightest hesitation in her voice as she spoke.

"If that is what you would like to do, Patti, I don't mind." He got up and pulled out her chair as she stood up. Before leaving, he placed a ten-dollar tip on the table. At the dance floor, he took her small hands in his large ones and started moving. His touch was very tender and caring. The suit he wore was spotless, and when she looked at his hair, not one seemed out of place. The cologne he had on drove Patti wild with desire. A current seemed to start from his hands and enter into her. It warmed her whole being, and she found herself leaning in closer. She laid her cheek against his strong, massive chest and let him carry her around with the rhythm of the music. They danced for half an hour, and then he asked her if there was anyplace she needed to go. She told him she was open.

"How was your cake, Cal?" He had gotten too close to that emotional retreat she reserved for herself. She needed to cool down the environment.

"Patti Cake, you are the best baker in Santa Rosa. I started eating it and couldn't quit. It is a third gone. It is so delicious! We used to go to Grandma's house when I was small. She had a strawberry patch there. I would go out and snitch berries when I thought no one was looking. Your cake tasted just like the biggest, juiciest berry I have ever eaten. But it was much better. When you eat strawberries, they make a little crunchy noise when you bite down on the seeds. Your cake literally melted in my mouth. I fell in love with your cake, and if you are anything like it, I think I could easily fall in love with you."

Patti blushed a little. She wondered if she wasn't falling a little bit herself. He drove her to a little hill overlooking the city. His strong arm reached over and drew her close. It was nice. Cal opened up and talked like a boy would talk to his best friend. He laid out his goals and interests in a way that painted a picture of love and security this woman had never known. She in turn opened up and talked more about her personal life than she had with any other man. He seemed to understand but more than that, care. This was a bit scary. He had a way of drawing her out that made her feel vulnerable. She liked to feel vulnerable, but at the same time, it was a dangerous place to be. Realizing she had talked too much, she drew back into her shell, putting more distance between them. She needed more time to evaluate this. There was something about Cal that pulled at her, tugging like a gentle stream that pulls at the banks it passes.

The evening ended all too quickly, and soon she was back home again. He had been a perfect gentleman all the way and not one bad thing had happened to either of them. He again got out and opened the door for her. They walked to the porch together. She quickly climbed on the lower step and before he had time to think, planted a soft, warm kiss on his firm lips. Startled by this, he leaned in for more, but that was all he would get from her this time. She dashed up the remaining steps and turned before opening her door.

"Thank you, Cal. I had wonderful evening. When you get home, you had better not get into the cake. Too much of a sweet thing just might not be good for you, especially being a dentist and all. The strawberries will be okay for a couple of days yet if you place the cake in the refrigerator."

From the window, she watched as he opened his car door and drove off. The scent of his cologne still lingered on her clothes.

It had been a while since Patti had talked to God. She thought of Him now. Her relationship with Jesus was a little different than what others stated they experienced. She talked to Jesus as she would a friend who was right there beside her. She had always looked at Him this way. Now she started talking to Him again.

"Jesus. You have always been there for me. When I had a bad experience, You comforted me. In college, You kept me from doing foolish things like partying and doing drugs. You guided me into a career that I dearly love. I have a confession to make to You tonight. I have never trusted You with choosing a husband for me. I am sorry. Perhaps I wanted to make that choice on my own. Now two men have been introduced into my life. I do not know much about either of them. You do, Jesus. Perhaps one is a husband You would like me to have. Perhaps not. I really do not know now. In James 1:5, You promise to give wisdom if we ask. I am asking for wisdom now. I do not trust myself with my own future in this matter. Show me and guide me, so that I follow the pathways You have planned for me, okay? I love You and would never be happy to have that change if I ran headlong in the wrong direction. If Cal or Jim are right for us, you and I, Jesus, then show me which one. If there is another man or perhaps no one at all, I suppose I could survive so long as You are with me, but somehow, deep down inside, I do not think that is what You have planned. Thank You again, Jesus, for caring so much and coming to offer me a chance at salvation. This, after all, is the most important value in my life. If there is a man to share it, so be it. Amen."

A promise popped into her mind, but it was more of an answer from a very dear friend than a Bible passage.

I will bring the work I have started in you, Patti, to a wonderful and complete finish through My grace that is being demonstrated in you.

Chapter 7
A KITTY FOR LANISSA

Patti had another date with Cal a couple of days later. It was a lovely evening, and the warm air kissed her cheeks as she smiled at her dentist again. She could sense him pushing his heart toward her, and she knew it was within her power to take it. They walked hand in hand after the meal and let their feelings touch each other. He was so like an overgrown kid who was trying to deal with his emotional desires and the extra length to his legs both at once. But Cal was a man, not a boy, and his inner needs were screaming to be let free. He tried to woo her love and coax her. He even tried a little bribe or two, but he couldn't draw her out to his satisfaction. She managed to stay just out of reach. In his mind, he was taking her in his arms and holding her soft, warm body next to his own. His reaching brought back nothing though but the ghost of the woman he knew she was. He didn't know why she managed to slip out of his grasp time and time again, but Patti knew. Could she ever trust another man? She had only really loved one guy before, and it had turned out to be the worst nightmare of her life.

Then there was Jim. The time was nearing for her to meet him again. She dreamed of the moment he would be back in her sight. She scanned his well-shaped body in her mind, over and over. While in these moods, she felt her hands running over the ripples of his muscles, wanting to be possessed by him. At times, the vision was so real, she blacked out and was there, in his arms, trapped by their strength yet free. She needed to think of something else. She would call Nancy and the other two women to come over for a few advanced decorating lessons tomorrow. With this pattern of thinking, Patti was able to control her emotions while in the presence of this powerful man. He again delivered her to her door. This time she did not kiss him and she could not help but notice the disappointment on his face.

The next day there were three orders to fill, so why not let the ladies do the work? That would give her time to dream of next week while still managing to keep an eye on her apprentices. She set out all of the ingredients and had everything ready for them upon their arrival. Nancy came first and brought one of the other women with her. Then Trudy showed up. Trudy was the life of the party. She made a festivity out of everything, but that did not inhibit her efficiency. Patti saw great potential in her if she would only learn to control herself a little more and be less uninhibited. By the time an hour had passed, the ladies had done exceptionally well. Two of the cakes were ready for frosting, and the third was baking in the oven. Trudy had them all wound up, ready to spring, when the phone rang.

"Hello, Exquisite Cakes from Patti Cake. May I help you?" Patti answered.

The voice on the other end of the line was desperate.

"Hello. This is Judy Spencer. Can you make animal cakes?"

"What do you mean by animal cakes?" Patti questioned as several animals flashed through her mind.

"A cake that is in the shape of an animal, like a cat, for instance?" Judy was trying to envision what it was that she wanted but was unable to come up with it.

"Yes, I can make a cake of nearly any shape you want. What did you have in mind?"

"My daughter is having her fifth birthday today. Just a few days ago, her kitty died. We are getting a kitten for a present, but she told us she didn't want any other cat. She wanted Heidi back. It has been difficult for us to explain that her kitty will never come back. She cries a lot. We thought if her birthday cake was in the shape of a kitty and we made the birthday party special for both her and her new kitten, she wouldn't be so sad about losing her other pet. I was wondering if you had the time today to take on a project of this nature. You came very highly recommended from my dentist. He said you made the best cakes in all of California and were so well known that you even do cakes in LA. If that is correct, I hope I can afford you. Could I meet with you and show you kind of what I am looking for? At the same time, I do not want to influence your design too much. I am sure you know more about it than I ever will."

"Certainly!" Patti answered. "I'm assuming if your dentist told you about me, he also included my address. Do you live far from here?" The lady assured Patti she could be at her place in about forty minutes.

"Bring some pictures of your daughter's cat, and I will

make a cartoon cake that looks something like it," Patti suggested. She hung up the phone and told the ladies they would learn how to make specialty-shaped cakes. They were delighted. This would be a lesson worth its weight in gold. They would start right away on this new cake.

Patti chose a German, sweet-chocolate cake for her kitty cake. She looked at the recipe and decided to double it.

1 (4-ounce) package Baker's German sweet chocolate
1 teaspoon vanilla
1/2 cup boiling water
2 cups unsifted all-purpose flour
1 cup butter or margarine
1 teaspoon baking soda
2 cups sugar
1/2 teaspoon salt
4 egg yolks
1 cup buttermilk
4 egg whites, stiffly beaten

She measured out the water and put it on to boil. When the bubbles started coming to the surface, she placed the chocolate squares in the pan and then went to her mixer and creamed the butter and sugar. She separated the yolks from the whites of the eggs and added the egg yolks one at a time while the mixer was on a low speed. Next came the buttermilk alternated with the flour, having been sifted with the salt and baking soda. She then added the melted-chocolate-and-water mixture. She turned the processor up to full speed until the cake batter was very smooth. In a separate bowl, she beat up the egg whites until they were stiff. Then she folded them into the rest of the cake. Nancy and the other two ladies watched every detail.

To make a cartoon cat, Patti needed special-shaped pans. She had a number of them in her cupboard. She selected a deep pan for the main body of the cake from which she would sculpt the head, ears, and front portion of the kitty. She selected a large oval-shaped pan for the remainder of the body of the cat. The tail and legs would be added on. Before pouring the cake mixture into the pans, she sprayed them with Pam and dusted them with flour. This would allow them to easily separate from the pans after the cake was baked.

The cakes were out of the oven and cooling when the lady arrived with the pictures. When the cake was fully cold, Patti shaped the body and head of the kitty. It was a cartoon kitten, all right, looking up into the air with a little butterfly on its paw. She had sketched it out, and when the lady saw it, she told Patti it was perfect. The cartoon kitty would be frosted with gray and white frosting, like the colors of the deceased kitty, but being a cartoon cat, it should not remind the little girl too much of her departed pet. The mother decided if the cake came from Patti, the little girl would accept it better than if her mother brought it in. The little girl almost blamed her mother for the loss of her cat, so every detail was important for repairing her relationship with her daughter. They decided that Patti and her three associates would deliver the cake to the party. They were all excited about this and looked forward to it greatly.

Patti opened the door to the garage and loaded the cake into the van. She had a special seat belt that held the container in place. Two of the three ladies had come together so they entered their car, and the third lady got in hers. They followed Mrs. Spencer to her home. Already a number of the girl's friends had arrived for the party. The little girl's name was Lanissa. She was very cute, but Patti could tell she had been crying. All of the kids who had come to the party helped some. When the last guest arrived, Lanissa's mother and father brought the kitten into the room. It was pure white and had the cutest pink nose and pink ears. Lanissa looked at it and started to cry again. This was not what the parents wanted.

"I told you not to get me a new kitty. I want Heidi back, not this one."

One of the kids found a string and tied a safety pin to it. The little white kitten started playing. This caught Lanissa's attention. The little kitty chased the pin all over the floor. At one point, it landed next to the girl. She reached out and petted the kitten and stopped crying. In a few minutes, she was playing with the string, much to the relief of her parents. The other children brought her some presents, and soon she forgot all about being sad. It was so good to see her smile as she opened each gift. The little white kitten curled up in her lap and went to sleep.

Soon it was time for cake and ice cream. Patti and the other women crossed their fingers as they brought in the cake. Lanissa came into the kitchen carrying her new kitten. When the top came off the cartoon kitty and Lanissa saw it, she began to laugh and then dance all around the table, holding up her new kitten to see it.

"I'm going to call you Snowball. Snowball, see the gray-and-white kitty? That was the color of Heidi. Heidi was my other kitty, but she's up in heaven now, catching butterflies just like this kitty. Today is my birthday, Snowball, and I am five years old. See, that is this old." She held up five fingers so the little kitten could see. "Heidi looks so funny catching butterflies. I think she is very happy, and so am I now, Snowball, because I have you. Today we will have a birthday together."

The cake had five candles on it. Lanissa's daddy lit them and told her to make a wish before blowing them out. She started to say it out loud but put her finger over her mouth when she realized that everyone was looking at her.

"We'll just make another wish then, Snowball." She giggled. "Too many people heard that one." She bent over slightly and whispered in the kitten's ear, "What is your wish, Snowball?"

The kitten gave two short meows.

"That is a very good wish. That will be mine too." Lanissa blew all the candles out in one burst of air, and everyone clapped. She took the little kitten's paws and clapped them together also, and then told her mother she could cut the cake.

When the party was over, Patti called the ladies into a little circle before they left the house.

"Thank you for helping me to make this cake. I couldn't have done it without you. This is why I bake cakes. This little girl is so happy now, and to think I had a small part in it makes all this worthwhile. Nothing can bring happiness quite like something sweet, and my kind of sweet is cakes."

Lanissa's mother came over to where the women were talking.

"How can I ever thank you ladies for what you have done? It was so good of you to come on such short notice. When I saw my daughter laugh again when she saw the cake you brought, a heavy burden dropped away from me. She laughed a lot like that before Heidi died, and when we saw her crying all the time, we didn't know what to do. I am so glad Dr. Ripland recommended you. You have a very special gift, Miss Murray. You made this lovely cake, and you gave us our daughter back, all happy and laughing again. Thank you so very much. And I think you and Dr. Cal would make a very handsome couple. He thinks very highly of you, you know." She gave each of the ladies a hug and brushed a little tear away from her eye while following them to the door.

It was growing late by the time they left the house. Patti needed to pick up some fertilizer for her house plants, so she stopped at a florist shop on her way home. She found a gallon container filled with just the right blend of nitrogen, potassium, and potash. This was tucked securely under her arm as she browsed around the lot. The sun was nearing the horizon, and it was a most lovely evening. Patti got a lot of ideas for her decorations from places like this. She spotted some of the yellow flowers that had graced the frosting of the heart-shaped cake, and once again, her mind drifted to the golden-haired man she would see in just a few days. She hoped she could find these yellow flowers in Los Angeles. As she looked deep into the center of one pretty flower, her mind pictured his hands. They were strong yet gentle. She started stroking them while looking up into his laughing face. He was facing the setting sun, and flecks of gold swam in little circles around his eyes. He was smiling, and his lips were so close. She reached for them. Just one little kiss. A thought popped into her mind. "You are mine," the thought said. Yes. It was true. She was his.

"Patti Cake! Is that you? What are you doing?" The strong voice of Cal broke her trance. In a flash, the golden-haired, blue eyed man turned into the dark-haired, tall one. Patti was startled. She dropped the fertilizer on her foot and jumped with pain. There was a shelf of plants between her and Cal. She fell against it, and it in turn fell against him. He fell backward, striking his back on another shelf of plants. Three shelves broke on his way down. Patti closed her eyes. When she opened them, she was looking directly into the shocked face of the dentist. His eyes were as large as saucers. The little yellow flecks were no longer dancing around in any eyes, imaginary or otherwise.

"I am so very sorry, Cal," Patti blurted out, as she saw the astonished expression in his eyes. "Are you okay?"

"Yes, dear. Aside from a broken back, I am just fine. What are you doing here, Miss Murray?"

"I was about to ask you the same question, Dr. Ripland. I was picking up some fertilizer for my plants. I planned to feed them before I left, and you, why are you here?"

"Well, for your information, I was purchasing these roses to give to you before you took to the air. I was planning to stop by and surprise you with them this very evening, but just look at them now. They are squashed. You spoiled everything."

"Dear Cal, those roses in your hand are the most beautiful ones I have ever seen." She reached for them and cradled them in her arms like a mother cuddling a tiny baby.

"Liar," he retorted.

Just then, a clerk came and a few other people gathered around to see the two people facing each other with a bunch of plants and shelves between them. Patti tried to get up, but her top was all tangled up in some daisies. She tried to move her leg, but it was pinned down by something heavy. One of her hands was resting under Cal's head. The other one had a shelf between it and her stomach. She felt the back of her hand.

"Oh no!" she gasped half under her breath. She turned red again, but it was dark enough now that Cal probably didn't notice. She pulled her hand away and gently lowered her lips to his. Her kiss was lingering and wonderful, even though some potting soil managed to get in the corner of her mouth.

"Oh yes!" he repeated mockingly, when she finally removed them.

Soon the clerk had the couple untangled and the mess somewhat cleared up. The fertilizer and flowers were forgotten. Cal walked Patti back to her car. She reached up and picked a flower out of his hair and then brushed a speck of pearlite off from his nose.

"Shall we continue this conversation over hot chocolate at my house?" she asked casually.

"After what just happened? You'd better believe it!" he replied. "I would really love to hear you talk your way out of this one, young lady. An explanation of all this is definitely in order." He waved his hand around the yard, and they drove away from the florist shop.

The last man Patti had had at her home was Jim. Now Cal was there in the same place. He sat in the same chair as Patti brought in a steaming cup of cocoa. She wondered how to begin the conversation and what to talk about once it started. She knew he knew there was something holding her back. Should she tell him about Jim? She decided to go with it.

"I have a confession to make, Cal. The roses you were going to give me reminded me of the ones I received that first day we went out. I led you to believe they were from the wedding party in Los Angeles. That isn't exactly correct. I believe I said *client*. The man who gave me the roses is my client, but he is not getting married. His sister is the bride, and he explained that he learned about me from my website. He flew all the way here to order the cake in person, and after we agreed on the design, he offered to pay all of my expenses to make the wedding cakes on site."

Cal had a faraway look in his eyes when Patti turned to hear his reply. "I sensed there was something that was keeping you at a distance. The roses bothered me some, but you had a way of making it sound like it was nothing and your kiss in the flower shop got my hopes up. Do you think this man is interested in you? But more importantly, are you interested in him?"

Now it was Patti's turn to get that faraway look in her eyes.

"Yes and no. At times, I think he is interested in me, but then I have seen his personality type so often in the past. I don't know whether to take him seriously or not.

His type are flirts. They will flirt with any woman they fancy at any time. I just don't know enough about him to make a fair judgment."

"I appreciate you being up front with me, Patti. It took a lot of courage to do this. There is something I have been meaning to talk with you about for some time now, but after hearing what you had to say about your client, it can wait."

Patti took a sip of chocolate and then responded, "I will know a lot more by the time I get back, Calvin. The times you and I have been together have led to some of the most unexpected adventures I've ever had. I must say there's been nothing boring about our relationship so far. It has become quite a challenge to bring it down to some sort of normal level."

"I agree with you, Patti. I have never had such fun and pain all mixed together in one bundle. Being with you makes my tedious work at the office much more bearable. I think what you need to do now is go see your tycoon or whatever he is. If you two are meant to be together, then so be it. If, on the other hand, you feel like you could continue seeing an old recycled dentist like me, I would welcome the challenge, as you called it, of pursuing this friendship further. I am a firm believer in God. I can see by the picture of Jesus you have on the wall that you also are a believer. All my life, I have trusted in Him. He has seen me through some very difficult times. He has never failed to be there when I needed Him most. I think in the great courts of heaven, He has a wonderful future planned out for both of us. If we are meant to be together, it will happen and no one in all of California can prevent it. Deep down inside, there was some reason you stepped into my life in these various unusual ways. So go, but please, look at all the angles. Do not let your emotions overcome your reason. Do you think you can do that for me?"

Patti was quiet for a few moments before giving her answer. "I wish I had your faith, Cal. I do believe, and Jesus is a very dear friend. I claimed the promise in James 1:5 for wisdom just a few days ago. I know Jesus is working in all of this, but I keep finding myself trying to take control of my life. A lot can happen in a short time. I do not know if I can trust myself."

"I have been there also, especially when it comes to women. Some have tried to do bizarre things to entrap me into a relationship. I have had to turn my back and walk away from temptation more than once, but Jesus has seen me through. He has laid a hand on me, strengthening me at just the right moment. He will give you strength also to meet your strongest temptation if you allow yourself to trust Him."

The two finished their hot drink, and then Cal said he had better be getting home.

"By the way," he mentioned, "I took your advice on the strawberry cake. I placed the remainder of it in the freezer, and I am rationing it out a crumb at a time. I figure I should have it gone in about a year."

"Oh come on, Dr. Ripland. You are going to extremes now. First, you gorge yourself on sweets and then starve. Balance out, young man." It felt good to Patti to call him a young man. He was again looking sheepish, kind of like that overgrown kid she had seen before.

"I also figure that I will be starved from seeing your

sweet smiling face for at least a week, even though it has that smudge of dirt on it."

Patti gasped.

"How could you wait all this time to tell me? You don't mean I have been here having a perfectly good conversation with you while my face is all dirtied up with potting soil, Mr. Ripland, have I?"

"That is exactly what has happened, sweetheart, and as far as I am concerned, you have never looked more beautiful."

Patti glanced at the mirror and noticed that there was indeed a black smudge on her left cheek.

"Go on then, Doctor, and get out of my house before I throw you out."

"That will be the day, Miss Patti. Do we have a date then for that, at least? One more when you get back, to let me know how things went?"

"I just might not come back," she retorted and then felt bad about saying that when she saw the hurt look in Cal's eyes.

"It's your choice, Patti," he mumbled as he stepped through the door. She watched as he made his way back to the car. The spring had gone from his step. He looked sad and dejected. She noticed that he was limping slightly. What had she done? She started to give herself another lecture. Why was she talking to herself so much lately? If this Cal guy did this to her, how could they ever hope to carve out some type of normal life with each other? She would just have to gain control of herself before she went crazy.

Chapter 8
A FLIGHT, THEN PARADISE

The flight to Los Angeles was perfect. Jim had reserved a window seat for her, and it was first class. Patti had never flown first class before. A flight attendant bounced back and forth among all of the rich, elite passengers, fulfilling their every need. Out the window, the clouds looked like little sailboats floating on a translucent sea. Far below little postage-stamp-size squares of land covered the ground. The tiny ribbons of road often sparkled as the sun glinted off a windshield or two. Somewhere ahead in the haze was Jim. Why had she been so infatuated with him? Did the fact of his being a movie star have anything to do with it? The stars seemed to live such glamorous lives, but the tabloids often painted quite the opposite picture. There was always an announcement of one type or another. One star breaking up with another one, or a spouse, or there were fights between them, or one being caught in some affair. No, the tabloids did not paint the life of glamour that all too often appeared on the screen.

She remembered a magazine article once where ten of the top stars had opened up their homes to the photographers so the world could see how they lived and what type of architecture their house had and so on. It was a world about which Patti knew nothing. What would it be like to have thousands of dollars to spend on whatever one wished, whenever one wished? Any whim she desired? She was already getting an uneasy feeling about this whole adventure when the pilot announced they were about to land. Would Jim come in person? She didn't have long to wait for the answer.

Patti was one of the first people off the plane, and Jim was one of the first people she saw. She was so relieved she ran toward him and threw herself into his arms. He was surprised but recovered remarkably fast, almost too fast!

"Hello, darling," he said with a smile as big as California. "I have missed you." He planted a firm kiss on her lips, and she relaxed. He was so easy to be with. He turned and pointed out a couple of people who were with him.

"This is Bobbie, and this is Ted. Ted drives me around, and Bobbie is newly in my employ. I recently hired him as a bodyguard." Jim lowered his voice to a whisper before continuing, "Bobbie doesn't understand very much English yet, but he is very good at what he does. He will be starring with me in a movie over in Ireland next month, and I do have a confession to make if you have a few minutes."

"Comments would be welcomed, and should I call you John or Jim?" Patti was all ears and expectantly waiting, ready to hang on every word that would soon come out of his amazing lips.

"Jim will be fine. Let's sit down a minute. You look like you need a rest."

"A rest? Not me." Patti wanted to run circles around

him or just start hopping and skipping like a grade-school girl. "I have been resting for over an hour, but I am a bit thirsty. I know they say the airport is not the best place to eat food, but there ought to be something to drink."

"Yes, by all means." Jim was not as peppy as Patti. He had a faraway look in his eyes and was peering all around as if he expected someone to jump out at him. Patti wondered if something had happened between now and the last time she had seen him. His strong, confident nature was not rising to the occasion today. "Just name what you want, and Ted will get it."

"An orange soda would be nice." The answer came slowly out of her mouth. She stretched out the word *orange* as she spoke.

"Ah, orange," he hummed, "one of my favorites, too. Get us a couple of orange pops, Ted."

Patti and Jim sat down under the watchful eye of Bobbie. He didn't even look like he was watching, but his eyes saw everything at the same time they seemed to be looking at nothing.

"Here is my confession. When I came to order a cake from you, I did not want people to identify me. I have to be very careful when I go out in public now. I am Jim, the movie actor, but I was hoping you would at least give me a chance if you didn't think I was rich and famous. I tried to keep it down, but you saw through me. I hope this does not jeopardize our friendship. I am really attracted to you and can hardly wait to taste one of your cakes."

"I pretty well had you figured out as Jim. After you left, a friend of mine brought over a DVD of your last movie. Then I knew you were Jim. In the movie, my friend and I analyzed your producer. We pegged her to be a feminist. When I talked with you back in Santa Rosa, you also said your boss would have fired you if *she* could have. Do you work for a female producer, Jim?"

"Yes, and she is very much a feminist, really deep into women's rights. She doesn't plan to quit until a woman president graces the White House. She plans to run for president herself if no suitable woman can be found."

"We pegged her right then." Patti was glad at least she and her friend's analysis was somewhat right. "I don't see how you can allow a woman to dominate you so. You did come close to fooling me about this John who looks like Jim story. In the movie though, Jim had my John's moves, his voice, and his expressions. "When I told my friend you had ordered a cake, she didn't believe it. She asked why would a movie star come all the way to Santa Rosa to order a cake from Patti Cake? That alone would be enough evidence to prove you were not Jim. She said if you called yourself John, then you were probably John. What was the name? Stratton? How original. That is a good, old-fashioned Quaker name, and somehow you just didn't strike me as a Quaker type."

"I am sorry if I disappointed you, Patti. I mean Quakers, some of them, held prominent positions in our early society. I hear they were a little scary though when they got hold of the Spirit. They began to shake and quiver and quake. That is where they got their name, Quaker." While describing the Quakers, Jim had quivered and quaked, mimicking what he thought a Quaker would look like.

Patti couldn't help but laugh. He was so funny.

Ted returned with the orange pops, and after a few more pleasantries, they left the airport in a shiny black limo. People waved at them all along the way as they headed for the highway. The inside of the limo was very plush. There was a television set and leather upholstered seats that a person sank way down in. Jim's arm went around Patti as naturally as if they had been together for weeks. He was so easy to be with. His wit and humor were relaxing, and soon Patti's guard was totally dismantled. It would have taken weeks with Cal for Patti to feel this comfortable. They were like two kids out for a great time. Once out of sight in this luxury ride, Jim relaxed again and went back to his old, good-natured self.

"About your sleeping arrangements. I did not reserve a hotel for you, Patti. I hope you don't mind."

"No, whatever you have arranged will be fine," Patti responded without thinking. "I am not picky, and a sofa with a blanket is good enough for me if that is what you are offering."

"That is what I like about you, Patti Cake." Jim was very serious as he spoke. "You are not like so many of the others. You are not money hungry. You are easy to please and so very lovely I think I could spend the rest of my life getting to know you and enjoy each passing day more than the day before. I have recently put some earnest money down on a new house. There are twenty rooms in it, and I am sure there are several that will suit you just fine. The current owners still live there and are anxious to meet you. They are an adorable elderly couple who gave me my start in the movie business. I owe everything to them. You will love them. I will continue to stay in my penthouse while you are here so there will be no pressure for you to feel any obligation to me. I just want your stay here to be the best that you have ever had. If that happens, I, above all men, will be most happy. Once you get to the house, do whatever you want. Don't let anyone tell you what to do, not even me. I want you spoiled rotten while you are here."

"I have everything I need right here, Jim," Patti replied as she snuggled closer to him. His chin rested on her forehead. There was just a whisper of whiskers, and her brow tingled at the contact. She felt very safe in his arms. Along the way, he pointed out some of the more beautiful homes in the area with the residents' names, and to Patti, each was beautiful in its own way. Finally, Ted drove them up to an electronic gate. A gatekeeper came over to the tinted window and looked in. Then he pressed the button, and the door opened. The limo entered the long driveway of the most beautiful home Patti had ever laid eyes on. It appeared ancient and modern at the same time. The fountain in the center of the turnaround was elegant beyond words. Flowering shrubs were in full bloom all around it. Close to the ground was a carpet of blue evergreens so smooth they looked like a golf course. There was a tall pole and on the top rested a quaint birdhouse. Trumpet vines twisted all the way up. It was beautiful. Ted stopped the car and opened the door. He offered a hand to Patti, and she took it and then stepped out into paradise.

At the door, a silvery-haired woman greeted them. Patti fell in love with her right away. She was so motherly, and the many wrinkles on her face were all arranged in smiles. She had lived a happy life. This was rare. Most elderly people wore their life record on their face, and this lady had been blessed with happiness. Right behind her was her husband. He was smiling broadly and opened his arms to Patti as she came in. She couldn't resist. He was so gracious, kind, and gentle. Somehow amid all the glory and wealth, these two adorable people had found happiness—or rather made it. They animated it, and Patti knew right away that she would be at home with them.

Jim had watched the meeting from a slight distance, and that giant grin was again spread across his face. Finally he spoke. "Patti, these are the parents I never had. I call them Mom and Dad. So Patti, meet Mom, and Mom, meet Patti." He continued, "Patti meet Dad; Dad, this is Patti."

It was Dad's turn to talk now.

"Jim, my boy, why have you kept this lovely lady from us all of this time? I have not seen such honest eyes in a woman since Mother." He reached over and squeezed Jim's hand and then whispered just loud enough for Patti to overhear, "If you let this one get away from you, don't come back to me for any help with another. She is a priceless gem, lad, and more beautiful than any I have seen. I think you know that." He winked at Patti as he said it. Mom came to Patti's rescue and placed her arm around the young woman as she ushered her off.

"Men will be men," she quoted. "Put them in the presence of a pretty woman, and they all lose their senses. I will take you to your room first. You can freshen up a bit and then come down and I will show you around." The lady Jim had called Mom took Patti to a large room. It did not look like a bedroom but rather a large living room. There was antique furniture of the most elaborate design Patti had ever seen. Chairs, sofas, dressers all matched and were trimmed with pure, fourteen-carat gold paint. One of them had a brass plate that said "Chippendale" on it. The bathroom was as large as Patti's kitchen, and there beside the softest, plushiest bed Patti had ever seen were her bags, all neatly arranged from the largest to the smallest. She wondered how they had gotten there ahead of her. Then she remembered talking to the lovely couple and figured the two men must have been busy behind the scenes with her luggage.

"You will find new towels in the drawer there and a robe if you care to bathe. Don't be afraid to call if you need anything. The intercom is right by your bed." The motherly woman pointed out the object and gave Patti a reassuring pat on the arm before excusing herself. For a moment, the young lady just stood there looking around at everything. It was all so ancient and beautiful. She then stepped back and took a flying leap through the air onto the bed. She sank down, down, down like a rock settling slowly into the water. It was so comfortable; she looked up at the ceiling and imagined the golden-haired man looking down at her. He winked and blew her a kiss. She must be dreaming, or was this really paradise?

Chapter 9
TO BED OR BE WED?

When Patti awoke, she didn't know where she was. All around her was this soft, plush cover. On top of her was another. It was as light as a feather yet thick and warm. Outside, a darkened sky hung thick with a few stars smiling down at her. In a corner next to the bathroom door, a night-light burned. Then Patti remembered. She looked at her watch. It was three in the morning. What had she done? She had been with Jim and then been introduced to these two wonderful people. The confused guest tried to sort out the remaining details in her benumbed mind. She remembered being shown to her room and then flying through the air only to land on a bed so soft it put her instantly to sleep. She felt the covers at her sides. They were hugging her stiff muscles. Was this heaven? Three? Patti was glad it was that time. She had a good four or five hours to rest yet before she need do anything. Jim's adopted mother must have brought this blanket and covered her up. There had been no cover when she fell asleep. She rolled over and was soon in dreamland again. The same dream that was given her the night after Jim ordered the cake came again. This was the very house and the very woman she had seen. Was it an omen?

Jim waited three hours for Patti to come out, but she never did, much to Ken's and his disappointment. Jim had an elaborate evening of entertainment planned for them. They were going to go to a fancy restaurant and then to catch a little entertainment with drinks and finally some dancing. He figured he would get her back by one in the morning or so. He was a night person and was at his peak. She seemed to be at the opposite side of the spectrum. He played Ken a few games of cards. Later they went to the pool room and shot a few rounds. All the time, Jim hoped to see Patti's pretty face silhouetted in the door. Finally around ten at night, he excused himself from Dad's presence and looked up. Mom was standing in the door, not Patti. He shrugged his shoulders as he came up to her and then gave her a warm hug.

"What do you suppose happened to her, Mom?"

"She has gone to sleep, Jim. The poor girl was plum tuckered out. I saw it in her face the moment she arrived. When she got into the room, all the stress just passed away and she fell asleep. I checked on her not fifteen minutes ago. I'll be real surprised if she wakes before morning. I can understand how disappointed you must be. You had a lot planned for this evening, but go home or you are welcome to stay here if you prefer. She most likely will not be doing any socializing until tomorrow. The rest will do her good. So what will it be? You can have the room there to the left if you wish."

"No, thank you, Mom. I am a long way from tired. The night is still young. It has not even begun yet. I think I will go and catch a little R & R. Call me on my cell phone if she wakes up in the next half hour or so; otherwise, I guess, let her sleep. One final question before I leave. You are a woman, and so is she. What do you think would tucker a young lady like that out? How exhausting can cake making and decorating be? It is not like she is a world-class Olympian straining her muscles and all attempting to beat some world record."

"I personally think she is long overdue for a vacation. At her place, she keeps a tight schedule, I expect. She has a list of things she must do to get everything done. Now that she is away from all of that, she can relax. She has nothing that she absolutely has to do for the next few days. I imagine it took a while, but once all of that 'I must get this done, then that, then I really have to do this other thing,' once that is no longer pushing her, she really can and it looks like did let it all melt away."

"Come to think of it, right after she got off the plane, I told her to do whatever she wanted to do once she got here. I also mentioned to her to not let anyone tell her what to do. Not even me. I didn't expect her to do this though." Jim called Ted and Bobbie. They were there in a moment. They headed out of the door, got in the limo, and left.

Patti awoke early. She looked at her watch and then at the large clock in the corner of the room. Both of them read a quarter after six. The sun was just coming up. She stretched and yawned, pushing her soft, warm hands into little fists before putting them over her head. She rolled toward the edge of the bed, and the covers rolled with her. They deposited her softly on the thick, plush carpet. She rolled over on her back. Why hadn't she gotten out of these clothes? She jumped up and went to one of the large windows. It looked out over a beautiful pool. There were vines with deep purple flowers framing her view. A ruby-throated hummingbird was seeking an early breakfast of nectar. Hummingbirds, they were here too. She wanted them on her wedding cake. Was this another omen? She stripped down to nothing and headed for the bathroom. There was a hamper by the door. Without thinking, she placed her discarded clothes in it and entered the shower. The towels were there along with shampoo and conditioner just like a hotel.

After bathing, she opened one of her suitcases and selected her clothes. She chose a soft white blouse and some silky blue jeans. The blouse was long and loose. Patti liked them this way. She would take up the slack with a knot tied at her left side and slightly back on her hip. This gave her top a pronounced look. She peered into the mirror. Her hair was a mess. She opened up one of the smaller cases and in a few minutes had it done up in the back with little strands of curls coming down on each side of her face. She had seen a number of brides do their hair this way on their wedding day. The transformation was amazing. Now all she needed was a little makeup. When the finishing touches were placed on her appearance, she ventured out the door and began her own private tour of the home. What had Jim said about this house? It had twenty rooms. What would a person do with so many?

For the first five minutes, she did not see a soul. Perhaps they were all still sleeping. She paused in front of one room that dazzled her senses. In its center was a giant white grand piano. It was trimmed with gold also. *This must be the music room.* There was a large open area where a person could set up several chairs. A concert pianist could perform quite nicely there. Patti had always wanted to play the piano. Perhaps she could go over now and strike a few notes, but no, if people were still sleeping, wouldn't that wake them up? She was about to leave the room when the piano suddenly started playing all by itself. Patti was startled yet curious. The music coming from it was so very soft and beautiful she was compelled to venture further. As she turned left a little, she saw the sweet little lady playing. She was so short her head had not been visible over the stand. Her eyes were closed, and she seemed to be playing a tune from a distant world, as if she had tuned into heaven and brought it to earth. The young woman found a chair and sank down in it as she let the music soothe her soul. Then a beautiful voice started to sing along with the sound. It was angelic.

Patti listened for a full fifteen minutes. Then the music stopped and the little lady got up. She was startled when she saw Patti.

"Oh, pardon me, Patti. I hope I didn't wake you. I usually play a little in the morning when my mind is fresh."

"Not at all. I was up early today and started for the kitchen when I saw this lovely room and had to see what it was all about. It is the most beautiful music room I have ever seen. Did you design it yourself?" Patti was sincerely interested in hearing the answer. It was very, very lovely.

"Yes, I did," responded the older woman. "I used to

travel all over the United States giving concerts. That is how Ken and I got our start in the movies. It was a natural next step. We realized that after we were asked to star in back-to-back musicals. I sincerely hope I did not bother you in any way. I mainly play for my own enjoyment now. I am getting well up in years, and I have lost my voice."

"It sounded angelic to me, ma'am. It was truly the most beautiful music I have ever heard. Your voice was perfect." Patti was silent for a moment and then asked a question. "Pardon me, but I don't know what to call you. Jim introduced you as Mom. Is it okay if I call you that, or is there another name you would prefer?"

"My name is Betty Sears. You certainly can call me Mom if you like. It is kind of nice, in fact. Jim spoke so highly of you, it is like you are part of the family already. So call me Mom or Betty. Mrs. Sears is too formal though. Please don't call me that."

"Mom it is then," responded Patti. "And what name does your husband answer to?"

"You can call him Dad or Ken, whatever you are most comfortable with. You must be starved, dear," interjected Mom. "Let's get you down to the kitchen and pump some food into you. You are much too skinny. A little meat on your bones would make you as plush as a peacock. What would you like for breakfast?"

"I am not picky, Mom. Will you make breakfast, or do you have people who do that?"

"We used to have a cook, but after Ken retired and we stopped traveling with our concerts, I took over the job. Every now and then though, when we have company, I call her back. Jim enjoyed her last meal so much, he has hired her part-time, but no cook can make food taste as good as the queen of her own kitchen. We do have a live-in house cleaner. You will most likely run into her while you are here. Her name is Barbara and her daughter, Lacy. She and her daughter live in a furnished apartment joined to the house with its own outside entrance. She also is a great cook and can get up a meal in a pinch if we have unexpected company. Would you like scrambled or fried eggs, waffles, pancakes, hashed brown potatoes, dried cereal, cooked cereal, sweet rolls, sausage, bacon, doughnuts? You just name it, and I will set it before you."

"That is quite a menu you have, Mom," replied Patti. "Today I am your guest. Fix me whatever you were planning for your own breakfast, and that will be just fine."

Betty went to work quickly. In no time, she had some crepes made up and brought out some fresh raspberries with whipped cream to put on them. She poured Patti a glass of orange juice and polished the meal off with some dainty pieces of toast—or at least that was what Patti thought they were. They were made from small loaves of bread but sliced very thin and then dipped in some sort of mixture before being toasted. They had the taste of tangy lemon and powdered sugar. It was a simple meal but very delicious and satisfying.

Patti looked around at the kitchen. There was a copper rack with a number of copper kettles. They were arranged from large to small. There was a giant oven, fully three times larger than Patti's. It had several settings arranged in a series of buttons. You could use the infrared setting, microwave setting, convection setting, regular setting, or a combination of any of them. It enabled the owner to bake things much faster than in conventional ovens. Metal pans could be used in this oven if the microwave setting was not selected. Betty explained that Patti could bake her cakes in about half the time and they would have the maximum rising capability possible. To activate the technology, one only had to select the desired combination and push the power bake button for the process to begin.

Patti thought of the pans in one of her luggage bags. Perhaps she would be able to bring them down later and have Betty show her how this worked. That would be exciting! With an oven like this, she could turn out twice the number of cakes in the same amount of time. If she married Jim, this would be her kitchen. What a wonderful place to work. It looked out over a private garden. There was an English-style fence enclosing it. On the left was an assortment of herbs. In the middle were some vegetables, and the rest were flowers. Patti looked at the flowers. She was surprised to see the very same dainty yellow ones she needed for the cake decorations. In the distance, tall palm trees towered into the sky. They held what looked like strings of dates. As she was dreaming about the future, a tall man stepped into the garden and began to pull some of the small weeds that had recently sprung up.

"Do you have a gardener, Mom?"

"Yes, Manuel comes in three days a week to care for the yard and gardens. He is a skillful horticulturist and also maintains our arboretum. We can go there later this morning for tea. We have music piped into it. There is a sound that makes plants grow. That is going all the time. The arboretum is lighted with fiber optics. This blocks the UV rays. We also have increased the oxygen levels within and atmospheric pressure. You can't imagine how big things grow in there. Ken raised a seven-pound tomato just last year. They also sprayed the plant with some sort of solution that infuses carbon dioxide with growth hormones. He literally grew some cherry tomatoes as large as tennis balls. You can ask the gardener about it when you see him. He will talk for hours on the subject if you let him.

"We also have water pumped over the top of the arboretum. This does something to the gravity. The plants are uninhibited in their growth. Ken gave some fancy name for it. Let me see what was it? Hydrotropism, I believe. It has something to do with the plant's response to water. Manuel also breeds prize-winning flowers. He has several hybrids to his credit, yet he is perfectly content to remove weeds, mow lawns, or prune shrubs. He will be maintaining our gardens in Palm Springs as soon as we are settled there. His nephew is into electronics. They recently brought a high-tech mower to the yard. They placed little sensors all around the grass, and this mower mows the lawn all by itself. Ken really likes that too, and he will talk about it to just about anyone who will listen."

"When might I expect Jim back, Mom?" questioned Patti suddenly. In all the excitement of the large kitchen, she had forgotten about him. That was probably not very courteous of her. She should have been ashamed of herself but was not. No, not in the least. Why?

"I would guess he will show up around four … His producer works him hard, and sometimes he has long days. They shoot trial runs of the movie they are working on so the animators and special effects experts can do their thing on the giant computers. Then when they get to the location of the film, they shoot the real scene, but the modifications are all ready to go. It works like a template. The modified areas are superimposed in just the right places, and the actors then have less time to wait for their films to be released to the public after the shoot. It is a lot different from what Ken and I were doing making films. They even figure with the powerful memories in the computers now that in a few years or so, actors will not really be needed. They will make computer-generated, virtual actors who do not make mistakes. They do not complain about the conditions they are exposed to, and they cost a whole lot less. So if Jim doesn't make his mark in the next five years, he may be out of a job. But even if that were to happen, he has enough money stashed away to support a hundred average families in America. He just might get a chance to retire at thirty years of age. To me, that is too young. A man should work at least until he is fifty."

The morning went fast. Ken came to breakfast shortly after Patti and continued his flattery of the charming young cake decorator for fully half an hour before going into the city for a meeting. Around ten, Patti brought down her cake pans and the two ladies made a sample cake. It was a lemon heart-shaped one just as Jim had requested. The oven did well. The cake did exactly what Betty predicted it would. It raised fully an inch and a half thicker than any Patti had made before with the exact recipe. When they had a piece of it for lunch, it proved to be a cake of dreams, one of those divine creations that few bakers realize in this world. Jim had wanted to sample one of her cakes, and she had made none better than this. Betty had every ingredient known to cooks and then some. She knew tricks that only the old-school cooks and bakers knew and could well have been the chief cook for the commander in chief of the United States had she wanted the position. To Patti, it was like going to heaven.

The telephone rang. Jim was on the line. He asked to talk to Patti.

"Sleepyhead, I decided to call and see if you had gotten up yet."

"I was up hours ago, Jim. I took a shower, listened to a concert, had breakfast, and made a cake. Now we are about to have lunch. I'm sorry about last evening. I wasn't planning to go to sleep. Once on that bed though, and I must have been out in a couple of minutes."

"You won't go to sleep on me this evening if I come over, will you?" he asked.

"No. Not this evening. What time will you be by?"

"Sometime around four thirty. There is a fundraising dinner, and I want you to be my date. There will be a lot of important people there. Did you bring some formal clothes?"

"I don't know what you mean by formal, Jim. I have some nice dresses, but I don't know what they wear to banquets in Hollywood."

"Don't worry about it, Patti. My sister has tons of them. She is exactly your shape and only a couple of inches taller. I will have her select five or six that would be nice, and then you can choose one of those, if that is all right?"

"I usually don't wear other people's clothes, Jim, but

if this banquet is that important, then I will accept your offer."

"I'll bring them with me when I come. I have to stop back at the penthouse anyway to get my clothes. I will have Kathy meet me there. Good-bye, my lovely. I can hardly wait to be with you."

"Good-bye, Jim," Patti responded, trying to imagine the evening he had planned. "I will be looking forward to seeing you, too."

Patti was smiling broadly as she hung up the phone. Betty pulled her aside.

"You appear to like Jim very much." Betty was suddenly very serious. She seemed to be seeing a vision of some events either in the future or in the past. There was a faraway look in her eye, and some of the sparkle faded. The little smiley wrinkles even seemed to turn down. Patti prepared for the worst before responding.

"Yes, I do. We seemed to have hit it off great, right from the start. Is there anything I should know about going to a formal dinner with a movie actor, Betty?" Patti was wondering if that was what had brought on the change in her.

"Not really, Patti. Just be your own, sweet, beautiful self, and you will get along fine. I can help you out with your makeup, and I have some lovely jewelry that would make you look like the Queen of Sheba, if you don't mind wearing it."

"I was trying to tell Jim that I don't make a habit of borrowing others' clothes. Borrowing jewelry is even more out of my comfort zone."

"Don't think a thing about it. I have so much that I

never will be able to wear it all again in this lifetime. Plus, I seldom get out anymore. I think I am becoming a bit of a hermitta when it comes to social events." Betty made up a word from somewhere that tried to give a view of a female hermit. "You are welcome to it. I want you to keep whatever jewelry you wear this evening. Remember to take it with you when you go home. With your looks, you will wear it much better than I ever could."

"Oh, but you're so beautiful, Mom. When I saw you with your eyes closed, sitting at the piano, I thought you were an angel. Your beauty is ageless."

"Thanks for the vote of confidence, Patti, but my looks went away years ago. I have far too many wrinkles. This old skin just doesn't do much for me anymore." She sighed, remembering the bygone years when she could capture the attention of any man in any room.

Patti wanted to run into the city to gather a few supplies for the cake and decorations. It would be several hours before Jim came by. She wondered how she was going to manage it.

The two women had a light lunch in the arboretum. The place was beautiful. There were tropical flowers on all sides. The water running over the top made it quite cool inside. In the center, there was a cluster of palm trees. These were framed on either side with banana trees. One of the banana trees had small bananas growing on it. Patti realized that many of these plants and flowers could be used if needed along with the dainty yellow flowers she had spotted in the garden. She would also stop at a florist and see what else might be available in a city several times larger than her Santa Rosa. She needed to spend tomorrow morning shopping. She decided to ask Betty how to go about it.

"Jim asked me to order the flowers that will go around the cake." Patti piped out the comment with a little bit of enthusiasm. Perhaps this would bring the sparkle back into the face of this little mother. "I have a picture of what he wants it to look like in my room. I saw some yellow flowers in your garden for starters, but do you think I could somehow get into town in the morning to order some other arrangements?"

"Certainly, Patti. Jim is planning to take the day off tomorrow. He will take you wherever you wish to go. He also wants to show you off down at the studio. I think you will have a great time."

Patti smiled as she heard these plans. It would be nice to go around and see some of the sights, and it would be especially nice with Jim taking her. She went to her room and brought her portfolio down for Mom to see.

"Here is the cake I am making for Kathy's wedding, Betty. Jim liked this heart-shaped one."

Betty looked at the pictures and gave a number of exclamations as she saw the detail Patti exercised in decorating her cakes. She made that frosting do impossible things.

"I have never seen finer cakes than these, Patti. You have a rare talent and the touch of an elegant artist. If you showed these pictures around here, you would soon have more orders than you could fill. These cakes must go for thousands of dollars."

"Not really, Mom. I don't usually charge more than seven hundred fifty dollars for the largest ones."

"Seven hundred fifty, Patti?" Mom questioned. "You could get two thousand around here for some of your simpler designs. You are underselling yourself."

"Do you really think so, Betty?"

"It is usual for cakes at a fundraising dinner, such as you will be attending this evening, to go for less than five thousand, even ten thousand or more. What were you planning to charge Jim for his sister's cake?"

"Since he was so kind as to fly me out here and see that I was comfortable, I was only planning on charging him twenty-five hundred for the cake. That is a good wage for a couple of days' work back in Santa Rosa. This is more of a vacation for me than a business trip."

"I hope you haven't given him your price yet; you would be foolish to charge him less than five thousand for the cake you plan on doing. The flowers alone will cost a lot of money."

"Are they really going to be that expensive?"

"Yes, but you won't have to pay for any supplies. Jim told me he was taking care of everything. Don't skimp on anything, Patti. Do whatever you want to do, and don't even consider the cost. He would be hurt if you tried to skimp on anything. He is very close to his sister. She really has been his whole family. We tried to fill in, but Jim and Kathy have a bond that is closer than any other brother and sister I have ever known. When you make her cake, make it as if you were doing it for the person you loved most in the world. Let your heart make this cake. Fill it with love. Jim has a lot of love inside. All he needs is to find a woman like his sister, and he will be one sweet, loving husband."

Patti smiled softly to herself as she heard the older woman speaking from her heart. She would follow her advice. She would make this cake and cover each inch of it with all the love she could muster.

"I have a serious question to ask you, Mom. Jim has a large following of fans. There must be thousands of women who would do anything to have him pay attention to them. Do you really think he is capable of loving one woman more than all the others?"

Mom pondered the question for a few moments before answering. "Yes, I really believe deep down inside that Jim could love one woman more than all the others. I think there is a woman who could hold his love forever. She would have to be a very special woman though. She would have to realize that Jim was not solely hers. She would have to share him with his fans and the world. She would also need to be willing to make sacrifices for him, realizing his career was very important to him. There are a lot of women who could not share him. In his movies, for instance, he will often kiss and even be shown in bed naked with some of the other stars. This would be hard for a possessive woman to take. The lady Jim marries must not be possessive or jealous. This is very hard, I know. Ken and I had to share each other and sacrifice for each other over and over again. But in the end, our love was strong enough to hold us together.

"Hundreds of movie stars marry and get divorced. They do not have what it takes to make their love last. Love has to be more than passion. It has to be more than looks. No matter how good a lady is in bed or how pretty she looks, there will always be some woman who will be better and look prettier. No matter what your personality, there will always be someone who will shine a little brighter. But true love can bind the heart and soul. And yes, Jim is capable of that kind of love. I can see it in him. He is ready to settle down and raise a family, but I would almost be willing to say that his wife, whoever she will be, will have to consider having an open marriage with Jim. He will most likely have physical relations with other women, probably for the rest of his life. It would be a lot to ask him not to. He belongs to the world, yet when it comes to true love, he will love one the best, and that will make all the difference."

Patti was quiet after she heard the answer Betty gave. It was not what she wanted to hear. It went against everything she had been raised to believe. A woman and man who planned to unite in marriage were to be bound together, holding to each other only, as long as they both should live. She had heard it a hundred times or more in all the weddings she had made cakes for. Yet she knew deep down inside that Betty was right. Jim would not hold only to her. She did not know how she had known it, but it was there all along. This was why she was so comfortable with him. She could enjoy his companionship without commitment. She was afraid of commitment. Too many of her friends had tried and failed, and when she had given her all, it had nearly destroyed her. This was also why she was slow to open up to men like Cal. He was looking for commitment. If Jim was also looking for a wife, it didn't seem to be in his top priorities now. In some ways, he seemed ready, but in others, he was still a kid chasing his dreams. True love had not come to him, at least not the kind of love Betty had claimed he showed toward his sister. He might be committed to his sister, but he was not committed to marriage yet. Patti did not want to be the one who forced it on him either. She didn't realize it, but that was one of the main reasons Jim was so attracted to her. As Patti pondered this further, she realized that was why Betty had become so serious when asking if Patti was really interested in Jim. She had sized her up in just a few minutes. She probably even saw her through to her conservative religious viewpoints. Betty was nobody's fool. Her concern had been well founded.

Patti took another slice of the cake and let her taste buds savor each tiny morsel. She wondered why she did not get tired of tasting cakes. Most wedding cakes were so sweet and stacked with so much frosting that a person could only choke down one piece—and not one that big either. They were more for looks than for eating. But Patti had overcome this. She had found one cake early in her career with just the right blend. The baker had shared the recipe with her. She had analyzed all the ingredients and transferred them over into her own cakes, changing her recipes until each captured the magic formula. Then she had worked on just the right frosting mixes to make certain sweet was not too sweet or sickeningly sweet. This cake had it all. It was perfect! She watched as Betty cut another slice for herself while continuing to go through her portfolio of pictures.

"How did you come to choose a career in cake making and decorating?" Mom asked as her eyes were drawn to an orange-cream-colored cake that looked like a giant marshmallow with little fancy swirls all over it.

"I think it was my aunt that put me on to it. My mother's sister would borrow me quite often when I was growing up. She made cakes on the side but was really not all that good at it. Oh, she could make a normal wedding cake as good as the next person, but it was always that sweet, sickening type of cake with frosting and decorations sometimes an inch thick. I saw a number of weddings where people would scoop off all the pretty flowers and frosting and dump them in the trash while eating only the cake portion. I thought to myself that was a real waste. Aunt Julie spent hours trying to make each little flower perfect, and to see them tossed in the trash upset me. I ask her once if I could experiment with her frosting recipe. I found a filler besides sugar that I use to this day. My aunt was so impressed she purchased a bunch of decorating implements for me, and when she had to take Uncle Ben to the doctor unexpectedly one day with an unfinished cake, I was left to finish it. My cake made it to the third page in the local paper. My aunt realized my ability in this area, and after that, I was hooked."

Betty was silent again for a few moments and then expressed to Patti what was on her mind.

"You clearly have the gift, Patti. God has given you amazing talents. He has also blessed you with good looks. I am sure if you and Jim get together, you will be able to hold his love. He will always love you more than all the others. In time, you could even come close to matching the affection he holds for his sister. If you do this, make certain you marry him because you love him and not because of all this glamour you have been thrust into. Tonight you will catch it. You will be in the spotlight. It will be all grand and glorious. But deep down inside, you need to look beyond the illusions and see him for what he is. He is just a man like every other man. Fate has given him more than the average man; that is all. In the end, it will come down to love. Do you really love him? Could you see yourself loving him no matter what circumstances you find yourself in or what circumstances he finds himself in? Examine your heart. Talk to your God. I can see you are a Christian and have rather high standards. Ask yourself if you would be willing to compromise your standards? Will your sense of right and wrong get in the way of your love if you see Jim doing things that do not measure up? If you can live with that, then I can certainly give my blessings and best wishes for your future together." Betty had a sad look in her eyes.

Patti knew she had hit her in a sensitive area. Would she, Patti, be able to overlook what was just below the surface of his charming, bubbling, gracious, fun-loving personality? Would she really be bothered when he showed that same charm to woman after woman? He would always be a flatterer. Women would be drawn to him like a magnet. He had the charisma. It flowed out of him whether he wanted it to or not.

Chapter 10
A QUEST FOR GOD

Cal had to get away. Shortly after his last dental assistant quit, this new one came waltzing into his office, looking for employment. She had responded to an ad he had placed in the local newspaper. Her name was Brenda. She had all the qualities he was looking for; plus she was very cute. They hit it off right from the start. Then she became possessive. At this point in their relationship, she was driving him bananas. She was putting the pressure on him to take their relationship from one of business to pleasure. He had been startled just the other day when he went to the staff lounge and saw her dressed only in panties and a bra. It seemed she had purchased a new outfit and was changing when he passed by. She did not even seem embarrassed by the incident. In fact, she appeared to enjoy seeing the color that was even then creeping up his neck into his face. She just stood there in all of her bare splendor and smiled.

"Pardon me, Cal. I was invited out to a party this evening and needed to change into something more informal before meeting up with my girlfriends. Now that you have had a look at me in a more informal way, what do you think? I've been following some great exercise classes on television, and they appear to be getting my tummy back to where it should be. Oh and my buns too. There is this little exercise that really rounds them out." She turned just enough to show her cheeks off.

Cal cleared his throat and then responded, "I'm so very sorry I walked by when I did. I didn't mean to intrude while you were changing. I have to be leaving now."

With that, he quickly moved on down the hall. As he was going, he heard her respond, "The party is not till seven, Cal. It has been a long time since I have been, you know, with a man. Perhaps ..."

But Cal was out the door, running toward his car. He would come back later—yes, later would be a good idea—to check and make sure she locked up everything when she left. Then, what he needed next was to get away! When it came right down to it, the location didn't matter. Perhaps he would retreat to his favorite place—on the mountains. The newly bought and already packed backpack in his trunk would serve him with all the necessary supplies for a three-day getaway. He would have a great time, although bittersweet, since the last time he had taken an outing like this, Linda had been with him. How he missed her now. He remembered the pouring rain during the last day of their mountain campout. As they became drenched, they shared an intimate kiss. He remembered the taste of her lips and the smell of her hair and skin; all the while, the showers came down upon them. To be able to caress her in his arms once more would be like going to heaven, he thought. Just to take a woman in his arms again like, like Brenda, even, and feel her soft skin next to his would be marvelous. He pondered the mental image only a moment before feeling guilty.

Heaven? What about that? If God were up there somewhere pulling the strings, why had He let Linda die? Why? He remembered getting the call. She had been traveling on Interstate Highway 1. It had been raining, and when she drove around a corner, a deer standing in the middle of the road caused her to swerve. She avoided hitting the deer, but the watery roadway created a hydroplaning effect, and the car plummeted off the road, crashing headlong into a tree and flipping over into a deep ditch. Such a small, unexpected event had caused his beloved to have a fatal accident. Several hours passed before they found her. Cal shook his head, trying to remove the vivid memory and graphic pictures from his mind.

"God!" he cried out. "You could have saved her. You have angels looking over us to lift us up lest we dash our foot against a stone. You have saved my life at least a hundred times. You could have saved hers this time also. I don't get it, God. I just don't understand. The way in which You brought us together was so beautiful. We did all of the right things. Not that we were perfect, Lord. We are human, of course. We made mistakes. But we always gave You thanks. Every meal, we thanked You for Your bountiful blessings. You brought a little package into our life. We were so blessed. I had a good job. We were in love. We had it all, and then I had nothing. I lost my first practice because I was such an emotional wreck; then life with its many stresses piled onto to my shoulders. It was like the entire weight of my world came crashing down upon me. Still, Lord, through it all, I never gave up on You. In looking back, though, my faith weakened, especially in myself, and when life got me down so low, it was easy to give up on myself. That is until Dad shared that sermon with me. I swear, God. He should have been a preacher. He would have made the saints tremble in their seats. Forgive me for blaming You. I know You are busy with running the universe and all. A little prayer like this probably never even gets to Your ears. But somewhere I read that You hear all prayers and that the prayer of a righteousness man avails much. Dad is a righteous man, if I have ever met one. Was he praying? Was he meddling in my life? Did You give him that sermon that got me back on track? I really believe You did. Well, whether You gave it to him or not, it worked. At least I think it worked or is working. I am back in business. I have my own practice again. I have a good house now. I was able to keep a lot of Smith's clients. Then when Grandfather left me that money, I knew You had a hand in it. So forgive me, Lord. I'm sorry that I got so distressed. But could I give you a little hint, Lord? That woman in my practice just about got to me today. She would have let me have my way with her. She invited me to … to give in. You know I am a weak one when it comes to that area of life. Have her lay off, okay? If that happens again, I am afraid of my human nature—I guess the Bible calls it fleshly passion or something like that—is going to win over reason. I can't trust myself. One more temptation like that might overpower me. That is why I am getting away. I want this to be a time to reaffirm my faith in You. Help me to this end. Amen."

At home, Cal placed the stuff he had packed in the back of his Jeep. At least he still had this much to remember his first marriage by. Linda and he had picked it out together.

Though used, it had had only thirty thousand miles on the odometer when they purchased it. He remembered the many weekends they had headed for the hills with it. Now he was heading for the mountains. He intentionally avoided the last camping place they had been. There were just too many memories. He would go up higher, nearer the timberline. He might even do a little skiing. Nothing was quite like cold snow dusting one's face as one raced down a steep, frozen, mountain hillside. Yes, skiing would definitely be on the menu. Backpacking up to a glacier lake would also be a part of this trip.

The flatter lands lay out behind him as he started climbing into the hills that would eventually give way to the mountain. He had stopped at the last gas station and filled up. He had also purchased some energy bars and one Babe Ruth candy bar. He would indulge at least once during this trip. It couldn't be any worse than cutting into Patti's delicious strawberry cake. But that was what was unique about her cake; it was not that sweet, or perhaps it was a natural sweetness. He would pack the candy with him. Perhaps it would be on a windswept knoll overlooking a crystal lake where he bit into it. Perhaps it would be at sunset beneath a brilliant pink-and-orange sky. He would know the right moment to open the wrapper and enjoy. Being a dentist, he had to be careful though. Too much sugar was not even good for a dentist's teeth.

Finally the camping area was before him. He paid his dues at the gate and entered. He and Linda would always drive around the entire campsite before choosing a place to pitch the tent. They had decided to do that after taking the first one available one fateful day shortly after they were married. Later, they had seen this fantastic place overlooking the valley. But that time, as they were close to the road, noisy vehicles passed by during all hours of the night and morning. Plus, the neighbors loved their boom box and did not like it turned down. It went for over half the night. Both had awakened the next morning with deep circles under their eyes, as tired as old horses after a twenty-mile run. But they had survived. They had each other; they had love. But this was not to be about Linda. This was to be about God and Cal.

Cal would set up a large tent by his Jeep. Then he would backpack up to some site above the crystal-clear reservoir. Here he would set up his smaller tent. From there, it was about a three-mile hike down to the lake. He and God would walk it together. Finally, all was ready. As he was about to leave, he spotted his small Bible. God might be more apt to respond to his railings if he carried the Word of God with Him. It was kind of like taking the guidebook or map to show what destinations were available. Yes. The Bible was not a bad idea.

It was early afternoon when Cal started up the trail. The day was quite warm. The insects were not bad; they were a bit worse than in Santa Rosa though. The reason? More moisture, probably. A Bible passage popped into his mind from somewhere back in his boyhood days. *"I will instruct you and teach you in the way that you should go. I will counsel you with My loving eye on you" (Psalm 32:8 NIV).*

A strange thought came into Cal's head. Did God only have one eye? It was a silly question to ask. Why not say, "I will counsel you with My eyes upon you." Then he thought of another Bible passage that stated a person was to have an eye single to the glory of God. Did the writer of that only have a single eye? That led to Paul. Supposedly from what he had gleaned from some preacher, Paul had poor eyesight. It came to him after seeing the brightness of the Lord on the road to Damascus. Strange thoughts to start out a trip into the wilderness with God. He was glad he had good eyes. He was thankful he did not need to wear glasses. With his eyes, he looked up at the snowcapped peaks high above him. Another passage came to mind. *"I will lift up mine eyes unto the hills from whence cometh my help, my help cometh from the Lord" (Psalm 121:1, 2 KJV).* Well, he certainly needed help in the form of strength-in the emotional, physical, and spiritual areas of life. Did he miss any? Cal knew he needed help and strength from without to arm him with what he needed within, most especially if he was going to stand against the temptations of the world the old devil was putting in his path. Then another crazy thought came to mind. At least David had two eyes.

"Help me, God," he whispered as he climbed ever higher.

He did not know why at that very moment Patti's name came up. Perhaps it was the candy bar cake thing? He believed he loved her. He believed that included loving all of her. He even loved thinking of the trouble she had given him. Now that he was removed from the incidents, they actually seemed funny in a way. His sympathy for her had reached its peak when he had nearly destroyed her teeth on that most unfortunate visit to his office. Yet, during that chaotic visit, for some unknown reason, Cal momentarily stopped thinking about the unprofessional events around him and he found himself considering the possibility for Patti to be his wife and the mother of his child. She appeared to be genuine, no phoniness in her demeanor or words. And if children were present or the subject came up, it was obvious from her behavior and the little bit she dared share with him, that, yes, she was interested in a family. *Yes,* Cal thought. *Patti could be a very good mother.* Carissa really needed a mother now more than anything at this time in her life. Cal pondered this situation, wondering if it were to present itself, would it be a problem? Patti knew nothing about Carissa. How would he bring up the subject to her? And when? Would he have an opportunity at some future date to introduce the subject of children to her? Patti had run off to LA, chasing cakes for that—that cad. How could she? How could she abandon him so quickly after those wonderful dinner dates? He was going to tell her about Carissa the day she announced her intent. Well, this trip of his was not supposed to be all about Patti. Cal's purpose was to commune with his Lord and to learn how to know his God in a deeper relationship. But if Patti were to be in his future, could it not be about her too? Patti, Cal, Carissa, and God—or should he change the order. Yes, definitely! God first and foremost, then the others, Patti, Carissa, and himself.

"I suppose we could talk about it, Lord, if You are not too busy. I wanted to impress Patti, so I emphasized myself as if I were this great Christian with my entire life figured out. None of the plans were incorrect really, because everything I said is really what I want and dream. So, considering the facts in that respect, I do not believe I was lying. What about Patti? Did I ever tell you that she looks just like …?" Then, all of a sudden, a large doe dashed out of some brush and continued on up ahead of Cal without seeing him. She was on the run, but from what? Without rustling even so much as a blade of grass, Cal edged over and hunkered down behind a large stump. He wasn't sure what he was waiting for, but his unspoken question was answered within seconds. A grand buck with a bunch of antlers bounded out from the same bushes from whence the doe had emerged. His rack must have been five points or more; it all happened so fast it was difficult to count that quickly. *Surely this majestic creature must be Bambi's dad or maybe even Bambi himself,* Cal thought. And what a beauty! Although Cal was not a hunter, he did want to get a shot of this beauty with his camera! Whenever Cal was in a place to watch these woodland creatures in their natural environment, it was just awe-inspiring. Words did not really do justice to how his heart and soul would soar when he had a chance to admire God's creatures in their natural habitats of beauty. Cal could not even fathom how some could think it was a sport and take great pride in killing the innocent woodland creatures just so they could display their heads on the wall somewhere. And all the bragging, as if this was a vital part of this same ridiculous ritual, some half-truth story about some hunting luck that was had during an exciting adventure. As if killing in any form was an adventure, let alone exciting.

In a split-second hesitation before a big jump, the buck froze in his tracks and looked directly at Cal. He slowly reached for his camera. Behind the creature, the sky was just beginning to darken. A few pink, wispy clouds were dancing in the wind, being blown about this way and that until they settled above the stud's head, forming the perfect shape of a heart. Although the entire scene was only a moment paused in time, the cameraman was quick to recognize the opportunity of a lifetime and seize the moment. Click, click, click went the shutter, and instantly, the moment was interrupted by the continued chase. Again, as if right on cue, the very small voice once more shared this same quote with his heart: *"I know the plans I have for you, Cal. Plans to prosper you, not to harm. Plans to give you a future filled with hope and prosperity. Higher than the highest human thoughts can reach is My ideal for you."*

As quick as the voice ended its quote, the tone abruptly changed to reason, appealing to the mind of the man. Cal had heard of God talking to people in the Bible. This was not that kind of talk, where holy men of old spoke or wrote as they were moved by the Holy Spirit. No. This was an inner guiding voice like that still small voice of conscience, revealing right from wrong. Yet it was more. A conversation was going on somewhere deep in a corner of his mind. He tuned in with a spiritual ear to listen more closely.

If you could see the end from the beginning, Cal, as I see it, you would not question Me. You would not wonder why things turned out like they did for you and Linda. There is an enemy in the world. He hates all that I have created. He hates to see two people in love. He hates it when My children are happy. You and Linda were a thorn in his flesh. He tried to destroy you and your marriage over and over again. My angels were by your side. They diverted his blows many times. Actually, Cal, every blow that he hurled at you fell on Me. I was there with you through it all. I felt your pain and anger. I know your loss. I also know what the future holds for you. You have heard the story of Job. You know what My Word says he went through, don't you?

"Yes, Lord. Is that You talking to me?"

Yes, Cal. I am talking to you.

"How can this be? Why haven't You talked like this to me in the past?"

I have, Son. There was one problem though. You were not listening. You never heard Me. I have tried to talk to you on several occasions. But you never seemed to have need or at least you never expressed your need of Me when you spoke to me … that is, not until last week.

"So why now, Lord? Why are You doing this now? And what do You mean about last week?"

What did you plan to do this weekend?

"Get away and try to find myself and get better acquainted with You."

Have you ever done that before?

"No. Now that I think about it, no. I pray often, but more in the form of requests. I have not really spoken with You. Nor have I waited for an answer from You."

You made time for Me, Cal, and so I made time for you. We could do this every day if you trusted Me. About Brenda. Had you been in a conversation with Me before passing that room, would your thoughts have been different?

"Oh! Yes, I'm sure they would've been, Lord. I might even have had her soul's salvation in mind rather than that red bra she was wearing. Should I have mentioned that to You, God? I am kind of new at this. I never thought of talking to You about … I know it is not what I should have said, Lord. Forgive me."

Do you not think I can read your thoughts, Cal?

"Well, when You put it that way, if You can read my thoughts, why should I speak? But now that we are on this subject, what am I supposed to do about her?"

She will be quitting your employ soon. Even now as we are talking, a man has come into her life, and she is quite taken with him. You will not need to worry about anything happening in the future with her. I am going to send you a blessing in the form of an older assistant. She has a rather motherly appeal about her, something you will need close by in the near future. Since those younger girls seem to cause you to lose your focus, this will be a bit of a change, but a good one, I can assure you. Now back to Patti. What do you think of her?

"I was wondering if You had anything to do with our encounters, Lord. If so, You sure must have a sense of humor at my expense, I might add." Cal thought he heard laughter coming from his invisible companion.

While we are talking about Patti, you were not exactly a saint once you had her under your control at the clinic.

"You do have a sense of humor, God. Why, some people I know, like my neighbor Reata, would consider such a thought as that blasphemy, to think that God might enjoy a laugh once in a while."

170

Another chuckle seemed to come from somewhere into his mind.

"What do I think of Patti? Why are You asking me that question, Lord? You are supposed to know everything."

That is the problem, Cal. You have not taken a whole lot of time to form an opinion of her. So I am kind of at a loss here. I know what you could think if you were to choose the direction of light. I know you will choose wisely.

"Now this is getting complicated, God. Should I call You that, or do You have another name You would rather I use during this conversation?"

"I can't believe this is happening," Cal muttered to himself.

What is that you said, Cal?

"Never mind. You weren't supposed to hear it. It wasn't that important."

Wasn't it? Everything about you is important to Me.

"You know all things, Jesus. You know what I really want to talk about. She is on my mind all the time. Things are getting desperate with Carissa. I have to make the final decision soon. I was hoping I would not have to. That is why I came out here, at least in part, to get some answers from You or whomever. I am afraid Patti will run away just like Darla and Sammie. What kind of parents would name their daughter Sammie anyway?"

To answer your question, Cal, her legal name is Samantha. But back to our conversation. I know this is an area of life weighing heavy on your mind, Son. I understand. I wish I could give you a vision and show you the future, but at this time, that would not be the best for you. You are going to have to wait on Me. You are going to have to come to the point where you trust your future with Me completely. Once that happens, you'll know the right decisions to make. Until then, we can continue communicating just like we are here today … that is, if you will just take some time out to listen.

"I would like that," Cal responded.

Later that evening, Cal broke open that candy bar and offered some to His Lord as he looked out over that grand valley with the glorious sunset painting the heavens around him. One thing about Jesus, He provided His own food when you went backpacking with Him. Only His kind of food is a bit different from candy bars. His food was of a spiritual nature. He was, after all, the Bread of Life. And for this weekend, He was the Bread that came down from heaven. A song passed through the dentist's mind on several occasions. "Heaven came down, and Glory filled my soul."

So the three-day jaunt passed. Somewhere in the mountains of California, a troubled man found the answers he was seeking. Cal and his Lord Jesus linked up, arm in arm. High in the highest heaven, the angels rejoiced that another one of the lost human souls had found its place within the great plans of God as well as a reason to keep moving forward in the hope of the Lord.

Chapter 11
FOR LOVE OR MONEY?

Jim left the studio and had Ted stop by the store to pick up a couple of things for him. He called Kathy on his cell phone and told her about the dinner. She told him she would be at the penthouse to pick out the dresses.

"What are your plans for tomorrow, Sis?"

"I really don't have many except to do my last-minute shopping for the wedding. Why do you ask, Bro?"

"I am taking the day off to show Patti around. She needs to purchase some supplies for your cake and possibly pick up some flowers. Would you mind going with us? We could add your shopping to everything else and make a swell day of it."

"That would be nice, Jim," Kathy responded. "I am dying to meet this woman who has captured the heart of my hithertofore uncatchable brother. I want to know how she did it. Heaven knows that hundreds of others have tried. What is it about her that has stopped you in your tracks? Why do you think she is the one, Jimmy?"

"I have tried to figure that out myself. I think it has to do with the fact that she is not chasing me. She likes me for who I am, not for my money."

"I have heard that one before, but if that is true, I will

have to see it to believe it. Most every woman I know is trying to marry a rich man. Do you love her?"

"How can I answer that, Sis? I deal with love every day. I have played it over and over again in movie after movie. Each lady I star with is the one true love that every man is looking for. I suppose I love her more than most of the others."

"You mean you are not sure she is the one?"

"I am quite sure but not one hundred percent certain. I have only seen her twice. Last evening, I had everything all planned out for us, and she fell asleep on her bed. I waited over three hours for her to wake up, but she never stirred. Any other woman would have been so obsessed with going out with me she would not have been able to sleep a wink. Patti is different that way, and I like that about her."

Kathy broke out laughing at this comment.

"You mean to tell me that your girlfriend went to sleep on you? I can't believe that one. She must find you extremely boring if she runs off to her room and goes to sleep on you. Where is that woman wooer that drives all the ladies crazy?"

"Come on, Sis. I'm not that bad. Patti was just tired. She even apologized to me about it when I called her. She said she never realized she went to sleep. She had no intentions of it. The bed was so soft, when she laid down, that was it and she was out like a light. That's all I know right now, but the more I am with her, the more she grows on me. She is awakening feelings in me I never knew I had. I find myself wanting to protect her from all the evil I see around. I want to keep her innocent like she is and never let anything hurt her. If that is love, Kathy, than I am falling in love and am helpless to do anything about it. When Betty told me she fell asleep on that soft bed, I couldn't get that picture of her out of my mind. I saw her there with soft blankets cradled around her face, and I loved her."

"You mean to tell me that you went to her room and saw her sleeping?"

"No, Sis. I pictured her there in my mind. It drove me crazy with desire. On the set today, that passion overpowered me. The star I am showing with started getting the hots for me right there on the screen. My director praised us on that passion. It was Patti who created it. I want to possess her totally and hold her near my heart forever."

"I think you are falling in love, Brother. Yup! My little brother is going to get caught, and he won't be able to say I never told him so. You are going, going and will soon be gone if you let those kinds of thoughts keep overpowering you. Do you think you are ready?"

"No, I'm not ready! That is what scares me. Love, if that is what this is, isn't supposed to come like this. I expected something totally different. I pictured some exotic woman in an island paradise, sweeping me off my feet, similar to a movie I starred in not long ago. I never imagined a photo on the Internet could turn out to be something like this. When I saw the photo, I wanted to meet the girl. When I met the girl, I wanted to meet her over and over again. She was too far away to do that, so I brought her out here. I don't understand it. It is too deep for my comprehension. I do know this though; she makes the fanciest cakes I have ever seen. She could make a fortune selling them around here. I also know that she is sweeter than any cake she ever dreamed of making."

Kathy went to her closet and picked out half a dozen dresses. Jim went over to look at her selections.

"Which of these do you like best, little brother," she asked, holding up a selection of very lavish outfits. Some were very, very expensive. Jim looked at the assortment and immediately pointed to a black one.

"You like that one? You always like your women in low-neck dresses. This one doesn't have a low neck."

"I know, Kat. That is why I like it. I don't want all those other guys looking down her dress to see what they can see. I haven't seen her yet, and it'll be a cold day in hell before I let someone else get that privilege first. I don't want any portion of her cleavage exposed to lustful eyes. The rest of the dresses you have chosen are too revealing. Select more like this one."

"My, but you are getting protective all of a sudden. I have never seen this side of you. Did you learn that from some new script in your movie?"

"You know better than that, Kitty Kat. You know my producer's views on women's clothing. She says if they got it, they need to flaunt it. It gives them that much more control over men."

Kathy put three of the dresses back in her well-stocked closet. She replaced them with some multiple-colored designs.

"Your Patti Cake probably likes color. Her cakes show it. I can't imagine her choosing that old black dress, so here are a few bright-colored ones to give her some variety."

"I appreciate your input, Sis, but I think I will make up some excuse to only get her the black dress. I don't want her all decked out like a lit-up Christmas tree."

"Jimmy Boy, let me tell you something about women. I would have thought you would have picked this up by now, but since you haven't, let me tell you plainly. Women like to be in control, especially of their wardrobe. Women also know what colors they look best in. Most men don't have a clue about that. Just take the whole lot of them and let Betty put them in her room. Then leave her to choose the one she wants, okay? She probably feels intimidated enough to have to wear borrowed clothing to this ball or whatever thingamajig that you are going to tonight. If you give her the courtesy to choose and if she likes you like I think she does, she'll make herself look very nice for you. You'll be the proudest man at the dinner, running around with her on your arm. Just let her do her thing. I have full confidence that a cake decorator and an artist like her can do that and so should you."

"Okay, Kat. You win this time, but if I see that she is raising too many eyebrows, I will leave early and take her out somewhere so we can be alone."

The ride over to the new house took longer than Jim wanted. He had been away from Patti all day, and he really wanted to be with her as much as possible while he had the chance. The traffic was extra heavy, and time seemed to crawl by.

"Is there any way to make this crate go a little faster, Ted?" Jim asked.

"No, the traffic is real heavy. We are making progress

though. As soon as we pass this bottleneck up ahead, I think we will be back to normal."

"I sure hope so!"

Finally he could see the house up ahead. Ted pulled up to the gate, and the keeper let them in. Jim jumped from the car and literally ran up to the house with the dresses in his hand. He didn't even wait for the chauffeur to open the limo door. Bobbie even had a hard time keeping up with the star. At the door, he didn't even knock but barged right in. Patti was sitting on one of the leather chairs with her bare feet propped up in the air. She gave him a big smile when he entered. She gracefully bounded to her feet and met him as he came toward her.

"You get more beautiful every time I see you, Patti!" he said as he put his arms around her, dresses and all. She gave him a quick kiss and then slipped out of his grasp as quickly as he had gotten her into it. She ran to the kitchen with him following at a trot. About the time he reached the tiled floor, she whirled around and popped a piece of lemon cake in his surprised mouth. That stopped him dead in his tracks. The flavor was so delicious. He gulped it down and muttered while trying to point to his mouth, "Moe?"

"Later, big guy."

"No, really, Patti. That cake was absolutely the best I have ever eaten. Is that what Sis's cake will taste like?"

"It is the very recipe," she replied and returned with another piece. This time, it was on a plate and she had a fork with it. She traded it for the dresses. While he tended to the cake, she looked over what he had brought. They were her size all right, and they were beautiful. There was a light, pastel-green one that had little sparkles all over it. It complemented the color of her hair perfectly. It was a bit modest but would look gorgeous on her. Her second choice was a black one with soft lace around the neck. Jim was still occupied with the cake so she slipped silently away with the dresses without him even noticing. When he turned to praise her on the cake again, she was nowhere to be seen. Without thinking, he sped down to her room. At the door, he caught sight of her backside with only a bra and panties. He was about to burst into the room when Mom came up the hall from her own room.

"Hi, Jim. I am so glad you made it. I was just watching the traffic report, and they showed an overturned semitruck. It was on fire, and the traffic was being rerouted down another road. You must have missed the accident."

"Yes, Mom. I am sure we did, but the traffic was slow and it took forever to get here." He placed his arm around his little mother and walked her back to the kitchen.

"Patti gave me a sample of Kathy's cake. It was delicious. It is truly the tastiest cake I have ever eaten. I don't think a cake for five hundred will be enough. Everyone is going to want a second piece. Did you help her bake it?"

"No! She wouldn't let me, but I did help her frost it. She is talented. I told her a couple of cakes like that around here and she would be swamped with orders."

"I believe you are right about that. I do think we will need a bigger cake though."

"Patti already thought about that. She will be making a couple of side cakes. She will also add layers to three of the center cakes. She said there was a strawberry cake that would go nicely with the wedding colors. Then she plans to make a chocolate one also, since that still remains a favorite cake of many people."

Betty excused herself and went to Patti's room and knocked. She entered and helped Patti with some makeup and then opened a small box of jewelry. After a few minutes, she returned to Jim. The two talked for about ten minutes before Patti emerged. When Jim saw her, he just stood there, gazing at the most beautiful creature he had ever laid eyes on. She had chosen the pastel-green dress with the shimmering sparkles. Around her neck was a gold necklace with a series of dainty diamonds. In the center of the necklace, just below the hollow in her neck, a giant diamond sparkled with rainbow colors. Her hair was set back a little, exposing her elegant skin. She was smiling and seemed to float toward him. His knees went weak for the first time in his life. Lucky for him there was a chair behind him. He sank down into it and stared some more. She was within reach now, but he was paralyzed. Patti's expression changed to one of concern.

"Are you okay, Jim?" she questioned. "You look like you have seen a ghost. I hope the cake didn't have anything in it you are allergic to."

After a few moments, he finally found his tongue.

"No, Patti. The cake was marvelous, but the dessert is so much sweeter."

"What do you mean, dessert? The cake is the dessert."

"Not in my book. You are so beautiful, you are the dessert. I have half a notion to take you back to your bedroom and not let you leave for weeks."

"You'd be cruel enough to make me a prisoner of my

own room, Jim?" she asked again as she took a couple of steps closer. She placed a mock fearful look on her face that gave her the appearance of a scared little girl.

"No, you wouldn't be the prisoner, dear. I am the one who would be imprisoned. You have already made me a prisoner of your beauty. I will forever be your humble servant. Just let me live in your presence forever, and I will be eternally happy." A quote from one of his movies slipped out of his lips as he continued to stare at this fairy princess before him.

"Okay, Jim. That is enough. Your flattery exceeds your common sense. How long will it take to get to the fundraising dinner?"

"I am serious, Patti. I love you."

"Yes, and I am sure you have said that to a string of other women. Now answer the question. How long will it take?"

"Ted can have us there in half an hour if the traffic has cleared up, so we still have plenty of time." Jim sighed. "I'll have him bring in my clothes so I can get dressed. You really are beautiful. And I do love you." He rose and gave her a kiss so gentle her willpower began to melt.

Why go to the dinner? She would just follow him to his changing room and help him undress. To cover her feelings up though, she faked a hard look and commented as he headed for the room, "Love can fool a man sometimes so you had better be careful what you say. You may regret it someday."

Jim mumbled something to himself as he took the clothes from Ted and headed in the opposite direction from Patti's bedroom. Betty came over and checked Patti out.

"You really do look beautiful, Patti. That dress complements the color of your hair perfectly. You will be right in style at the dinner. I will be surprised if you don't get at least a half a dozen proposals for marriage this evening."

"You're not serious, Mom, are you? Proposals don't come that plentiful anywhere."

"They do here. You will be evaluated by both men and women. Jim has received hundreds of proposals for marriage by some of the prettiest girls in the country. I would love to go along and watch. When those girls see you, they will know you are way above their class. You will get a number of them who have set their mark on Jim extremely worried. So be careful. Tomorrow you will be in papers all across California. Your picture will be on over ten thousand Facebook listings. Don't be surprised if you find out things about yourself that never were. There will be a lot of stories fabricated by people. Don't talk much. Just smile your pretty smile and let them think what they will. The more you talk, the more your privacy will slip away. If they find out you bake cakes and live in Santa Rosa, they will blow the story all out of proportion. Let them think you are from London or Spain or some exotic, faraway country. If you know any peculiar accent or a foreign language, use it when you talk. Keep them guessing. Celebrities have no privacy anymore, so whatever you do, don't let them know much about you."

"You are serious, aren't you, Betty? I had no idea

this would be such a big deal. We're just going out for a fundraising luncheon.

"The fans love a story. They will go to impossible feats to get one even if they have to make most of it up. They will have you secretly married or say you met on some paradise island or a hundred other possible explanations of why you are with Jim tonight."

"Will Jim keep quiet too?" Patti questioned.

"Normally he would, but he is so taken with you this evening, he might be vulnerable to some unsuspecting reporter. I will have a little talk with him and hope the message gets through. He is pretty gone though. You shook him out of his comfort zone, and I love it. He always did come across like he was too sure of himself. This is good for him but also dangerous."

"I speak some French. Will that help?"

"You really do? That would be perfect. Speak mostly in French this evening. When you do speak in English, make it broken with a little accent. That will throw them off from your trail quite a bit. It will also keep Jim from losing his composure. I will tell him that. He will know how to play the game. He is a good actor, and if he can keep his head about him, he will pull it off handsomely. It will be a way to protect you more than you probably know."

Jim returned from the room dressed in a tux and a light-green, pastel shirt to match Patti's dress. His long blond hair literally shone, and his expensive cologne permeated the air with a smoothness akin to his manners. His beard was trimmed perfectly, and he smiled broadly when he saw Patti again. Betty took him aside and let him in on the French plot. He loved it. He came up to Patti and whispered in her ear, "If you can speak French so fluently, can you French kiss equally as well?"

Patti blushed a little before answering. "If I did, I wouldn't let you know about it. Now let's get going, *monsieur.*"

"Okay, *mademoiselle.*"

Chapter 12
MADEMOISELLE PATRICIA

The trip to the luncheon was quite nice. Patti again rested in the arms of this handsome man. His charm and cologne made her feel right at home. She felt so complete when she was in his arms. He was tender and gracious and a perfect gentleman. She sensed he had a tender regard for her and a deep caring that changed him, made him all the more appealing. Was this love? She had sensed it only in one other man, Dr. Cal Ripland. Whatever these two men had, she liked it. It made every inch of her five-feet-two-inch frame feel every bit a woman. She stretched her face up toward Jim and gave him a sweet kiss on the lips. He blushed even as he allowed his lips to linger on hers. This was her man. She knew it at that moment and sensed that the feeling was mutual. Jim knew it too. Here at last was a woman who could hold him. A broad smile crossed his face as he looked into her eyes.

"Has anyone ever told you that you were beautiful?"

"Yes, Jim," she responded. "But none have said it in the tone you just used. You said it like you really meant it."

"I do mean it, Patti. You are beautiful in so many ways. Your appearance though is not to be surpassed by your inner beauty. You are beautiful from the inside out. Your inner beauty is what makes your outer beauty so exceptional. I have been trying to figure out why you are different from the others, and now I know. It comes from your inner beauty. I have gone out with a number of women who are classed among the prettiest ladies in the world, but none of them had that inside beauty that you have. I believe I could marry you and love you for all time. Your innocence and beauty are ageless. I could wake up next to you fifty years from now, and you would be just as lovely as you are tonight."

"Fifty years is a long time, Jim. I am sure any beauty you might think I have now would be completely gone by then."

"No, Patti. Take Mom for instance. She is beautiful, don't you agree?"

"Yes, she is a very pretty woman. She has wrinkles, but they are happy, smiley wrinkles."

"That is the kind of beauty you have too, Patti Cake. It is ageless, like Mom's."

Patti snuggled a little closer to Jim and placed one of her hands under his tux. She could feel the ripples on his muscular chest beneath her fingers. Her hand felt warm. The ride to the hall was far too short. Patti looked over at the body guard. He had a way of disappearing. It was like he was never there. She was with Jim in their own world. She had thought the presence of another man would make her feel uncomfortable with Jim but found that she actually took comfort in the fact there were two men near her. She felt safe, and that was wonderful!

Inside the building, there were at least two hundred people. They were all dressed nicely—not all of them as formal as Jim and Patti, but very nice. A small blond lady came bounding up to Jim and was about to give him a kiss when she spotted Patti. She slowed down and came to a complete stop just inches away from his face. She first looked at Jim and then at Patti. Then in a sarcastic voice spoke.

"Jim, darling, I see that you brought the cleaning maid from your house. What a shame that you wasted that diamond necklace on her."

Patti flushed with anger. She was no maid. She was about to respond when she remembered her French. She would tell this rude woman that she was no cleaning maid and that he was the one she intended to marry.

"Je ne suis aucune bonne. C'est l'homme que j'ai l'intention d'epouser. Je l'aime," she said so sweetly that at least fifteen people turned her direction when they heard her speaking.

Remembering that she was supposed to be a Frenchwoman this evening, Jim turned to the small crowd that was gathering around them and introduced Patti.

"This is mademoiselle Patricia. She has come a great distance to be here this evening. I would appreciate it very much if you would show her how nice America is. She understands English very well, so be careful what you say. She is more comfortable speaking French this evening so don't try to engage her in conversation unless you speak French. She is my date, and I am seriously interested in her."

"If she is from France and does not speak English

that well, how will you ever communicate with her, Jim?" asked one of the men nearby.

"We are studying each other's language. Since I made her acquaintance several weeks ago, we have been communicating back and forth. My command of French is growing better with each passing day."

"Prove it," replied the man with a hint of sarcasm and disbelief in his voice.

Jim looked at Patti and then at the man who had asked the question. He searched his mind for any French words he could remember. He had starred in a movie once that had a few French phrases. He could almost remember them. He had to do something so he let it fly.

"Jeune homme, vous serez requis d'apporter aux vaches dedans du pâturage chaque soirée," he replied without blinking an eye.

Patti smiled a very beautiful smile when she heard the phrase. It was something about bringing the cows in each evening. She decided to respond once again in her own sweet way. She would add that they were not to forget to bring in the jackasses too.

"N'oubliez pas d'apporter les ânes de cric, aussi!"

The man who had asked Jim to prove himself was very defensive now. He asked Jim a question. "Did she just call me a jackass, Jim?"

"You mean to say that you don't know, Scott? If you don't know what she said, perhaps you had better brush up on your French. I certainly am not going to interpret her sentences to you."

"That's probably because you don't understand what she is saying yourself."

With that, he left the couple and was followed by several of the others, including the rude blonde. About that time, the master of ceremonies announced that the meal was about to be served. The seats were assigned so Patti and Jim started looking for their places. They found them at the end of one of the rows of tables. Patti looked over the people who were nearby. She saw several looking their direction and watched them whisper back and forth to each other. Her appearance with Jim was certainly causing a sensation. One of the distinguished-looking guests rose from his seat and went to the back of the room. Patti watched him make a phone call on his cellular. She was startled when one of the ladies across the table asked her a question.

"There is a rumor going around that you are from Paris. Is that correct?"

Patti did not know how to answer. She did not want to tell an outright lie, and yet she did not want to start a counterrumor either.

"*Non*, Eii haff spend some time there bud no much. I no much gooot at Engliss. I learn, *rapide* though—how you say, fass?" She motioned to the lady like she was searching for the word.

Jim decided to enter the conversation now. He turned to the lady.

"Patti comes from a long line of influential people. She is actually related to Louie IV. I am scheduled to go to Ireland to film portions of our new movie. Patti will be accompanying me there. She understands the culture there much better than I. She even knows some of the language, don't you?" Jim turned toward Patti, anticipating her response. If they were going to play the game, he at least needed to make it convincing and give a reason for her presence.

"Non molto," she replied in Italian. That hushed up the woman, and the caterers started to serve the food. Patti looked around at the place. It was lavishly decorated. There were expensive flowers at each section of table. The tablecloths appeared to be handcrafted. She could tell that a lot of money was represented there that evening. There was more money represented there than most people would ever see in ten lifetimes. Everybody who was anybody seemed to be present. She recognized several of the stars who graced the big screens and even the TV shows in her living room. If there were all of these celebrities present, surely her appearance with Jim could not be as involved as Betty had made it out to be. She sank her fork into the potato salad. It was tender, sweet, and melted in her mouth. She looked over at Jim. He too was enjoying the salad. She noticed a small chunk of potato caught in his beard. She gently removed it with her napkin. He noticed and thanked her.

"I appreciate that, Patti. I have to keep up my image. There are several eyes on us this evening. You are managing to fit in splendidly. I am so very pleased that you are here. This is my world. Do you like it?"

Patti brought out a small pen and wrote on her napkin. "How do you want me to talk now? In French or broken English?" she wrote.

"Just respond in French, and I will nod with understanding even though I don't have a clue," he wrote in response.

"La nourriture est très bonne, monsieur," replied Patti.

"It is very good, isn't it mademoiselle?" came back Jim's reply.

"How did you understand that, Jim? I thought ..." Patti had forgotten to speak in French. She put her hand up to her mouth and quickly looked at the woman who had been talking to them moments earlier and then sighed in relief. She had not noticed the slip but was busily engaged in conversation with the couple on her left.

"C'était étroit," she responded a little louder in French. No one seemed to notice. They must have come to the conclusion she was genuine and accepted it.

After the wine, appetizer, bread, and salad, the main entree was served and then dessert and espresso or coffee. The dessert was cake and had been displayed on the counter near the front of the auditorium. Patti remembered passing by it while she and Jim were looking for their places. It was decorated quite nicely. Four years earlier, she would have been proud to have turned out a cake like that, but now she was much better. She prodded Jim to come close as she whispered in his ear, "Could you find out how much they paid for the cake? I would really like to know."

Jim looked at her and whispered back, "Most everything here was supplied at cost or donated. I overheard the cake decorator say that she normally would charge seven thousand dollars for a cake like that if this had not been a fundraiser at fifteen hundred a plate."

Patti looked at the cake again and shook her head. "I supplied one about the same size as that for a wedding about a year ago. I only charged them thirteen hundred," she whispered. "I could make a killing selling cakes here."

The lady turned in Patti's direction and looked at her. Patti blushed and decided to speak in broken English.

"Do haff *pièce de dames*? How you say room?" She pointed to herself before saying "room" to indicate that she wanted the ladies' room.

"Ladies room?" queried Jim. "Yes, there is one over there." He pointed to the restrooms.

This seemed to appease the lady, and she went back to her conversation with the others. Patti got up and went to the restroom. When she returned, the evening program was already in progress. She was tiring of the French game. She hoped she would not have to keep it up all during the time she socialized with Jim. She could hold out for the duration of the evening though and so far seemed to convince several of her genuineness.

Patti sat down next to Jim and looked around for Bobbie. The bodyguard was standing several feet away but well within reach if needed. He had a way of disappearing into the background. Patti remembered how Jim told her Bobbie did not understand much English and wondered what nationality he was. She took out her pen and wrote on the back of the napkin. "What nationality is Bobbie? Also, I am tiring of this French game. I hope I don't have to keep this up all the time I am out in public with you."

Jim read the note and responded, "It is kind of foolish but don't make such a big deal out of it. The Good Book says our speech should be 'yes, yes and no, no, that everything else can lead to evil. So now that they know you won't speak much English you can act like your sweet self. Be bubbly and laugh and smile and nod your head up and down for yes or back and forth for no. If they are rude, just smile and act all happy, and no one will be able to resist your charm. I know I can't when you are that way. Your smile alone will help you sail through the rest of the evening with ease."

A great dread dropped away from Patti as she heard what Jim said. She felt bubbly. She was happy. She could laugh and nod her head, and that was what she did. After the program, several ladies came and talked to her and she used the technique with all of her charm. The little curly swirls of hair on either side of her face bounced this way and that as she laughed and smiled. It was stunning, and it worked. Any hostility that might have been trying to claw its way to the surface melted right in front of her. It was amazing. Besides, by the time it was over, most of the people there were so soused they didn't know much. Patti could never understand why people did it. They made fools out of themselves when they were drunk. There were some men who came by also. One even commented on her shapely body, and she told Jim to slap him in French. After applying her charm and nodding techniques, the rest of the evening was a smashing success. She did receive one proposal from an Italian gentleman who spoke French. She realized his mastery of the language immediately and kept a tight lip whenever he was around. One slip and he would see through her disguise, but he apparently noticed nothing and took the whole story without any suspicion. He asked her to dance with him in French, but she told him no. At the end of the ball, the master of ceremonies mentioned that over $200,000 had been raised for the humanitarian project they were promoting, and everyone applauded. It really had been a wonderful evening.

As they were leaving the building, Jim told Patti that Bobbie was from Russia. He had been trained to be a bodyguard for some of the leaders of that country but had been relocated to the United States after his employer had married an American woman and taken up residence in the States. After he had been here a couple of years, there was no longer any need for his services since his employer was no longer in a leadership position in Russia. He had been recommended by one of Jim's close friends and so far had not needed to show his abilities. The three were about to get into the limo when an avalanche of people and several members of the press surrounded them. Cameras flashed, and Patti was blinded by all of the action. Microphones were planted in front of her mouth, and the questions were flying to both her and Jim so fast she became confused. Bobbie now took in the scene and with a look as mean as that of the meanest of men opened his massive arms and singlehandedly pushed the whole group back quite forcibly. His strength was amazing. Jim grabbed Patti and pulled her into the limousine. Bobbie followed, and the door was quickly shut as Ted roared off. Several cars followed but soon started to fall away as they neared the outskirts of the city. Ted actually went in the opposite direction for a while before turning down a darkened street where he shut off the lights. He stopped the limo and watched his mirror. The last of the cars tailing them sped by. When there was no sign of any others, he continued to drive up the street without his lights on. At the next intersection, he turned left and then right and then left again and was soon on the road home. It had been a grand and glorious evening. Patti leaned up against Jim and spoke softly into his ear.

"I had a very lovely time, Jim. Thank you for inviting me to the ball."

"Did you really have a good time?" he asked. "I am gladder to hear that than you can know. I was hoping you would not be intimidated by this type of life. It is not always easy to be in the public eye. You were wonderful— no, not *were* but *are* wonderful and when you are bubbly like you were this evening, you are lovelier than the prettiest flower I have ever seen. Everyone was charmed by you. I watched them. It didn't matter if they were men or women. Your gracious beauty outshone all of them. Will you marry me?"

"Oui." She smiled and gave him a soft kiss on his lips.

This time, he took her into his arms all the way and really showed her what a passionate kiss was all about. Patti was lost in the embrace but suddenly realized what he had said. Had she heard him right? Had he asked her to marry him? She pulled away and shrank down into a small ball.

"What is the matter, dear? What happened?"

Patti remained quiet for a while and then responded in a tiny voice, "Did you just ask me to marry you?"

"Marry?" he questioned. "Bobbie did you hear anything about marriage?"

Bobbie grunted some response, and then Jim smiled and took Patti's face back into his hands.

"You did accept my proposal. I heard it with my own two ears even though you answered in French."

"But, Jim, you can't be serious. We have just met. I hardly know you, and I am sure there is a lot about me you don't know. I didn't mean ..." Her voice trailed away as she pondered a new thought that flashed into her mind. Mrs. Patti Callahan? Callahan is better than Stratton. Stratton is really heavy on the Ts. Yes. To be Mrs. Jim Callahan was much nicer than what it would have been had the lie not been a lie. Mrs. John Stratton? She didn't think so. Then a dangerous thought came into her mind. If they did indeed marry, she would not take his name. She would forever and always remain Patti Murray.

"Two Ts in Patti and two in Stratton," she mumbled under her breath. Bah-humbug.

"What about Ts?" Jim asked.

"Oh, nothing. I was just thinking of something; that's all. Nothing important."

"Well, honey, what is our next step? We are engaged to be married. Do we set the date or move in together?" Jim was grinning mischievously as he queried.

"Not so fast, guy. You're not going to hold me to that yes, are you?"

"I sure am, Patti. You accepted even though it was in French, and I expect to hold you to that."

"Then we are only partly engaged and a very small part at that."

"What do you mean, partly engaged."

"Just the French part of me is engaged to you, Jim, and that is a very, very, very small part of me. Only a couple of courses in college. Certainly not a big enough part to have me shack up with you. You will just have to wait on that."

Jim became very quiet. His happy, good-natured self

slipped away, and he took on a mood that seemed to Patti to be uncharacteristic of him. He was not used to having people tell him no. He allowed that when working with his director and then only because she was who she was. If it had been any other woman he knew, she would have gladly jumped at the chance to marry a rich, handsome movie star such as himself. But this Patti Cake was not like that, and that was what attracted him to her. He thought of some of his fans. He expected if word got out that he was looking for a wife, hundreds if not thousands of women would come flocking to the area to offer him their hand. The Facebook and Twitter accounts would be screaming with comments and responses. Who did this town girl think she was? He only let the thoughts brew in his mind for a few minutes before turning to Patti for another try.

Jim glanced at her. She was looking out the window. The soft glow of the passing streetlights lit up her face every couple of seconds. A beautiful smile transformed her into an angel. Her eyes appeared almost dreamy. Somewhere behind that pretty face was a very special woman. This was not just any small-town girl. She was the nicest apple on the highest branch of the tallest apple tree. She was the one in a million, and he knew she would be his. He turned her head toward him again and gave her another kiss. This time, his lips lingered long and tender on her soft, moist ones. She did not resist.

Chapter 13
AN UNEXPECTED TURN

Patti couldn't rest. Her mind kept going back to the events of the evening. Was she engaged or not? One part of her mind told her she was, but the other assured her that it was not possible. Jim had dropped her off at the big house, walked her to the door, and kissed her again before leaving without a word. She could still feel his lips on hers. It was like heaven to be in his arms. She could still feel the sensation of her breasts pressing up against his chest as he drew her toward him in a passionate hug. She wanted to melt down into him and become one, closer, closer, closer to this man who held such magic over her.

Mom had gone to bed probably a long time ago. Though it was after two in the morning, sleep was the last thing Patti wanted to do now. She paced around her room like a caged lion. Then her eyes caught a note on the foot of her bed. She looked at it and read.

Patti, dear. You probably have a lot on your mind and are unable to sleep. A night out with Jim is not easily forgotten. Feel free to inhabit the kitchen. I have found in the past on nights like this, that cooking or

*baking is a great way to help me settle
down. If you are like me—and I sense you
are—nothing would be a better deterrent
than a couple of hours in front of the
oven. Help yourself.*

Love, Mom

Patti smiled softly to herself. This lady knew. She was one special woman. How did she know that baking was what Patti needed to do to get her mind back to reality? She slipped out of her silky dress and donned some shorts. Her bra seemed to limit her freedom, so she took that off and placed it in the top of her suitcase. Next she pulled out a T-shirt and stretched it over her head. There were some hard-soled slippers under the edge of the bed so she sat down to put them on. She looked at her toes. Some of the polish had worn off a couple of her toenails. In a few minutes, she had them recoated and the others touched up to match.

In the kitchen, she decided to bake an apple pie. There was a special cookbook she used for all of her pies. It was one her great-grandmother had used. It was called *Fanny Farmer Cookbook*. The cover had worn out long ago, so Patti purchased a large roll of Scotch tape and laminated it. Now she looked around for Mom's cookbooks. She found them in a cupboard next to the stove, and there nestled between two hardcovers was *Fanny Farmer*. She took the book in her hand. Mom's was not damaged like hers, but Patti could tell it had been used a lot. The pages were yellowed, and here and there, food stains still showed up. Patti opened to page 438 and started placing the ingredients for the plain pastry pie crust recipe in the bowl of the mixer. She really didn't need to look at it. She had it memorized, but why not? She needed to kill some time, and this was one way to do it. She measured two cups of flour, taking care to level the top with the back of a butter knife. The recipe called for one and three-fourths cups, but Patti always added a little extra, especially when using the bigger glass pie pan. She would add extra shortening and butter to make up for it.

The mixer had a pastry attachment. She placed it in the socket and added one-third cup of shortening. In the refrigerator, she found some real butter. She took a little over a half cup of it and placed it in the microwave oven. It was best for the setting to be on defrost. After a few seconds, the butter was as soft as butter was famed to be. Next came an oversized teaspoon of salt and then a half teaspoon of baking powder. Fanny Farmer did not have that in her recipe, but it would assure a flakier crust. Lastly the recipe called for one-third cup of ice water. Clear soda pop was better, so she looked in the refrigerator and found a can of Squirt. She measured out a little over a third of a cup and set it aside. Soda pop also helped to make a flakier crust. The mixer whirled and soon turned the flour, shortening, and butter into pea-sized balls. With the pop added, the crust was given a final mix and was ready for the pie.

Mom had a pastry envelope to roll the crust out, but Patti preferred waxed paper. A short survey of one of the drawers found a roll, and soon the crust was placed in the bottom of the pie pan. Again, to make it even flakier, she looked for some I Can't Believe It's Not Butter spray and lightly sprayed the crust. Patti peeled the apples and placed them in a bowl. Typically a pie took six medium apples, but after baking, there was often only an inch of apple at the bottom of the pie. To avoid this, Patti microwaved ten peeled apples and watched through the window as they melted down in the bowl. After cooling them a bit, she packed them into the pan. Tapioca was Patti's first choice for thickening. After a little looking, she found a box way back in the corner. There was some apple juice left in the bowl after the apples were cooked down, so Patti used this to mix with the tapioca and cooked it on the stove until thick. Then she layered it in with the apples, sprinkling a little cinnamon on each layer. She sprayed a few squirts of lemon juice over the apples along with a cup of sugar. Next she scattered a quarter teaspoon of nutmeg to top it all off. Finally she sliced some slivers of butter off a frozen stick and put them on top with a sprinkling of salt.

On the counter, she saw a glass jar with gumdrops in it. She selected six lemon ones and sliced each one into four pieces. These were nestled down into the apples. As the pie baked, the slices of gumdrops would melt and form a very nice syrup. They also helped thicken the apple juice along with the tapioca and added a special lemony taste to the pie that kept people guessing. Next she rolled out the top crust and wet the edges of the bottom crust before sealing it all in. The pie looked wonderful. Her aunt used to double the pie crust over and cut slices in the top before placing it on the pie, but Patti was more creative. She carved an outline of three apples on the top and wrote with a sharp knife the word *apple* above them and *pie* below. The oven was preheated already, and soon the pie was baking. Mom's special oven could bake a pie in twenty minutes with the infrared and regular setting selected. So Patti looked around for something to do while waiting.

Her attention was drawn away by a strange sound coming from Betty and Ken's bedroom. There was a thump, and Mom screamed. Patti ran to the door and entered. Dad was on the floor. His face was turning colors. Patti ordered Mom to call 911 and went into action. In a few minutes, her patient was breathing more normally, though he kept his hand pressed tightly against his heart.

"What do you think happened, Patti?" Mom asked through tear-filled eyes. "I have never seen him like this."

"I think he had a heart attack, Betty. Hopefully it has not caused too much damage. We won't know for sure until he is examined. How did he come to fall down like that?"

"He got up to go to the bathroom, started coughing, and then he turned sort of gray and fell over. He hit his head on the floor quite hard, but thank God, we have plush carpet in this room."

The window suddenly became lit with flashing red lights, and an ambulance with its siren going full blast sped up to the gate. Betty bounded out of the room and down to a panel on the wall by the front door. She pushed a button, and the gate opened. The medics were out of the vehicle within seconds, and soon at Ken's side. Their assessment was the same as Patti's—a heart attack. Soon they had him on a gurney and into the back of the ambulance. Patti rode in front with the driver while a couple of medics and Mom rode by Ken. He was mumbling something unintelligible as they hurried toward the hospital. It wasn't until half an hour later that Patti remembered the apple pie still baking in the oven. Fortunately she had adjusted the oven to shut off when the time was up.

Jim had a message waiting for him on his cell phone when he woke up in the morning. It was from Patti. It was short and urgent sounding.

"Ken had a heart attack early this morning. He is in the hospital. Please come as soon as you can or call me. We don't know yet how serious it is."

Jim broke all his former speed records getting to the hospital that morning. It was a grim-faced group of people who met him in the lobby. Ken's younger brother had been contacted and was there with his wife. All of Ken and Betty's children were there with the grandkids. After a few minutes, Jim was admitted to the room. The man he called Dad was fighting for each breath. He had tubes hanging every which way in and around him. Aside from the incoherent words he had been mumbling, Ken appeared to be comatose. When Jim entered the room though, his eyes focused. Through the respirator over his mouth, he spoke as clearly as possible.

"Take good care of Mother, Jim, and don't let Patti get away from you. She is your girl, Son." With that, his eyes grew very wide and then glazed slightly. "Marry her, Jim. Marry he—" The heart monitor that had been showing a much too irregular heartbeat leveled out, and a buzzer sounded. Two nurses and a doctor came flying into the room. They tried everything to revive the man but were not successful. Ken died, and it was all over that quickly.

Patti cried in Jim's arms for half an hour. Jim, himself even came to tears a couple of times. He said very little, but when he spoke, it was always the same question.

"Why, God? Why did this have to happen now? Could you give me an answer?" Jim was not a religious man by any means. God seldom came into his thoughts, but during this time of grief, it seemed that was all he thought about. And why did God allow Ken to die at this time? He really was not old, old as in really old, only seventy-nine. Many men who looked twice his age had lived a full ten years more or longer. Throughout his life, he had always been healthy. It didn't make sense. Mom was heartbroken. This had not been on her agenda either. The two of them had plans together that took them well into their nineties, but it was not to be. It was a long ride home. Jim took Patti and Betty to the house in his limo. Patti suggested to Mom that she take a hotel room and leave the house to the relatives, but she would not hear it. She clung to the younger woman as if fearful of losing her, more so than even her own children. At some time in the past, the relationships with her family had been strained. This was easy enough to see. Something had happened to rip this family apart. It wasn't until Patti was at the doorway that she remembered the pie. Several hours had passed. She feared the worst, but when she entered the kitchen, she saw the pie sitting on the counter with a clean white dish towel over it. Then she remembered these people had attendees looking after things. In her room, she found her dirty clothes all washed and ready to wear. Her pants and blouse had been steamed and hung neatly on a hanger in the closet. Could she ever get used to this?

Chapter 14
PALM DESERT

The next couple of days went by slowly. Patti busied herself in the kitchen as much as possible, trying to keep out of the way of everyone. She cooked and baked and cooked and baked some more. She had donned an apron and wore slacks. Most of the guests thought she was the cook's helper or a maid. News of Jim's engagement had hit the papers the very next day. Patti saw herself with Jim in a couple of photos. In the first photo, she had her neck arched up and Jim was bending down to kiss her. How had they gotten a shot like that? The last photo showed her leaning on the arm of the handsome blond movie star, looking off toward the platform. She was smiling very sweetly in that one. Needless to say, she was very pretty, even by her own standards. The fundraising event and the couple's engagement was dwarfed by an earthquake that hit San Francisco that same morning. It toppled several buildings and some overpasses. Six hundred people were reported dead or missing. It was so big that Patti and Jim showed up on the fourth page of the paper down near the bottom. That was fine with her. The caption in bold letters caused her to smile even though her heart was sad. "Hollywood's Most Eligible Bachelor Falls for a French

Beauty. Gossip has it she is of royal blood. Will they tie the knot? Close friends of the Hollywood star say they will or already have." The story went on for about seven more paragraphs, and that was all.

Patti looked out the window just as a van pulled up with another group of relatives. Perhaps this would be a good time for her to look up her old roommate, Pam, in Palm Desert. She left the kitchen and looked for Betty. She was in the music room with some of her friends. Patti went up to her quietly and then started to speak.

"Mom, I would like to go out for a while. I have a friend in Palm Desert, and I need to do a little shopping. I will be back in time for the funeral if that is okay with you?"

"I understand, Patti. There are a lot of strangers here, and I should have noticed you were not comfortable. Please help yourself to one of the cars. Take the little convertible. It will get you there quickly. It is easy to maneuver in and out of traffic also. You will find the keys in the garage. Tell the caretaker you will be using it and that you have my permission."

Patti bent down and kissed the sweet little lady on her forehead.

"Thank you, Mom. I will be very careful with it. Here is my cell phone number if you need to contact me." She wrote the number on a piece of paper and placed it on the piano before leaving the room.

Patti went to her bedroom and called Pam. She was home.

"Hi, Pam." Patti held the phone close to her lips as she talked. "I am in the area and was wondering if you had some time to hang out for a few hours."

"Patti! Is that you?" The voice on the other end of the line sounded very excited.

"It is the one and only, Pam. I am here on business. I am baking a wedding cake for a wealthy client. They paid all of my expenses to fly out here."

"I saw your wealthy client, Patti. And you can't tell me you are here on business. I saw your engagement photo in the paper. Well, it really wasn't an engagement photo but a picture of you with Jim. When did you meet up with him?"

"I would love to tell you all about it, but it would take too long. Are you doing anything this afternoon? I could drive over, and we could go out or just stay in and catch up on all of the gossip," Patti replied with a touch of hopefulness in her voice.

"It is your lucky day, Patti. I took the day off from work. I have a dentist appointment in the morning and do not want to go around the office acting half drunk. Call me when you get to Palm Desert, and I will tell you where to meet me," Pam replied.

Patti spoke again, laughing this time. "Dentist, eh? Do I have a whopper of a story for you. Hopefully your trip to the dentist will be more pleasant than my last encounter with one."

"What happened?" returned Pam. "Don't scare me off now. I am jittery enough as it is about them poking that needle in my jaw."

"I will tell you all about it," Patti replied. "I do not want to spoil your visit now though. Have a good time at the dentist. I will call you when I get near Palm Desert."

"Yeah, like I am supposed to go off and have a good

time at the dentist's office with the old guy putting his fingers and all sorts of stuff in my mouth. Yuck!"

It's not always an *old* dentist." Patti emphasized the *old* as she spoke. "Sometimes they can be quite handsome. And by the way, they do use sterile gloves, you know."

"Talking about handsome, Pat. It looks like you got a handsome dude on the string. You are going to have to tell me all about your wedding plans, how you met him, when the wedding is, how they made you into that gorgeous creature in his arms. That bit about being from France was real rich! I nearly didn't recognize you. Please hurry. We have a lot of catching up to do." With that, she bid Patti good-bye and hung up.

It was a rather nice drive over to Palm Desert. Aside from the traffic problems, Patti did not have much trouble getting there. The car she drove had a GPS system in it that could tell her turn by turn how to get to her destination. It showed the shortest route and even gave the options of a live feed to help avoid traffic problems if she knew how to access it. When she did manage to get it talking, it was in French. The French female voice started talking. It prompted her that a software update was available. Patti did not mess with the updates, but the map was helpful. The French just added that much more allure to this fascinating, almost virtual adventure. She punched in her destination and watched as the monitor searched and then produced a route to Palm Desert from her current location. The convertible was fast. She actually made good time. Soon, Patti saw the sign for "Palm Desert, Next 4 Exits" loom up before her. She took the second exit and called her friend. A voice recording came on, and she left a message.

"Hi, Pam. Patti here. I just want you to know I am in the city. Was hoping to hear your voice, but I suppose you do not sound like yourself so probably chose to let your voice mail take the call. Give me a jingle as soon as you can. I am near one of the malls so will do a little shopping until I hear from you. Hope that is soon."

Patti parked the car and went up to the mall entrance. She needed to look for some shoes. She would need them for the funeral. The ones she had packed did not go with black. They were a little too colorful for a funeral. Black heels would be the best. She needed heels also to gain a little height. She would find some that gave her a couple of inches or more if possible. Five feet four with heels was still short, but it was sure better than the other option.

The saleswoman was very helpful. She found just the right pair of shoes and though the price was a bit more than Patti was used to paying, she splurged. Earlier in the week, Jim had handed her an envelope with a few thousand dollars in it. He said it was an expense account for her to get what she needed. She needed shoes. By the time she had the shoes purchased, a half hour had passed and still no call from Pam. That was funny. Patti took out her phone and noticed it was shut off. She turned it on and got the low-battery message for a moment, and then the phone shut itself off again. The charger was not with her. She had left it at Betty's house. Now what was she to do? She did not even remember the number. There was always Radio Shack. She could go there and purchase a charger that would work in the cigarette lighter. There was a register of the stores in the mall. Patti looked for Radio Shack and found one at the other end of the building.

On the way to Radio Shack, Patti stopped at a small gift shop and purchased a crystal mouse for Pam. Her friend loved mice, or so it had seemed. She had kept a couple of them in a cage in college during part of their time as roommates. Pam had stolen them from the lab where they were destined to be given an injection of cancer cells. One of Pam's professors was doing research, and there were two mice that never came under the needle. During a holiday vacation, Pam had taken them home and released them in a field. Who knew? Perhaps the white mice found gray mice mates and lived happily ever after?

Patti finally reached Radio Shack and found a charger that would work. By this time, an hour had passed since she had reached Palm Desert. Back at the car, she plugged in her phone. She turned it on, and the phone turned back off again. Surely Ken's car had a working cigarette lighter. The guy didn't even smoke. What would she do now? Without the phone, how would she find Pam? She started up the car. *Might as well drive around a little.*

"I suppose a car of this caliber would take super-unleaded," she mumbled to herself. There was a chirping sound, and the dial on her phone lit up. So that was it? The car had to be running for the charger to work. Patti looked at her messages. There were no new ones listed. So Pam had not called yet. She dialed the number again and got a recording again. Pam was not married, so Patti felt that a phone book would probably not be much help. Usually single women did not list their address. She would check though. At a phone booth, she looked up the number. There were two Pamela R's. and a Pam R. The Pamela R's did not have an address, but the Pam R. did. She punched the address into the GPS and was given a map to the woman's home.

Palm Desert was quite a place. Everywhere she looked, it seemed there were golf courses with palm trees and fantastic landscapes. The entrances to the various housing divisions had luxurious designs with waterfalls and exquisite landscapes. One even had a putting green. She wondered if either Jim or Cal were golfers. This would be a golfer's paradise. If she did marry Jim, would he ever go golfing? Some celebrities did. She would have to ask him. Cal surely looked like the type who would enjoy this sport. She had never tried it though, so whomever she married, Cal, Jim, or someone else, he would have to teach her the game if he really wanted her to tag along.

She spotted an outlet mall up ahead. They had a kitchen supply store. Well, while she was waiting to figure all of this out, why not grab a few more supplies for the cake? Inside she placed some much-needed baking things in a cart. The prices were great! It seemed like they were coming up with more cake-making ideas every time she turned around. There were the cake pops, which had recently become all the rave. These she knew could expand her services a lot. Just before she left Santa Rosa, a strange cake request had come in. The girl was going be three years old. She was kind of a tomboy type that liked rough and tumble things. Her parents had a small drainage ditch that crossed the back half of their property. Kindra had discovered frogs there. So when her mom had asked her what kind of cake she wanted for her third birthday, she had responded, "I want a froggy cake. There will be one big frog with a lot of little frogs crawling all over its back. That's what I want."

Patti wondered how she was going to manage that one. Could she make cake-pop frogs? If so how would she go about it? Should she purchase some of the modeling sugar and mold the little critters? How would she make the tiny balls on their feet? Fortunately she had nearly a month to figure it all out. She would be long done with Jim's cake and back in Santa Rosa by then unless ... She didn't want to think of the unless. Should she respond the way Jim appeared to want her to respond? She was almost engaged to him, wasn't she, at least in French? He told her he wanted to her to go to Ireland with him on his shoot. How would Ken's death affect Jim? Would he ever come to trust in God? She remembered her prayer from a few weeks ago. She had specifically prayed for the Lord to send a man in her life who had a deep love for God. Jim did not. But he had prayed. She had heard him. Was this God working things out in His own way? Then a thought crossed her mind, she had not prayed much lately especially since getting to LA. "Sorry Lord," she whispered.

"A tall, dark-haired man came into view a few rows ahead of her. She could just see the back of his head. He had broad shoulders just like Cal. In fact, she did a double take. She knew Cal would never be here, but could he have a twin brother? It was not impossible. Then he turned, and she saw his nose. There was just something wrong about that nose. No man should have a nose that long and that ugly. Why, how would he ever be able to kiss a woman? That nose would, would just … She shuddered at the thought. Cal? What might he be doing now?

"God, I have a problem. I need You to work it out for me, please. It is beyond my ability. I hate to say that, but this time, it is so. I have always felt I could take care of myself and make my own decisions, but this is different. We are talking about commitment here. I can't see into the future, but You can."

At that same moment, somewhere on a mountain trail, a tall, dark-haired man thought of Patti.

The GPS directed her to an apartment complex. It required a security card to get in. While Patti was standing by the door, an elderly lady came up. She looked at Patti and smiled.

"Were you looking for someone?" she questioned.

"Yes," replied Patti. "I am looking for a Pam Richards. Do you know if she lives in these apartments?"

The lady thought for a few moments before replying. "Not that I recall. I could check though. Are you a relative of hers?"

"No, just a friend. We were roommates in college. I tried to call her but keep getting her voice mail."

"You might as well come in while I check," the lady said as she placed the card in the slot.

The apartments were arranged on four levels. At the desk, the lady inquired for a Pam Richards. The receptionist looked up the name but did not show any residents by the name of Richards.

"I am sorry. What was your name?" the receptionist asked.

"I'm Patti."

"There is no Pam Richards registered here. Palm Desert is a big place. There are probably quite a few Pamelas in town."

"I am sure there are," Patti replied as she headed for the door. She went back to the convertible and looked at her phone again. This time, she was rewarded with a message sign. She saw that it was a number she had not seen before. She listened to the recording.

"Hi, Patti Cake. This is Jim. I went out to the house to see you, but Betty told me you went to visit your college roommate. Don't stay too long. I miss you. Call me as soon as you get back. We'll go out to eat or something. Don't forget to remember Ireland is calling us. It will be the most romantic vacation you have ever taken. Give me a chance to prove it to you."

Patti called her friend again and was rewarded this time with a live voice at the other end.

"Where have you been, Patti? I have been trying to call you for the last two hours. Has your phone been shut off or something?"

"Yes, low battery and I forgot the charger. I purchased a new one at Radio Shack and have been trying to call you also. Where have you been? How was the appointment with the dentist? Where do you want to meet up?"

Pam answered, "One question at a time, roomie. The

dentist appointment was crummy as always. I have been waiting for you to show up. Where are you now?"

"I just came out of an apartment complex where I thought you might live. It had a Pam R. listed there, but the R did not stand for Richards." Pam gave Patti her address, and she punched it into the GPS unit and was soon headed for her roommate's place. It was another apartment building across town. By the time Patti got there, it was nearly three in the afternoon. She was famished. The two girls met and hugged as Patti got out of the convertible.

"That is a very nice rental car, roomie. Since when did they start renting BMWs like this out to women drivers?"

"Oh, this isn't a rental car, Pam." Patti smiled a response.

"Does it belong to Jim then?"

"Nope, wrong again. It belongs to a very sweet lady who was kind enough to let me use it even though she lost her husband a couple of days ago. I was staying at their house. Jim introduced me to them. He was thinking about purchasing their place. I think he made them an offer. They were the people who gave him his start with the movies. It was so sad when Ken died."

"What made you decide to leave?" Pam asked.

"I felt like I was getting in the way. They have a lot of relatives coming in. A whole vanload of them arrived just before I left. The house is huge, but a death in the family is kind of a private matter. I was getting a bit uncomfortable. I was hoping to spend the night here and go back tomorrow. The funeral is the day after, and I will have to start the cake then because the wedding is the next day."

"What is this wedding, Pat? If you are engaged to Jim and he hired you to bake the wedding cake, is it for your wedding or his? If it is for his wedding, then why are you engaged to him and who ever heard of a bride baking her own wedding cake? I am dying to get some answers here."

"Let's go in and get something to eat, Pam. I am famished. I will tell you all about it."

"Every juicy little detail, roomie?"

"Yes," Patti responded, "if you want to stay up all night."

Pam's apartment was compact and cozy. It had a small kitchen and only one bathroom. There were two bedrooms and a living-dining room combination. Pam had converted the spare bedroom into a sewing room. She had a beautiful embroidery sewing machine that created very pretty picture designs. The room was littered with three or four projects in various stages of completion. Pam's latest project was an embroidered quilt design that only needed about half a dozen blocks to finish. She had chosen a nature theme. Some of the quilt blocks had trees; others had flowers. There was a diagonal line of blocks that had embroidered animals on them.

"Who is the quilt for?" Patti asked as she saw the work.

"It is for my hope chest," Pam responded. "One day, I hope to find a suitable mate who is somewhat compatible with me. Then we will move to his big house or build one, and I will set up housekeeping. I am hoping the house we build will be a log home. That is why I chose the nature theme."

"Do you have any prospects yet?"

"Almost. There is this executive in the building next to

the place where I work who has asked me out half a dozen times or so. He makes good money. He is a landscape architect. He helped design one of the golf courses here in Palm Desert. He also draws up designs for some of the celebrities over in Palm Springs. He is kind of cute but is already beginning to bald. I wish he would go get some hair implants before he loses much more. I never pictured myself settling down with a baldy. I always saw this tall, dark, and handsome man with a full head of hair. How about your man? Jim isn't balding yet, is he?"

"No way, Pam!" Patti commented as she reached for an orange from the fruit rack. "Jim has enough hair for any three guys, but he is not my man. I am not engaged to him."

"What about the article in the paper then? It clearly stated that you were engaged."

"He ask me after the fundraising dinner we attended. I did say yes in French, but it was just a joke."

"Are you putting me on, Patti?"

"No. Not at all."

Pam grabbed an orange also before continuing the conversation.

"Where did you meet him then? Did he see you at some convention or go to Santa Rosa for some reason and you just bumped into him? How did you meet in the first place?"

Patti had her orange peeled now. She divided it into sections before continuing, "His sister is engaged to be married and asked Jim to look up cake decorators on the web. He was looking through them and found my website. He saw my picture and a cake I made for a wedding, liked what he saw, so flew down to arrange for me to make the same cake for his sister. I was fortunate to have just had my website submitted to the top search engines. I was on the first page. He used Goggle, and, presto, my site popped up."

"Don't you think fate was working for you, Patti?" Pam asked as she popped a section of orange into her mouth. "What are the chances that a movie star like Jim would see your website and even take the time to fly down to make the arrangements? Is he more feminine than he appears on the screen?"

"No! Not a chance. Believe me; he is all man."

"You sound like you know him quite well, roomie. Just how intimately are you acquainted with him?"

"Not that intimate! He tried, but this girl was not going to warm his bed on the first date. I don't even think I would do it after five or six dates, though the temptation is very real. In fact, after he showed me to the house of his friends, I fell asleep on him. He waited three hours for me to come out of my room, but I didn't wake up till early the next morning. It was very rude of me, but he seemed to forgive me."

"You fell asleep? Unbelievable! What a slap in the face, roomie. And of all people to do it to, Jim—how did the papers put it? 'Hollywood's Most Eligible Bachelor'?" Pam finished her orange as Patti responded to her last statement.

"Betty, the lady of the house, showed me to my room and told me to freshen up a bit if I liked. I saw this gigantic bed and did something I have always wanted to do. I took a running leap and dove into the middle of it. I settled down, down, down into that plush bedspread and was out like a light bulb. I haven't enjoyed such a comfortable sleep in years. Poor Jim. He was very disappointed, but Betty, or Mom as we call her, would not let him wake me. He finally got tired of waiting and left. I think he was a bit upset but seemed forgiving enough by the next day when I showed up all decked out for the party. So now you know how we met, as incredible as it seems, and you know how I came to be in this part of California. You also know that I am not engaged to Jim Callahan, although sometimes I think I wouldn't mind it. He really seems to care. I think part of him wants to marry and settle down, but there is still another part of him that is a little boy who wants his freedom from commitment."

"That is some story, roomie. You were pretty convincing. I almost believe you. Do you think you will say yes if he really does propose to you?"

"I don't know. I love the house he is thinking of purchasing. The kitchen is a dream come true. Mom has everything a baker could want and a whole lot more. The place is completely surrounded with an eight-foot wall for privacy. There's a gatekeeper, a caretaker, a housekeeper, and a cook who makes the meals. I could get spoiled real quickly with such service. I don't know if I could keep up the pace of his night life, though. I never was much for partying. He comes alive at night. It's his time. He loves to be in the spotlight. I'd rather hide out of view the prying eyes of high society. Give me a few wedding or birthday cakes and a couple of kids to care for along with a simple lifestyle and I'd be the happiest gal in the whole of California. Of course, there are some advantages to marrying a guy like Jim. He is so incredibly handsome or perhaps 'beautiful of form' is a better way to put it. To be in his arms is wonderful, too. He's a perfect gentleman and very tender. And talk about muscles. He has a golden set of them. Plus being rich and never wanting for anything has a lot to add, but I do not know if I love him. I kind of do, but there's not that magnetism or whatever you call it … chemistry … Help me out here, Pam."

"Soul mate feeling?" she questioned.

"Yes! That is what I was looking for. I do not think he could ever be my soul mate. We come from different dimensions. He belongs to the world, while me, I'm just little old, simple Patti Cake."

"Do you have any other suitors, roomie?" Pam asked as she pulled some graham crackers out of the cupboard. Then went to the fridge to grab the milk. She poured a glass for Patti and then herself before sitting down.

"As a matter of fact, I do have another prospect."

"Who is this one?"

"He is just my dentist."

"So that must be the whopper you were going to tell me about. Let's have it, Pat."

"I met him in Safeway. As you well know, I am short. There was a nearly empty shelf of the flour I needed, but I could see one sack on the top corner in the back. I was balanced precariously on a shelf, reaching for it, when he happened along. He is very tall. He asked if he could help, but I told him no because I already had the sack in my hand. Then disaster struck as my foot slipped and I fell backward into his arms. He was caught off guard though and fell down. I landed on top of him, but the flour hit the side of the grocery cart and broke all over him. He was powdered from head to toe. Acting quickly without thinking, as I sometimes do, I grabbed a paper towel and looked around for some liquid. The nearest thing was a jar of pickles. I opened it and proceeded to wash the flour off his face with the pickle juice."

"Tell me you are joking, roomie!" Pam was laughing hysterically as she commented.

"No jokes, Pam. It really happened just like that, and he did not appreciate it. No, not one bit, but that was only the beginning. The following week, I decided to visit my parents and had a flat tire. Of all people to stop and help me at that point in time and that place ... well, it was incredible when it was he who came along and asked to help me. However, he asked before he saw and realized who it was. When I turned around, he was really surprised. He said, 'Oh, it's you.' And he sounded a bit disinterested for sure. After putting the temporary little spare tire on my car, he received a phone call, and while he was talking, I accidentally dropped the greasy, slippery jack on his toe."

"No! You didn't?"

"Yes! I did. And his anger with me was very apparent. He was in such a hurry to leave, he even drove off without one of his socks. Then, a few days later, I felt a sharp spot on one of my teeth and called my dentist. Who do you suppose had taken over my dentist's practice?"

"It had to be this guy. Right, Patti?"

"Right! Well, the appointment did not go well at all. He really messed up my mouth, and I got his assistant in trouble because I baked him a cake and brought his sock back all washed and clean." Patti was laughing now as she remembered the incident, though it had not been a laughing matter at the time.

"They got into a fight. He spilled Novocain all over inside my mouth, forgot to fill one tooth, and gave me whiplash when the chair went out of control from the remote—up and down and back and forth. I was very glad when the appointment was over and I could leave, but there is a bit more and he is a brave one; that's for sure! When he walked me out to my car, he proceeded to ask me for a dinner date for the next evening."

"That takes the cake, Patti Cake." Pam laughed as she dipped another cracker in her milk. "He really had the guts to ask you out after crucifying you in the dentist chair?"

"Yup!"

"Surely you didn't accept, did you?"

"I told him I would love to go to dinner with him, though I do not think by then I was speaking very clearly. I couldn't feel anything in my mouth. Anyway, we went out the very next evening and had a wonderful time. There were no mishaps, not even one. He limped a bit when we danced. But, Pam, he is tall. He must be six foot four at least, maybe six foot five. He has this thick head of black hair, and he dresses immaculately. I swear there's never a hair out of place unless, of course, I dump flour all over him."

Patti and Pam both laughed at that.

"In the mall, I picked you up a little gift, Pam," Patti said as she pulled a small package out of her purse. "Do you remember the mice you rescued from the lab at college?"

"How could I forget? Do you remember how the cage started to smell after the first week? That is why I took them out to a field and let them loose. I always wondered if they survived. They were white albinos."

Patti handed Pam the package. The sales clerk had wrapped it very nicely. Pam ripped it open.

"Oh, Patti! It's a darling little mouse. Oh, thank you so much!" She went over and gave Patti a hug as she carefully examined every detail of the little glass figurine.

"I wonder how they make these things. I watched a glassblower work once but could not understand how he had such a master's touch and control of the glass and could create such artwork. It was amazing."

"It is quite an art, Pam. I have seen them work also, and the pieces can just be exquisite in their final form. I don't think I've ever seen any rejects, but I'm sure there have been many over the years."

Pam placed the crystal mouse on a small stand she had mounted to the wall. It was perfect timing. A ray of sunshine shone in through the window and sent rainbow colors flickering all over the wall.

"This is so cute, roomie. I will always cherish it. Thanks again. I love you, my friend."

The rest of the evening went great. Pam and Patti went out miniature golfing and then took in a movie. It was one of Jim's earlier ones. It was really weird to see this larger-than-life man up on the screen, the very one in whose arms Patti had felt so comfortable only thirty-six hours earlier. After the movie, they returned to the apartment for the night. It had been good for Patti to get away. She had been able to sort out things a bit better and have some time for clear thinking. Being away from his mesmerizing personality really was a blessing in a way. Seeing Jim on the big screen again had helped a lot, also. As much as she was attracted to him, she was beginning to realize that life with Jim was not one she would covet. He was just too big. Some distant thought deep inside her came screaming to the surface. She wondered where that came from.

Patti! Do you know what you are doing, thinking like that? This is your chance. It has been handed to you on a silver platter. Do you think all of this is just happenstance, that fate is not pulling some strings for you here? Wake up and smell the roses. This is a once-in-a-lifetime opportunity. Reach out and take it before it is forever gone! The last portion of the thought was pleading with her very loudly.

Chapter 15
THE COOK'S HELPER

The trip back to Betty's was uneventful. Patti hadn't seen much of Jim. Between work, the funeral, and Kathy's wedding, he was kept very busy. He did drop by for a few hours the evening she returned. It was after most of the relatives and guests were in bed. He spent some time with Patti out in the arboretum. This particular night though, his thoughts were far away. He had stopped by the funeral home and had seen Ken. It was very difficult for him. He held Patti tenderly like a parent would hold a precious child. Patti saw tears stealing down his handsome cheeks. She kissed more than a dozen of them away.

After looking off in the distance, he asked her a question. "You wouldn't leave me like that, would you, Patti Cake?" Then he answered it himself. "No, you wouldn't. I know you wouldn't. You couldn't because I wouldn't let you. I would never let you go." Then his eyes moistened, and he held her close again. After a while, he fell asleep in her arms, exhausted like a tired little boy. He was truly grieving and deeply so, but not the same as Mom. She was completely heartbroken. She appeared lost. She'd walk through the large house talking to herself. If you got close to her though, you could tell she was carrying on a make-believe conversation with Ken. At times, she was in denial of his passing, and then at other times, she wept controlled tears. She too found comfort in Patti's arms. And her other comfort was the piano. Occasionally she would go to the baby grand and repeat a certain mournful song. She touched the ivories with her soul as she played the doleful music, and any who chanced to pass while she was playing would surely shed a tear or two as they heard the music from the brokenhearted woman.

The funeral was scheduled one day before Kathy's wedding. It would be tight, but with proper organization, they all could pull it off. Patti would have to bake the cake though on the day of the funeral. She had it all planned in her mind. Mom had given her the use of the convertible. She had an unlimited budget for the cake preparations. While in town, she wore one of Kathy's black wigs and put light sunglasses on her face. Aside from her small stature, there was little resemblance to the current Patti and the glamour girl seen in the newspapers and on social sites like Facebook and Twitter throughout the world. The reporters had been hovering around Jim's penthouse every day, hoping to get a glimpse of his princess, but she never showed up. Finally a paper going back to the fundraiser commented she had secretly flown back to France on a private jet the following day. They showed the back side of a small woman with light, long hair, heading up to the counter. She had three armed bodyguards surrounding her. Who would have guessed this was not Mademoiselle Patricia?

The day of the funeral dawned sunny and warm. Ken was well known, and hundreds thronged the hall where the service was held. Mom held on tightly to Patti during the entire drive there. She insisted she sit by her at the service also. Patti wore another of Kathy's dresses. It was a black one, and the shoes she had purchased in Palm Desert were just right for the occasion. If anyone suspected that Jim's fiancée would be sitting beside Mom, they never mentioned Mademoiselle. She appeared as if she were one of the family members, perhaps a granddaughter. The whole event was very solemn. He was placed up in heaven, looking down on his own passing, feeling unhappy in the sadness his death had brought to his loved ones. There were testimonials by friends and family of the wonderful and kind acts he had shown them throughout his lifetime. It was heartrending and uplifting at the same time. Then, in a moment, it was all over. Patti excused herself from the meal following the service and raced back to start the cake. Mom's little sister had shown up a bit late and took over the spot Patti had abandoned. Patti honestly felt that Mom never noticed the difference. Jim was there, but everyone could see it was difficult on him. He was grieving to his heart and soul. Patti appeared to be the last person on his mind. Bobby trailed him and at times supported him as he doubled over with sobs of emotion. He was despondent, and Patti was glad to take her leave of it for a while. A person can take only so much sorrow and heartache before a breath of freshness, a change in scenery, is needed for emotional and mental well-being.

Back at the house, Patti flew through the cake making. Within two hours, the cakes were baking nicely. Everyone in the home was gone. They were all at the meal that followed the memorial service. This was just what Patti needed, something to put herself into in an attempt to erase from her mind all of the hustle and bustle of the last few days. She drifted through the process likes hundreds of times before. Beep! Beep! A buzzer from the timer brought her back to the present. The largest bottom layer of the main cake was finished. Then another buzzer sounded, and one of the side cakes was done. Patti placed the remaining cake mixture in the middle and upper layers and put them in the oven the other cakes had vacated. She looked around for something else to do. She was famished. Her taste buds were craving something, but what? What was it? Then she knew. Fresh, homemade bread. That was what she wanted. She went to a recipe in her mind. Of all the breads she had ever made or eaten, this was her favorite. It was called heavenly white bread. She looked around for an electric bread maker and was not disappointed.

The machine was under a plastic cover on the large counter by the window. She uncovered it and lifted the lid. It had not been used for a while. Patti turned it to the dough cycle and let the canister warm for ten minutes. From the sink, she drew a cup of hot water. There was about half of a cup of condensed milk left over from the strawberry cake, so she emptied that into the water. Then she added a half cup of corn oil. Next came a half cup of sugar and a teaspoon of salt. She looked around for some eggs, but there were none to be found. She had used them all in the cakes. The recipe needed two eggs, though. She remembered seeing some egg-replacer powder in the cupboard and added a couple teaspoons into her mixture. Then Patti pulled the dry yeast out of the refrigerator. The yeast needed to be mixed with water so she placed three tablespoons of warm water in a cup, mixed in a level tablespoon of yeast with a little sugar for yeast food, and let it rise. There were a few ingredients that always made the bread soft and a little spongy. She needed one cup of oat flour, a few tablespoons of gluten flour, and some dough enhancer. She found the familiar round can back in the spice cupboard. Patti checked the mixer and made certain everything was working. Next, she exited to the bathroom. Inside, she surveyed herself in the mirror. Her hair was disheveled. There was flour on her nose. She washed it off but still felt she looked a wreck. What would people think of her if they began returning and she was such a mess? So, Patti took a couple of minutes and tidied up and then returned to the kitchen. The yeast was bubbling in the cup so she made a hollow in the top of the flour and poured it in just a few seconds before the slow mixing cycle started. After two hours passed, she'd divide the dough and place it in three one-pound bread pans.

"Two hours?" she exclaimed out loud. "I'll be starved by then. I think I'll let the bread mixer mix the dough till it looks good and then mold it into loaves without the first rise." Just then, another buzzer sounded, and Patti removed two more cakes from the oven. It was time to begin frosting the first covering of the first cakes. She went to the freezer and removed the layers of the two main cakes. While the next couple hours passed, she hardly noticed the time. This was Patti at her best. She loved her work. She knew she could spend the rest of her life baking cakes and enjoying the sweet journey, but was she a bride-to-be now? What would that do to her career? Would Jim want his wife baking cakes? Probably not. From some of his conversations, he'd probably want to keep her pretty as well as keeping up with his social life. And there were kids. He said he wanted lots of kids. Suddenly she was a little girl again and very homesick, homesick for her little kitchen and the business she loved so much. She went there in her mind and looked at the chair where Jim had sat. She mentally placed him there. Did he fit? Next she placed him in her bed with bared chest, leaning on one elbow, looking at her. No. She could not picture him in her bed. It was not a good fit. Perhaps she could see him in the giant soft bed. Yes, that was better.

"Oh well!" she exclaimed. "This too will pass." By the time the relatives started arriving back at the house, Patti had all of the cakes decorated and placed in a large, portable cooler she had rented from the city. She had eaten half a loaf of bread, and once again, the recipe had delivered the most exquisite loaves imaginable. The sweet, warm scent of fresh bread still lingered in the air. Before too many minutes had passed, the fresh bread was all devoured by people who should not have been hungry after stuffing themselves at the memorial dinner. They would have started in on the cakes too if Patti had let them. Some of the people were there for both the funeral and the wedding. All of the rooms in the big house were full. However, there were many guests who began packing and leaving for their separate homes. Mom's little sister agreed to stay on for a few weeks if need be to help the little woman get back on her feet. So

Patti pretty much had all of the privacy she needed. She decided as soon as the wedding was over, she'd take the return ticket and head back to Santa Rosa. Jim was due to fly off to Ireland the day after the wedding, giving her an easy way out to return home. And Patti believed with Mom's sis and all, there was really no reason for her to stay. Her main concern was Mom, but things seemed to fall into place, and for now, all was settled. Patti would leave quietly as soon as she delivered the cakes to the great reception hall. She took out her cell phone and turned it on. She had shut if off the night she stayed at Pam's and failed to turn it back on. After a while, some notes came up, stating that she had eight unheard messages.

"Wow!" she exclaimed. "Who has been trying to get hold of me now—and why?" She hit the voice mail button and listened to the first message. It was short.

"Patti! This is Clara. Call as soon as you get this message."

Patti deleted it and listened to the next.

"Patti? What is keeping you, girl? I am dying to know what happened. I saw your engagement photo in the paper. You really landed that guy! I can't believe it. Call me any time, day or night. Hurry! I'm dying of curiosity, Kit."

Patti deleted that message and pushed the next. It was from Clara again. There were more calls from her girlfriends. There was one when all three girlfriends spoke in unison.

"We need you, Patti Cake! Get here as fast as you can! The historical society in town is having a cake auction. They need fifty cakes by Monday. Help! Help! Help!"

There was one last call. She was about to push the button when Jim burst through the doors.

"How are the cakes coming, Patti Cake? It sure smells good in here. Is there anything you need? My sister told me to get out of the house. I was slowing her down. She told me to be sure the cakes are ready, so here am I. Employ me. Put me to work!"

Patti smiled at his good-natured comment. It was good to see him smile again.

"They are all finished, Jim. They are ready to be delivered to the reception hall bright and early tomorrow morning. I am sorry, but I do not have any employment for you at this time."

"Good! Good! Sweetheart," he replied sweetly. "Then make love to me. We can go into your bedroom if you like," he hinted with a boyish smile written all over his face.

Patti was taken aback by his request. Somehow she knew he would get to this sometime, but it was totally unexpected at the moment. She turned her back on him and pretended she was tiding up one of the counters.

"You won't regret this, Patti. I will make you feel like no other man ever has. When I finish with you, you will know you are a woman." He came up behind her and started fondling her. His mouth found one of her earlobes. It sent shivers all up and down her spine. She wanted to melt into his arms and be taken completely.

Patti had time to breathe only a short prayer. "Help me, Jesus!"

Something came over her suddenly. She took Jim's

strong hands in her little ones and unwrapped herself from his grasp. Then she turned to face him.

"I am sorry, Jim, but I can't. Not now. I've barely met you, and we still don't know one another yet, either. I heard your sister say you were flying out to Ireland the day after tomorrow. I won't be seeing you for weeks, possibly months. When I do make love to you the first time, I want it to last for more than an afternoon or one night. I want it to be the first time of forever."

"Then marry me, Patti. Marry me tomorrow night. We can fly to Las Vegas after the wedding and do it up proper. I even bought you the ring. It is supposed to be this way. I feel it right here." He put his hand over his heart as he spoke earnestly. "I'll be losing a sister but gaining a wife, all in the same day. What could be better? After we are married, you can go with me to Ireland. I never want to be separated from you. It will be perfect. No publicity. No one will see us go, and when we come back, they can say we got married over there on some exotic island or whatever other story they want to concoct. Marry me. I love you. I want you to be the mother of my children. I want lots of them, at least half a dozen. We can get started on the first one right now." He headed toward her again. His face was so serious. He was as honest as he ever would be, and Patti wanted him forever, but she clammed up again like she always did when any guy got serious about her. Jim was reaching for her with every fiber of his being. She could see the love in his eyes. There was a longing there she knew she had the power to fill yet couldn't. Not now.

"I can't, Jim. I can't go with you. The girls need me

back home. There is a cake auction coming up Monday. I'll be leaving tomorrow just as soon as I deliver the cakes and get the flower arrangements set up around them. I've already called and made the flight arrangements," she lied.

Jim's cell phone rang just then, and as he answered it, he went into the next room for some privacy. It was ReAnna.

"Hear you're heading out, baby. I'm going to miss you. Please come over tonight if you can. I have a birthday present for you. I'll even let you unwrap it, personally."

Jim pushed the stop button on the phone in disgust and looked around for Patti. She had taken advantage of the call to slip away out the pantry door. She entered the gardener's building where she peered out of the window. Jim had not seen her, and that was good. She hoped he would not find her. She didn't know why she had run. Most any other woman would have been in the bedroom now with the man of her dreams. The thought of it scared her. It had been so long since she had held a man in that way.

Jim went throughout the entire house, looking for Patti. He asked anyone and everyone he ran into if they had seen her, but he always got the same response.

"Are you talking about the cook's helper? No. We haven't seen her lately." One lady remembered seeing her in the kitchen frosting a cake about a half hour earlier, but she was the only one who noticed. Jim went out to the swimming pool and looked all around the yard, but there was no Patti. After looking for half an hour, he signaled the limo driver and left. He didn't know where to go. His sister had kicked him out of his penthouse. Patti apparently didn't want him around. Then fine! He directed the driver to take him to one of his mother's private clubhouses. They had a bar there, and he decided that on this night, he'd get crazy, stinkin' drunk. As for his sister and Patti and even his dominating director, well, they could go to hell for all he cared.

Chapter 16
CAKES AND DREAMS

After Jim left, Patti called in her reservations and retired to her room. She was exhausted. As she looked around at this exotic place that had been hers for the last several days, she was saddened. She felt empathy for Jim and Betty, and for herself, there was a feeling of melancholy she was unused to. For a few adventurous days, she had lived the life of a star. She had risen high above her dreams. For a few illustrious moments, she knew what it was like to watch the world below from a pedestal. It had been a wonderful feeling, though short. Ken's death had come crashing down on all of them, shattering a hundred dreams.

"Poor Jimmy Boy!" she exclaimed out loud. "How I wish I could have reached out and taken you in, but you are too big for me. Your world is too far out of reach. Good-bye, Jim. I really did love you. Maybe in another life, it could have been different."

Patti booked the earliest flight possible going to Santa Rosa. She was on the plane by seven thirty in the morning. She had risen early and delivered the cakes. She had obtained a key to the reception hall from the janitor and had arranged the flowers in a perfect order. It was lovely. Normally she would have taken a couple dozen photos from as many different angles as possible, but not this time. She had placed some large plastic containers over the cakes and made her exit just as the decorators arrived to begin their work. She left too early to say good-bye to Betty, but she had written a note. It had taken nearly half the night to write, but when finished, it said all that she wanted to say. Patti wanted some of these memories to shine brightly in her mind over the next several months if possible. They would keep her going when things got tough. The other memories, the sad ones, she tucked way down in the dark closet with the rest of their kind and closed the door. She would move forward like she always had. She would leave them buried there and go on like they never happened. This was the only way she could cope with them. There was just too much hurt for one person to handle.

In Santa Rosa, a taxi delivered her and her luggage to the door of her home. It was late morning. She was exhausted; all she wanted was sleep. She would unpack later. She took a quick shower, pulled the plug on the land phone, shut off her cellular, and crawled under the covers. In less than five minutes, she was out. She slept away the rest of the day. She got up only long enough to use the bathroom and then returned to her bed and slept. It was six the following morning when she finally awoke refreshed. A brilliant sun was streaming in though a crack in her curtain. It struck a small crystal figurine on her dresser and sent beautiful rainbows all over her room. Patti realized she was happy once again. She managed to accomplish a dream she always wanted, and that was to create an exquisite cake for a top Hollywood movie star. She hadn't even billed him. She never would. The spending money Jim had given her for expenses was more than she would have charged anyway. The job well done was reward enough for her. And today she would launch into the cakes for the auction. With a little luck, she could put out twenty of them. With that much of a head start, she felt she could break back into civilization and reenter life in midstream. In the end, it was good to be home in her own kitchen again.

Patti had no less than ten cakes baked when she remembered the phone. She plugged it in and turned on her cell phone. There were three unheard messages. The first one was the last message, the one she had not heard in LA. And it was from Dr. Cal.

"Hi, Patti. I promised not to bother you out there, but something came up that I wasn't expecting. I happened to look at the digitals from your mouth again and am sure there is another cavity we did not catch. I am scheduling you for another appointment for the fifth of the month. Hope you are back by then. Call me. We have at least one more date scheduled, remember?"

The next message was from Kit. It was short and sweet.

"I know you are due back today. I will be by right after work. That should be around four. You had better be there or else!"

The last message was from Trudy.

"Nancy and Clara are here with me, Patti. We have forty of the cakes done and only need ten more. Hope you make it back soon. We have half of them frosted but are running out of ideas. Hurry! Please! We moved the kitchen over to Clara's house. Call."

Patti redialed the number. Nancy answered.

"I'm back, Nancy. I was so tired I shut off all the phones and slept for eighteen hours straight and then got up early. I have ten cakes ready."

"You are a lifesaver, Patti. We are out of ideas and out of cash. We used up all of your cake supplies and our ideas. Where can we get together?"

"What if I leave my cakes here at the house and come over there? We will go shopping and finish decorating the ones you have left, then head back to my house to finish up if you are not too caked out by then."

"That sounds good! We will be waiting for you. After shopping though, Trudy has an appointment and will need to leave, but I think the three of us can manage the rest, especially now that you are back."

"Great. I will be there in twenty minutes. Good-bye."

"Good-bye" came the reply as Patti pushed the end button on her phone. She grabbed a few items and pushed the button to open her garage. A mouse ran across the cement, and Patti nearly screamed but caught herself. So they were back. Just last year, they had eaten a hole through the rubber seal at the base of the door. It had taken better than three weeks to rid the place of the pesky rascals. She stopped further entrance by placing bricks at the corners of the garage. One of the bricks was out of place. The mouse ran out the door and disappeared under a bush. *At least that one is out of here,* she thought. Patti backed her car out of the garage, hit the remote, and then got out to put the brick back in place. She went to the other side and made sure that one was also tight. She reentered the car and was at Clara's in no time at all.

The scent of freshly baked sweet cakes reached her nose as she entered her friend's home. The three women each came and gave her a hug of welcome; then they led the way to the display of finished cakes. Patti was amazed, and if she had not known different, they could have passed as her own. They were all lined up one after the other and were so wonderfully done, Patti praised her friends most graciously.

"These are marvelous! Clara, Trudy, and Nancy, you've all created wonderful cakes, and I can tell from looking over these edible delights that you have worked very hard in making them as professional and beautiful as I would have. Yes! Absolutely you are to be commended on an excellent job well done. How many orders came in while I was away?"

Nancy answered, "We got ten calls and filled seven of them. Three of the clients would not let us do their cakes. They weren't interested at all in having us substitute when they found out you weren't here. However, we do have quite a few checks waiting for you from the completed orders."

"Here they are, Patti," Trudy said as she opened an envelope. "We took the liberty to up your prices a little. There is a little over five thousand dollars here." Nancy was beaming with pride, and so were the others.

"This is wonderful, girls! You have filled in wonderfully. I am so pleased. How much are the auction people paying for the fifty cakes?"

"They wanted to pay no more than thirty dollars per cake, Patti. We told them that would not be doable, but we could do the smaller cakes for forty dollars each and the larger ones for fifty. They agreed to the prices and stated we came highly recommended. Some of the cakes are quite complex while others are simple. I hope we can do it for those amounts? I hear it is for a good cause," Clara remarked.

"What is the cause?" Patti asked in response.

"The historical society wants to purchase one of the elegant homes in the area that was built over a hundred years ago and transform it into a museum. They have several businesses contributing to it. All of the contributors will have their names engraved on a brass plaque in the entryway. It will be very good advertisement. We have enjoyed making these cakes so much we are hoping there will be new orders for a little extra work now and then to give us a little extra money. Nothing steady but a cake here and there couldn't hurt; that's for sure."

Patti was smiling. She thought of the prices she would have been offered in Jim's city for her work. Perhaps someone would notice Kathy's cake and just maybe, she would get a referral or two from there. If so, she could turn the local work over to these promising coworkers whenever she needed to get away.

"I am so very, very proud of you girls. This takes a big load off of my shoulders—now that I know there is such talent here. Let's go shopping. We have some checks to cash and some cakes to decorate."

The afternoon went by quickly. Patti was just the catalyst needed to get the creative wheels turning, and soon all of the cakes in Clara's kitchen were finished. Some of the cakes really looked fantastic because of the creative talents of all the girls but especially Patti. For one of the delicious delicacies, Patti used a special frosting for forming, draping, and sculpting. It was called *fondant* and was a type of frosting with the consistency of a sweet dough. It was rolled out like a pie crust. Then the decorator could use it for a variety of forms and styles that would hold their shape. While in Palm Desert, she had purchased a gum paste and fondant kit. She had used it to create the dainty little yellow frosting flowers for Kathy's cake. Adding the paste to the fondant enabled the decorator to create paper-thin designs. She could even make ribbons of frosting now.

At Nancy's, she bought supplies that had been all but depleted from all the auction orders, and she was glad to be stocking up again. She chose some precolored pastel fondants and a five-pound bucket of gum paste. Patti had a few ideas that she hoped would evolve into specially made edible artworks. Upon returning home, she began decorating the cakes. Choosing one of the precolored fondants, Patti rolled it out until she was able to drape it over the entire cake. Then with a special spatula, she shaped and formed this pliable yet firm sugar sweetness until the entire cake resembled a small cabin. It was a home for Pooh Bear and his friends, all characters from the story, *Winnie-the-Pooh*. This cabin cake would include Pooh Bear, of course, but also Tigger, Piglet, Owl, and not to forget Eeyore, the blue donkey. For these characters, Patti used the gum paste and some coloring to create each one. She arranged the friends around on the cake and then made a little round bucket and dripped in some melted, liquid caramel for Pooh's honey jar. In the end, the cake was really cute and Patti took pictures for her portfolio. She hoped someone special would receive this one for a birthday or celebration for a youngster, granddaughter, or grandson.

Next, she did a cake that resembled a green meadow. Patti molded three horses from the gum paste fondant mixture and placed them on top. She added a fence, a barn, and to give more color, some wildflowers. No matter whether the buyers or receivers of these cakes were going to be teenagers, small children, or adults, every one of these fancies would be enjoyed by all ages.

Charlie Brown and Friends appeared on a cake made in the same manner as the others. After all, Santa Rosa was the birthplace of Charlie and his friends. Patti went a little further with an idea of a cake in the shape of a potato. It resembled the spud that Mr. Luther Burbank, the now famous man, had unearthed following one of his agricultural experiments.

The ladies loaded the cakes into a couple of vans and delivered them to the historical society's auction hall. A cooler with glass doors in front had been rented and placed conveniently for storing and viewing as well as for removing for sales. Most of the cakes were displayed on the shelves, except for a couple of wedding cakes that were too large. A chest-type cooler was ready for those, and some of the other baked goodies were stored there also. Trudy had to leave so Clara and Nancy went to Patti's house and finished up the ten remaining cakes. They were just loading them into the van when Kit showed up.

"You got a lot of talking to do, girl. Here you've returned and are keeping me in the dark about your big engagement. What a friend you turned out to be! Better start explaining."

"Engagement?" Nancy and Clara chimed together.

"You got engaged, Patti? Why didn't you tell us? We would have celebrated by baking you a cake … or something." Nancy came out with that comment while licking some left over frosting out of one of the bowls.

"Come out with it, girl," Kit prodded. "When is the wedding? How did he propose to you? What kind of a house does a rich Hollywood star like that live in? How is he in bed? You just gotta be in the most coveted position in the world!"

"Hollywood? Movie star?" Clara exclaimed. "Who? Which one?"

"One question at a time, girls. In the first place, I am not engaged."

"You are too, girl. I saw the article with my own two eyes and cut it out and posted it right on the front of my fridge. Then I made a special trip to the nearest newstand and bought ten more papers to make sure everyone I came across who knew you learned of your engagement to Jim Callahan."

"Jim Callahan? No way, Patti. Tell me you're joking!" exclaimed Nancy.

"Yes way!" Kit pulled the engagement photo from her purse and showed it to Nancy and Clara. "That is Jim all right, but what did they do to you, Patti? You're a living doll in this picture and as pretty as I've ever seen you.

Who fixed your hair? And did you get help with your makeup?"

The girls were eagerly peering over the picture, unaware that Patti seemed to be absent from them in mind and spirit. Her thoughts were a quarter way around the globe in Ireland.

"Poor Jimmy," she whispered. And then at the sound of Kit's voice, Patti was brought back to reality in a snap.

"Girl, don't you dare tell me you turned that hunk down. Say it isn't true. He could give you the world!"

"He tried." Patti's voice was very low and solemn. "He asked me to marry him three times, and after I told him I wouldn't be able to, I ran and hid."

The three friends plopped down in chairs and just stared at Patti. Kit was talking.

"Either you are insane, not in your right mind, just plain dumber than a stump, or you had one larger-than-life, out-of-this-world reason for doing it. Now do tell what happened—and hurry, please?"

"The first time he proposed to me, we were in the limo returning from the fundraising banquet that picture was taken at. It was the fanciest place I have ever been to. So many stars were there, it was difficult to keep track of everyone. There were flashes everywhere from the paparazzi when we were leaving the banquet, and it was crazy trying to get away from it all. That is where and when the pictures were taken. Before we left, Mom or Betty, bless her heart, advised me to speak as little as possible to keep the newspapers from prying. I spoke French most of the evening. I don't think very many people, if anyone, realized I was an American. Jim knows a little

French. Later in the limo, when he proposed, the word *yes* in French slipped right out of my mouth before I even realized what I had said. The moment was overwhelming. You have to know the power Jim can have over a woman. Like many others, I imagine, I simply melted when I was around him. If you could only experience that dynamic influence, then you'd all understand exactly what I'm talking about."

The girls were all listening intently with all eyes riveted on Patti while she continued sharing her dreamy experience with this handsome movie actor.

"The second time he proposed, it was the day before he was going to Ireland. Right now, as we speak, he is working on a big-screen movie located in the Emerald Isle for the next few months. He asked me to go to bed with him to give him something to remember me by while he was over there. I told him no, that I just couldn't. I explained that when I went to bed with him the first time, I didn't want it to be for a one-night stand but that I wanted it to be for real love and the first time of forever. Then he asked me to marry him and go to Ireland as his wife. He proclaimed his love for me, and then at that exact moment, his cell phone rang and he actually stopped midsentence to answer the phone, even leaving the room to talk with whoever it was. While he was answering the call, I ran out to the gardener's building and hid. He left about half an hour later. I never made an attempt to say good-bye because I knew that if I saw him just once more, we would march off to the bedroom, not to be seen for hours or days. He would even have missed his flight out. I am certain of that."

"You are a fool, girl, if I ever saw one!" Kit exclaimed, not being one to resist butting into a story. "Let me borrow your body and have a chance like that, and it would be bye-bye, poverty; hello, Hollywood! I'd trade my … uh, my … oh gee, Patti! I'd trade my most valuable whatever in my life for even one night with that hunk!"

"So what happened next, Patti?" Clara asked, and all the others leaned in closer, not wanting to miss one tiny morsel of this enchanting story.

"I came home. Slept almost an entire day, and now, I suppose I'm ready to begin baking and decorating my cakes. He was really nice. And I did love him, but it wasn't the kind of settling-down-forever love. I just couldn't say yes and be with him if it wasn't the forever kind of love. You know, he was even in the process of buying a grand and gorgeous estate for me. It was out of this world! It was the most beautiful home I have ever seen. And the kitchen! Oh, the kitchen is every woman's dream come true. My cakes would've sold for thousands of dollars over there."

"What compelled you to make such a decision, Patti?" Nancy asked. "Or rather, why didn't you do what you wanted to?"

"I want to hear the answer to that one too, girl," Kit chided.

"The house belongs to Betty and Ken Sears. They were well-known producers for many, many years and still are well known. They gave Jim his start as an actor, and when he got a little older, he simply upped and left. He was tempted by another producer with lots of promises for his future, and the winning note was a fatter paycheck. Betty and Ken never stopped loving him though, and when they listed their grand home on the market, Jim approached them to buy it. They gave him the most fantastic price on their house. They said they were moving to Palm Springs and wanted him to have the place all furnished and everything. Then, just a few days later, Ken died. It was so unexpected."

"No!" Kit cried out.

"Unfortunately, yes, he did. And his wife, Betty (we called her "Mom"), was devastated. She clung to me like the long-lost daughter she never had. Finally, her little sister arrived to stay for a while and I was able to get away in order to bake all the cakes for the wedding. Kathy, Jim's sister, had been planning her wedding for quite some time, and the schedule turned out so that the memorial for Ken was the day before her wedding. The house was full of people. It was very busy and somewhat confusing. Some were there for the wedding, others for Ken. Some for both. I kind of hid behind an apron and played helper to the cook. Mom was grieving too much to have her house taken away so soon after she lost her husband. The loss of her house at the same time would have been just too much to take. She was sleeping when I left, poor lady. I wanted to say good-bye so badly. She was a wonderful woman and host and musician ... just wonderful, but she hadn't slept for most of the week, and I didn't have the heart to wake her just to say good-bye, so I wrote her a love letter. I was up half of the night writing and rewriting till I said just exactly what I wanted to express to her. Later on, I'll call and see how she's doing. The entire experience was so deeply sad. Poor Jim cried like a newborn baby. He never realized how much he cared for and really loved Ken until he was gone. Ken whispered his last few words to Jim, uttering instructions to marry me and never let me out of his sight. And with the last word, he peacefully slipped away and was gone.

"So, as far as the future goes, I have no idea what will happen next. However for now, Jim is gone, and I have my work. We did not part favorably, you know, and I wouldn't blame him if he never contacted me again. Besides, he has more women after him than any five men would know what to do with. He doesn't need me. Mom told me I would have to share him with not only the entire world but specifically with other woman as well. And to be honest, I don't think I could do that now, not ever. I want the man I marry to be my one and only. I know it is old-fashioned, but that's what I need for my life, my heart, my soul, and my Lord."

Patti was rambling on and on, not aware that anyone was listening. She was talking to convince herself, really, more than explaining it to the others. Finally she stopped, and there wasn't a sound. Her friends and colleagues were silent. After what seemed like a lifetime of stillness, Nancy finally found her voice.

"Wow, Patti! You've been through trials, tribulations, a dream fantasy, and a nightmare, all wrapped into one package named Jim. And when you returned home without one word of what had happened from you or us ... I mean, we never asked a thing about your trip or experience there. Oh no! We just expected you to immediately jump right in and finish up these cakes for our deadline. How selfish of us! No wonder you slept for eighteen hours. I'm so sorry. I think I can speak for all of us when I say we apologize from our hearts. Please forgive our insensitivity ... How are you feeling now, Patti, after everything that's happened? Are you okay? Tell us, really, Patti. Please? If there is anything we can do, just say the word, and we're there, okay?"

"Nancy, thank you, but I'll be fine. Thanks all of you for caring about me. I just need to pick up right here where I left off. I'll always remember that fantasy week with a twist. I have placed all the warm memories where I can draw from them whenever and however I want. Out of the entire ordeal, I did accomplish one of my lifelong goals. And that is I had one of my cakes in the wedding of a movie star ... or at least his sister. That is something no one can take away from me."

It was getting late. Nancy and Clara left, but Kit hung around for a little while longer.

"What will you do if he comes back to you? He's going to have a long time to miss you, ya know. If he really loves you, like he said, I expect he'll not give up as easy as you might think. Do you think you could live that kind of lifestyle, the one you mentioned? Like, could you share him like that?"

"It would be hard, Kit. Betty told me that love would win out if it was true. I have to take her word for it. She and Ken were happy together for years and years and a lifetime. She was so sweet. All of her wrinkles were smiley ones. She had an ageless beauty that only true love could build. And for me, I believe that if the Lord wills it to be, then it is meant to be, and then I could handle it. I can handle anything with the Lord by my side. Besides, Jim said he wanted to keep me pregnant all the time and have lots of kids. He loves me and wants at least a half a dozen little Patti or Jims around the house. If things got strained between us, I could always pour out my love on our kids, but then, I'm afraid I might not be a good enough mother. Somewhere out there, I have let at least one person down in that area. I can never get that back, and I never want to go through that again. Ever!"

"Wow, Patti, that's an awful lot you have on your mind, girl," Kit said, pondering all of the most recent information given by her friend. Wondering if she should ask about that last comment, she had second thoughts since it appeared that Patti was really deep into some memory. Kit gave her friend a hug, said her good-byes, and then left for home. Patti barely noticed until the door closed, and then she snapped back to the present moment once more.

It sure had been a difficult week. And tomorrow morning, she would deliver the rest of the cakes to the auction hall and pick up the check. Her account was looking pretty good now. She wondered if she would ever get any more money for Kathy's wedding cake. She wondered how the wedding went—and the reception and if the people liked her edible creation. She had left without leaving a bill, and they never did talk about the price. Patti wondered a lot of things about what had happened lately, and then she realized just how tired she was. She was asleep less than five minutes after she hit the pillow.

Chapter 17
AN AUCTION AND A DATE

Patti awoke with another toothache. She remembered something about an appointment with Cal, but what were the details now? She fumbled around, found her cell phone, and went to the messages to listen to the information about her upcoming appointment. The dental office scheduled her for the fifth and—Oh boy! That was today. Patti had time, however, to get dressed, fix something quick and light for breakfast, and then deliver the cakes to the auction hall before seeing the dentist. After eating, Patti went to the garage to check on and deliver the cakes. Upon entering the garage, she noticed the van's dome light was still on. When she slid open the side door, Patti saw one of the front doors was slightly ajar. So that was what caused the dome light to be on. She looked over all the cakes, and they appeared nicely arranged on the shelves. She had installed the shelves herself and used little brackets and holders that kept all her baked goods steady and snug for the ride to their final destination. She was about to close the door when out of the corner of her eye, she spied a little hole on the edging of one of the cakes. On a very close examination, she found evidence that those pesky little critters had come to dine on her delicacies.

"Oh no!" she cried. "If that doesn't take the cake!" And she laughed halfheartedly at her pun and then went to work inspecting every detail of every cake. She discovered only the one was now fodder for the mice. As Patti contemplated the order, she remembered it called for fifty cakes, not forty-nine. Being able to assess a situation and think quickly on her feet, Patti decided to deliver the forty-nine and return home to produce the final one. She felt thankful the auction was scheduled for an evening event and confident there was sufficient time to finish the last cake before it began. Patti took the nibbled-on cake into the kitchen, removed the mouse's dining corner, and tossed it into the waste basket. The rest of the cake was undisturbed, and since it was one of her favorites, tangerine cream, Patti thought there was no harm in sampling her wares. She was not disappointed at all. The fluffy, creamy frosting combined with fresh, moist cake appealed to her taste buds immediately. In addition, the pastel, tangerine shadings of frosting and cut cake differed ever so slightly yet were in perfect harmony for a captivating visual appeal. Together, the edible artwork was a treat to the eye and a delicious sensation for the taste buds.

"This cake sure would have brought a pretty penny at the auction; that's for sure," Patti said, all in a whispered tone. She often kept herself company by expressing her views verbally when she was alone. She used to tell her friends that her talking to herself prevented her from giving in and getting a kitty or pup. No pet hair in this little home bakery, she declared.

"What kind of cake should I make to replace it? I guess

I'll decide that later. At the moment, I'll take these cakes down to the auction hall before any more of them get spoiled by those pesky little rodents. On the way, I'll stop by Nancy's and pick up a few more supplies." She covered the cake and advanced to the van. It was a quick trip, and in a matter of minutes, she was at the hall preparing the display of cakes. A couple of society members helped her bring them in.

"You really do beautiful work, Patti!" an elderly woman complimented. "These should be a real popular item at the auction. Last year, we only had ten cakes. We were surprised at the response. One cake, let me think … umm, I believe it was a red velvet cake. Yes. Yes, it was, and it sold for over a thousand dollars. Several of the others went for more than five hundred. We are hoping that fifty of them this year will put us over the top. We are only twenty-five thousand dollars short of our goal."

"I'm glad you like what you see … Sandra, is it?" Patti questioned as she looked at the lady's name tag.

"Yes, that is what I am called. They make us wear these tags so people can ask us questions, I guess. Do you have any questions about where the money is going?"

"No, my associates filled me in pretty much. I'm glad you've nearly reached your goal. When will the museum be open for tours?"

"They expect it to be ready by February. They have the opening scheduled for President's Day," Sandra replied.

"Well, I sincerely wish you the best of luck."

"Thank you, Patti. I suppose you would like to pick up your check?"

"Normally I would, but I haven't delivered all of the

cakes yet. It seems that I am one cake short. I plan to make it as soon as I return to my home bakery; then when I bring the final cake, I'd like to pick up the check at that time."

"You needn't bother, dear. I am sure forty-nine cakes will suffice any sweet tooth. Here take the check, now. Go home and get some rest. You must be exhausted after such a job as this. Did you say you have some associates, or did you make all of these yourself?"

"I have three very talented assistants. They did the base work while I was out of town. A client from LA flew me out to make their wedding cake."

"You do cakes out of town?" Sandra asked.

"Not usually but I do have a website and someone saw one of my wedding cakes and flew me out. It was to be quite the extravagant wedding."

"You mean they didn't invite you to stay?"

"Oh, I was invited to stay all right, but there was this order to fill and the ladies needed me here to help finish up, so I delivered my cake to the reception hall and took the first flight home."

"Would you mind my asking how much you got for that cake?" Sandra asked.

Patti responded slowly, so as not to let her ready-to-spill-over emotions show.

"I gave them a price of two thousand dollars, but the one who ordered the cake said it was way too low. He said it was worth no less than eight thousand."

"Did I hear you right, Patti?"

"Yes, eight thousand is what he would pay me; plus my

room and board were free and I had an unlimited budget for supplies."

"No! No! Not the price … the *he*. What kind of a man would make arrangements for a wedding cake? That has been in the ladies' department of the wedding as long as I have lived and that has been a long time. He was not … um, you know what I would say, but …?"

"Oh! No, he is very much a man," responded Patti. "It was his present to his sister. I guess she was the only family he had left, or so he thought until he ran into his old producers. Then he inherited a mother and a father."

"It sounds like a story I would love to hear, Patti. If this *he* had producers and you were in LA, then no doubt he must have been in the industry—a musician or perhaps a movie star—but for now, I have to go. Please, look me up at the auction. We want all or our contributors to tell a little about their business. There will be a lot of influential people here. You should have all the work you need right here in Santa Rosa. No need to run off to Palm Springs or wherever. There is plenty of business right here for a girl with your beauty and talent. Remember, be sure and look me up. I want to hear the rest of your most fascinating story."

"Okay, Sandra. It was a pleasure to make your acquaintance."

"The pleasure has been all mine, dear. The pleasure has been all mine." She patted the younger woman on the shoulder and then left.

Patti returned to the van, heading for Nancy's. She stopped there and picked up some red food coloring. She knew just the cake to make. It was one of her favorites, though she had at least a dozen of them. This one was called the Astoria. It was a red cake, hopefully better though than the one that sold for so much at the auction last year. Some fifty years earlier, when money was not so inflated, the original recipe had sold for $2,000 at a cake auction. That would have been like $20,000 or perhaps even $50,000 by today's standards. The recipe had been passed down from her grandmother to her aunt and was perhaps the biggest reason for Patti's choice of career. Most red cakes or velvet cakes were on the dry side, but this one was moist and delicious. When the Astoria's creamy white frosting was applied, it literally slid down one's throat like cool ice cream on a warm summer day.

The trip home was uneventful, but upon returning, Patti had a special surprise for the mice. She went out to the garage and set a few mouse traps after adjusting her bricks to help prevent them from entering the garage in the first place. This way, the ones inside, if there were any, would not be able to get out except through a trap door. Patti laughed again at her own pun. Then she returned to the kitchen to work on the Astoria. It was a three-layer cake. She remembered one birthday where her mom had made each layer a different color—red, white, and blue, for Old Glory's sake. Now, however, she made a double recipe. Patti had a special container in which she placed her cakes to cool. She looked at her watch and called to confirm her dentist appointment. It was a bit disappointing when the receptionist answered and not Cal. She asked how long it would take to fill the cavity, and the receptionist said to plan for no longer than an hour. She remembered her last trip to this dentist. Would her jaw be numb for the auction? She didn't want to be embarrassed when she was called upon to speak and not be able to say anything intelligible. So, she asked if there were any other openings and found out that a cancellation had just occurred, leaving an opening for the next morning.

"I'd like that time slot, if it is not too much bother," she requested.

"Okay" came the reply. She was just about to say good-bye and hang up the phone when the receptionist asked if she could wait a moment because the dentist wanted to speak with her personally. His voice was very warm and friendly when he spoke into the receiver.

"So how is the worldwide traveler? You must have decided to come home after all."

Patti smiled as she answered. "I'm back and ready to take what comes next."

"And just what do you expect that to be, Patti Cake?" Cal questioned with just a hint of mischief in his voice.

"So far, I am open to suggestions. Do you have anything planned for this evening, Mr. Ripland?"

"Not that I remember unless it was a date with this strawberry-blonde who has caught my attention." Cal was chuckling as he spoke. It was good to hear his voice.

"Doctor? Are you seeing a strawberry-blonde now?" she questioned. "Last time, you were chasing a semiredhead. Who is this strawberry-blonde who has captured your attention?" It was Patti's turn to be mischievous this round.

"She is a sweet little lady who makes the best strawberry cake in the world."

"Never heard of her!" Patti lied. "If you can forget her for the evening, Cal, I'd like you to come with me to an auction the historical society is hosting at one of the halls. My assistants and I have managed to put together fifty cakes, less one, and I hear the strawberry-colored ones bring the highest price."

"I wouldn't miss it for the world, Patti Cake. When should I come by for you?"

"About six thirty would be perfect."

"Okay, sweetie. I won't be a moment late."

With that, he hung up. Patti set to work on the frosting, and soon it was ready to spread. It was a soft and creamy frosting, so a decorator like herself could not use it to make any kind of decorations. There were some miniature red roses left over from the other cakes though. She took several out of the freezer and placed them in a beautiful bouquet on the top of the cake. After they were placed, she wished she had made up some strawberries. They would have looked equally as nice, she believed. If this cake was going to be the big seller tonight, though, she would hate to rob the dentist who would surely bid the highest for it.

Cal was prompt, right to the minute, and dressed to kill. He had spent no less than forty-five minutes making sure every hair was in place, every hint of a whisker vanquished, and every wrinkle in his expensive suit steamed smooth. When he showed up at the auction with Patti, Kit went nuts. She came running over to her friend and motioned for her to step away from Cal. Patti excused herself and followed her friend to a corner of the room. Kit was beside herself with excitement.

"Where did you pick up that tall, dark one over there? No wonder you don't feel bad about giving Jim the slip. If I had known you had him hiding around here, I would have moved into his house or apartment while you were gone chasing after movie stars. You wouldn't have had a chance."

"Let me see, Kit. Where did I run into him? To tell you the truth, it is a longer story than the one I told you about Jim, much longer. For starters though, he is my dentist."

"You have been holding out on me, Patti Cake. Friends aren't supposed to treat friends like that, especially *best* friends. They are supposed to share, you know, like the olden days. No secrets between. Now I am going to have to come over and get all of the facts. Where do you come up with these hunks, girl? You are like a magnet to attractive men. Every time I talk to you lately, you have a different one hanging on your arm or since you are so short, hanging on his!"

Just then, Clara and Trudy came up, followed closely by Nancy.

"Come over and sit with us, Patti and Kit. We have a couple of seats saved second row back."

Patti looked at her friends and then over at Cal. He was looking longingly in her direction. She nodded her head in his direction.

"I can't, ladies. My date is waiting." She took her leave, much to the amazement of the three, and when she reached him, slipped her hand around his arm. They moved over to the corner of the front row where their names had been placed.

"Who is he?" Trudy asked. "I thought you said that Jim, the movie actor guy, was a blond. What is she doing in the arms of that giant with the jet-black hair?"

"Beats me," Kit responded. "But I aim to find out. All I know is she said he was her dentist."

The auction started with flower arrangements and then went to decor items. There were some antiques next and some novelty items, and then they auctioned off some pies. After the pies came the cookies and other baked goodies. Then they brought in some electronic devices. There were gift certificates from various businesses in the city. Cal had managed to hand over a couple of certificates for cleaning teeth. Finally they got to the cakes. At the end of each section, the people auctioning their items got up and gave a little talk about their service or business. All in all, it was not too bad. There was enough food around so no one was hungry. Cal purchased a plate of cookies for five dollars, and Patti's sweet tooth craving was nearly filled when it came time to auction off the final tempting items. There were about sixty items. There were several custom piñatas of the Charlie Brown characters filled with all kinds of goodies, and then there were the cakes.

The historical society waited to auction the cakes last in hopes of keeping as many people there throughout the auction as possible. It appeared to work, and the cakes sold quickly. They were displayed on a long table. For some of the cakes, little pieces were cut from them. This did not happen to the Burbank, the Charlie Brown, Winnie-the-Pooh, or any of the very special cakes. For each sampled cake, a group was assigned. Then each group tried to make the buyers believe their cake was the best-tasting one of all. The group who tried their hardest to prove theirs was the best cake they had ever tasted was that of the sauerkraut cake, but still it sold for $300, which was the lowest price of all the cakes.

As Patti had predicted to herself, Cal bought the strawberry cake. He just had to have it, especially after the first one she had given him a while back. He paid a mint for it too. The former dentist who had sold his practice to Dr. Cal was also at the auction and bid it up to more than $1,000 before yielding the cake to the younger doctor. The cakes with the molded figures brought handsome prices. Charlie Brown and Friends brought in $1,500, and the final cake, the pièce de résistance was the Astoria with the dainty red roses. Some of the same people who sampled the other cakes came up again. They each took a piece and then called up some of the others. They called up still others, and soon a quarter of the cake was gone. The bid opened at $2,000 and kept climbing. Dollar by dollar, the bidders continued, each outbidding the other while the total amount grew and grew. Three thousand dollars came and went so quickly until it reached $3,500, at which point one little elderly lady held up $4,000, and the floor was quiet. The cake was hers. She went up front, paid her bid, was handed the cake, and cradled it like a mother would hold a baby. As she did so, a little bit of the creamy white frosting smudged on her sleeve. Someone brought her a Tupperware container, and they placed the cake inside. Patti went over to her and promised a whole, completely new Astoria since that one had a big hole in it.

The auction was over. The net worth totaled near $68,000, a much greater amount than anyone had dared to hope for. A good portion of the monies came from Exquisite Cakes, by Patti Cake. She was then asked to speak a bit about her business. Before the hall was emptied, she had fourteen new orders written in her notebook. Nine of them were for the Astoria. Finally, Patti was able to introduce her friends to her dentist and date. She was able to tell by looking at the girls they were mighty impressed.

"I had a truly wonderful time, Patti!" Cal exclaimed as he walked her to her door. "You are the most amazing woman I have ever met. Tomorrow I will try my best to make your visit to my office as painless as possible."

"You better, Doctor," she teased. "If you want me to patronize your facility in the future, you'll have to do a better job than the last time." She planted a warm kiss on his lips and let herself into the house. Before closing the door, she turned back to Cal. He was looking intently into her eyes. He appeared as though he wanted to say something but was afraid or uncertain. Patti grew a little concerned for him.

"What is it, dear?" This was the first time she had called him "dear," and it touched a warm spot in his heart.

"I was wondering what you are doing next Saturday."

"As far as I know, Cal, I have that day open. What do you have in mind?"

There was a long pause. Calvin thought long and hard before responding. He had come to love this little package. He knew what he was about to say could change the relationship forever, possibly even bringing it to an end. Finally he spoke.

"There's someone I'd like you to meet this Saturday, if you are not too busy, Patti. I'd like to take us all out to lunch. Would you mind if there was one more person to share the meal with us?"

Patti grew quite serious. She didn't usually mind surprises, but when it came to personal relationships, that might be a different story. Finally she replied, "That will be fine, Calvin. I could drive over to your house and save you a trip to mine. I could meet your friend there. Then we could go out for lunch, if you would like."

Cal looked relieved. He smiled a relaxed smile, as though a reserve he had been carrying for a long time had dropped away.

"I'll see you at my house around 11:00 a.m., Saturday, and I believe 9:30 tomorrow morning." He literally danced off toward his car.

Patti watched until his taillights disappeared around the corner.

"Who could this someone be?" Patti started talking out loud to herself again. "Perhaps it's his mother or maybe a grandmother," she speculated, speaking out loud again.

The tooth filling went off with perfection this time. There was no pain and no discomfort. Cal would not let the dental hygienist touch Patti. He did all the work himself, including cleaning her teeth. He was as tender as a mother caring for her newborn baby. And he was happy, happier than she had ever seen him before. It was a hopeful type of happy, like a small boy would have before opening up his

Christmas present. When no one was looking, Cal kissed his patient on the forehead and saw her eyes light up with tenderness even though her mouth was propped open. At the door, he whispered so no one in the office could hear, "See you Saturday, love."

Patti was walking high as she left his office. Then her mind turned to her friends, as they had insisted she tell them how she had met Cal and she had been putting all of the bittersweet details together in her mind. Before she finished with them, they would be rolling on the carpet with laughter. She knew she could pull it off. They would have a cake and storytelling party, of course. Part of their job was to help her polish off the tangerine cream cake that was slowly dwindling in size. Then with a cup of coffee in hand, she would let the story flow out with all of its amusing details.

It worked. Before the first story was out, they were in stitches, and as the drama unfolded with each exaggerated detail, they grew more hysterical. Finally, they came to the climax in the dentist's office, and that was too much for poor Clara. She was laughing so hard she needed to make an emergency trip to the bathroom. This added even more hilarity to the event, and by the time it was all over, all four ladies agreed they had never had such a laughing good time, ever. When Patti brought up the part about the mystery person she was meeting in the coming weekend, there was no need to ask their thoughts on who it might be. Everyone volunteered their ideas without a prompt.

"I think it will be his mother," Kit suggested.

"No," Trudy cut in. "More likely his grandmother."

"If it was his grandmother," Clara injected, "why

would he be so secretive about it? Why not just come out and say, 'I want you to come over Saturday and meet my grandmother'?"

Not to be outdone, Nancy decided it was probably a child from a former wife.

"It has to be that, Patti. No one can tell me that a guy that good-looking hasn't been with a woman before now. Besides he is at least seven years your senior. What would that make him? About thirty, I would say. Some men have gone through a couple of wives by that age. I think it's his son. He wants you to meet his son, who lives with his former wife. He probably has a big alimony bill to pay each month."

Everyone grew silent at this thought. Nancy's explanation seemed to be the most sound and logical.

"You'll just have to tell us as soon as you get back!" Kit interjected. "This one is full of more surprises than Jim or perhaps even Goldie Locks and the Three Bears."

They all laughed and made their way to the door. It had been a grand evening and most entertaining.

It was still two days until Saturday. The time seemed to pass so slowly. Fortunately, Patti had those orders from the auction to fill and buried herself in her work. Finally the anticipated hour arrived, and she found herself walking up to the door of Cal's suburban mansion. Granted, it was nothing like the one Jim had considered purchasing, nor was it shabby either. And that was a fact for sure. It was better than anyplace she had ever lived in. Her parents had done quite well for themselves, but even their home was not this lovely. She decided a few flowers scattered around the yard would transform it into a cozy place to live. She noted a tall privacy fence in the back and was pleased. She loved her hot tub. She hoped he had one back there somewhere. She would invite herself into it and him too if he cared to join her.

Chapter 18
ONE DARLING,
LITTLE PACKAGE

It was Reata who first spotted Patti. No sooner had she seen this dainty little lady exit her car than she called up her friend Ruby Sanford.

"Look out your window, Ruby. Tell me what you see."

Ruby ran to the window and pulled back the curtain.

"I see a tiny red-headed woman, or is she a blonde? You can't tell these days. She is going up to the door."

"Do you think she is the wife, Reata?" Ruby asked.

"I do indeed, dearie. She is a spitting image of the little girl. If I hadn't seen it with my own eyes, I just wouldn't have believed it. Did the little girl grow up real fast? No, I know better, and the only difference I can see is the color of the hair. The little girl has black hair like her daddy. Other than that, she is an exact miniature of her mother."

"Why do you think they divorced?" Ruby continued.

"Probably for the money. Women these days want money without commitment. She most likely nabbed him, robbed him, had the kid, dumped him, then dumped the little girl off at the grandparents, and ran. That is what they do these days. No decency to 'em. The whole lot of 'em is power hungry."

"You're probably right again, dearie. He probably had to bribe her to come and see her daughter."

Patti was ringing the doorbell. No one answered. She rang it again and then heard footsteps running. Finally Cal opened the door. She could tell he was frustrated. There was flour on his pants, and he had some on his nose. He apologized for his looks.

"Sorry for the mess, Patti. I wanted this to be so perfect."

"What are you doing, cooking dinner?" Patti questioned as she tried to peer into the kitchen. "I thought we were going out to eat."

"We are or were until a little accident happened. You came at the wrong time. If you had been a couple of minutes later, I think I could have cleaned it up."

"Cleaned up what? Who is this mysterious person you want me to meet?"

"Well, now that you're here, I suppose you will just have to see for yourself." Cal led Patti toward the kitchen. He blocked her view for a moment and spoke softly.

"Don't be surprised at what you see, Patti."

There sitting on a bar stool next to the counter with a rolling pin in her hand and a pile of flour on the counter was the cutest little girl Patti had ever seen. She had dark hair and very dark eyes that seemed to shine out from her face. When she saw Patti looking down at her, she smiled.

"I'm making a cake, Patti Cake. Daddy said you were

the cake maker from Paddycake, only a lady, not a man. See, I wanted to surprise you with my cake." She proudly held up a little handmade paddy she had created from a bit of flour and some liquid. Patti surmised this little doll of a girl probably found and used milk from the fridge. There was an egg still in its shell, rolling around on the counter. Another one lay broken, splattered all over the floor.

"A cake for Patti Cake," the little girl repeated. She placed the paddycake in a little decorative tin and then reached her hands, extra flour and all, up to Patti. Without giving it a thought, Patti lifted this darling little maiden up into her arms, giving her a big hug. Her daddy tried to prevent it, but he was too late. He stammered a little and then found his voice.

"Puh … pah … um … Patti! Please, meet my daughter, Carissa. When I told her you were coming over, she asked lots of questions about you. I told her you were the Paddycake lady from the nursery rhymes. I had her all dressed and ready to go. Then I went upstairs to shave and change my clothes. I was only gone but a few quick minutes. As I descended the stairway, I heard a thump in the kitchen, and wouldn't you know it? At that exact moment, the doorbell rang. So first, I ran to the kitchen to make sure Carissa was okay, and this is what was waiting for me. But since there was no harm done really, I then hurried to the front door. Now you may understand what made me appear so disheveled and rather flustered. I'm terribly sorry about your dress. I do hope it isn't ruined." While Daddy was explaining, his daughter, Carissa, was talking up a blue streak, and all the while running her gooey fingers through Patti's once squeaky-clean wavy hair.

"You have very pretty hair, Miss Cake. It is the same color as my dolly's. Would you like to see my dolly? Grandma gave her to me for my birthday." The little girl was squirming now. Patti gently let her down, and Carissa bounded up the stairs, leaving behind a trail of powered footsteps. Patti turned and looked at Cal with a quizzical face as she attempted to absorb the entire scene and information given so far.

"Why didn't you tell me you had a daughter?"

Cal hemmed and hawed around for a bit and then responded, "I tried before you went off to LA. When you returned home again, it just seemed as though there was one thing after another keeping us both rather busy. And, too, I really thought it best you two meet in person. It's kind of hard to describe her. Thank God for grandmas and grandpas. Ever since Linda passed away, I have felt so lost and not always sure what to do."

"It would have been just fine. In fact, I'd have preferred it if, from the beginning, you were simply open and honest about this, Cal."

"I know, Patti. And I agree. I realize it would've been best to come right out with it, but so much has happened. It feels almost impossible to return to those days when our little family was close and cozy. Then Linda was in an automobile accident. There was nothing anyone could do. In the months following, it was necessary to make the move here to Santa Rosa. I needed help with Carissa during the day while I worked in my new practice. I knew in order to get my practice up and running, I'd need a lot of help. I didn't want her shuffled back and forth every day from person to person, especially not with strangers.

Grandma and Grandpa were willing and wanting to have Carissa live in a safe and stable environment with family. No strangers yet. I had such a tough decision to make, yet knew it was best for my daughter for the moment. One thing led to another, and as you know, the circumstances under which we met didn't really open a great line of communication. Little by little, we have journeyed to where we are now. And I have been doing all the talking. So, tell me, what do you think?"

"I think your daughter is simply adorable. How can you possibly live without her?"

"It isn't easy, as with any woman." He chuckled. "Living with her is a tremendous endeavor that I take very seriously, and time is so necessary for raising a child. Then, to live without her on a daily basis is even more difficult. Still, I had to do what was best for her. After grieving a number of months, I kept hoping and praying Mrs. Right would come along and rescue us. A couple of others thought I was the man they had waited for until they met her; then one after another, each would make excuses and simply disappear. They didn't want to raise another woman's daughter. I didn't want to scare you away, too. It was hard for me to finally get up enough courage to introduce you two. But this was necessary. It needed to happen."

"Never mind about the mess in the kitchen, Cal. If there's one thing I'm very familiar with, it is a flour mess. You can hardly bake a cake without some of the white stuff getting out of the mixer and onto the counter, the floor, my nose. If I had all of the flour I have spilled over the last few years, it would keep me in cakes for several weeks, I think. As for raising another man and woman's daughter, I would have no problem with that. I believe it would be an invaluable experience and most probably a fun adventure!" Then Patti added, "And I realize the ups come with downs as well. All in all, being a mom is one of my dreams."

The little girl was coming down the stairs again, and she had made some changes. For one, her clothes were no longer soiled. Carissa had taken off her floured dress and replaced it with a T-shirt and a pair of jeans. She had one shoe on and one shoe off, leaving that little foot bare. Secondly, she brought along her most valued possessions. Held tightly under one arm was a nearly life-sized baby doll with a full head of hair. In her free hand, she carried a little suitcase. She placed her dolly on the sofa and set the suitcase next to her baby and then went over and took Patti's hand. She led her over to the doll.

"You're a mommy, aren't you?" The little miss looked up into Patti's eyes, searching for an answer to her question. There was a long pause of silence while eyes and hearts waited for a reply. After some thought, very slowly, Patti nodded yes.

"Carissa, I was a mommy a long time ago. I had a little girl just like you. In fact, I believe you and she would be about the same age now that I think about it."

Now it was Cal's turn to be silent, even though he very much wanted to point an accusing finger at Patti and tell her off. How dare she expect him to share his little secret? And she, no less, with a much deeper hidden past. He started to speak, but something stopped him. Across the room, Carissa was opening the little suitcase.

"If you were a mommy once, then you know how to dress a baby, don't you?" pleaded Carissa, her young, inquisitive eyes watching Patti's every move and listening as intently as a youngster is able.

"Oh, yes, Carissa. I have dressed more than one little baby over the years, honey."

The suitcase was fully laid open now, allowing Carissa full access to all her baby's belongings. She pulled out a cute, pink, handmade outfit. It was a crocheted one-piece and a newborn-sized sweater set with matching bonnet and booties. She gave everything to Patti.

"Will you dress my dolly, please? When we were in the kitchen making your cake, she got her clothes all messy with eggs and flour, so they need to be washed on laundry day. Grandma told me this outfit used to be mine and I could use it on my dolly since she is just the right size. Almost all my baby's clothes 'n' things are mine … er, uh, I mean they were mine when I was a little baby. Of course, you know that was a long, long time ago. Grandma and Grandpa told me when I was a newer-borned baby, I was teeny tiny. Daddy told me that too, and he even showed me a picture of a teeny-tiny baby. And, Patti, you know what? Daddy was holding the whole baby in just one of his hands. It sure was a little baby; that's for certain. I don't know for reals if it was me, 'cause I can't remember, but who else could it be?" And with that, Carissa paused for a much-needed breath.

While Patti was dressing her new little friend's baby doll, her hands trembled with every move. She could hardly think straight with the story she just heard. She tried to maintain a calmness and finished dressing the doll in the tiny pink outfit, but as she tenderly placed the soft booties on the dolly's feet, Patti felt overwhelmed and was strangely silent.

Cal noticed. He also saw her cheeks glisten as silver tears replaced her usual smile. She beckoned for little Carissa to come closer, and with a heart of love only a mother could have hugged the little girl very tenderly. Her tears were flowing much faster now. Patti reluctantly released Carissa after kissing the little miss on her forehead a half a dozen times or more. Then Patti picked up the baby doll and held it close to her heart before returning it to Carissa. Getting up slowly, she looked at Cal. He could see that a flood of emotions was on the verge of bursting forth, and he was at a loss as to what action he should take, if any. In the background, a radio was softly playing a country ballad. The words added even more intensity to the moment.

"I could build you a mansion, high on a hill and fill it with treasures untold ..." The music continued to the end, while the lyrics struck the heartstrings of the listeners, but only one heard a message in her soul

"If blue tears were silver, and memories were gold."

"I really have to go, Cal," Patti stated as calmly as she possibly could.

Inside, her heart was aching. As she headed for the door, she had every intention of leaving without any more words. She felt unsteady about what was about to transpire if this emotional encounter continued any longer. Cal beat her to the door, and it was opened and waiting for her before she got there. She stumbled out and then turned toward him.

"I had a wonderful visit with you and Carissa, Doctor. Thank you for introducing me to your daughter. She is so beautiful. Truly, I believe she is the most beautiful child I've ever seen. She is …" With that, Patti ran to the car and was in such a hurry she spun the tires as she backed out of the driveway.

Cal just stood there, looking on with amazement and wonder! Patti looked back in her mirror. The tall, dark-haired doctor was still standing in the door, and there, silhouetted between his legs, was the little dark-haired angel watching. Soon they were out of sight.

When Patti arrived home, she mechanically moved about, first parking the van in the garage and then shutting and locking the door behind her. Once inside, she bolted the front door. Then went the phones; she disconnected the cord to the landline and shut off her cell phone. Next, she flew into her bedroom and closed the blinds. Lastly, Patti jumped into her bed, diving under the covers and all the while rolling herself into a little ball. She sobbed for the next two hours straight and after that off and on all night. This was not a night for sleeping or resting peacefully. Occasionally, Patti would get up for a glass of water, but in the end, it seemed to only allow more tears to flow. She thought they would never ever end. All her deepest, darkest memories with their overwhelming feelings poured into her heart. She remembered every event and detail as though it was a movie playing over and over in her mind. All of this pain rose up from the place where she had so carefully buried it years ago. With each tear came a cleansing of her soul and heart. Patti was unaware of it though. They flowed on and on, one tear after another until there was nothing left. Patti drifted off into a deep and peaceful sleep. All the rest of the night and day, she slept right through until Sunday afternoon. When she finally woke up, her heart urged her to pray. Still confused about everything that had happened, Patti prayed to the Lord in an almost accusatory manner.

"God," she cried out, "You knew this all along, didn't You?"

Jesus drew near. This was a time when He would need to be very tender with her. A voice seemed to answer her question from somewhere in the back of her mind. *Yes, Patti. I knew this all along.*

"Why? Why did You knowingly let me go my own way with my own ideas, even going to Jim's place? Why?"

Did anything happen with Jim that I do not know about?

"No. You know everything, Jesus. But I almost gave in to him. I was just a few seconds from it. When he was pleading with me to marry him, I was going to say yes."

But you didn't, did you, Patti? Why do you think that is the way it turned out?

"I don't know, Jesus. Something stopped me. Was it necessary for me to go to LA? What purpose did it serve?"

Did you make some new friends in LA, Patti?

"I suppose it was nice to meet Ken and Betty."

You were a great help to Betty, Patti. The support you gave her following her husband's death and during the times surrounding the funeral was of a greater comfort to her than you can ever comprehend on this earthly plane. You made a choice to go. You have, at least in the past, made it a point to invite Me into your life every morning. Lately, however, I have been placed on hold. When you prayed that short prayer, "Help me, Jesus," I came immediately to your aid. You asked, and I responded. I love you, Patti. I have loved you since before you were born. I know that is difficult to grasp now, but just know that My love does not wax old or wane and will never, ever change. I love you more than you can imagine. There is nothing you have ever done nor anything you can do in the future that will cause Me to love you any less. On the cross, I took your sins on Myself. I bore each one. You were justified that day when I cried out, "It is finished." I won salvation for you then and there. When Our Father looks at you, Patti, He does not see your life with its human frailties, mistakes, and failures. He sees My perfect life imparted to you and in you. You asked Me for wisdom in selecting a husband. Do you remember that?

"Yes, Jesus. I remember." Patti was sobbing again like a little child.

Do you think I would abandon you after you asked Me for wisdom?

"No, I don't suppose You would. You would probably be looking for every opportunity to steer me on the right course."

So, Patti, do you think I would let you do anything foolish, like say yes to a man that does not even recognize Me as King of kings and Lord of lords?

"You probably would if I was determined to do what I wanted to do without asking You about it."

Yes, I will never make a choice for you, but I will give you every reason I can to aid you in making the right choice, especially since you asked Me to guide you.

"I love You, Jesus. And I am so sorry for letting go

of You most recently. Friends do not ignore one another, and I give You my heartfelt apology. Will You forgive me? Also, thank You for being there whenever I've needed You. Even when I have not been very communicative with You and then cry out when I need You most, You are there … Thank You, Lord. Thank You too, for allowing me to meet Mom and Dad, and if I was a help to Betty in any way, thank You for that too."

You are certainly welcome, Patti. I love helping you. When you hurt, I hurt. When you are happy, I am right there being happy with you. And I want you to be happy all the time. I want you to have a loving husband who will treat you with respect and care for you as he would care for himself. Cal loves you. And Carissa is a sweet, wonderful gift. She needs you so much.

At the mention of Carissa, Patti cried all the harder. When would the tears end? "When, Lord?" she pleaded silently. She was unaware that her silent prayer had been heard. The tears subsided, her breathing became more regular, and once again, she slept in a peaceful rest.

Monday was a holiday. Cal's office was closed. But that was tomorrow, for now, it was still Sunday night. Patti undressed, took a shower, and then put on a light-green outfit. She checked herself in the mirror. There were deep, dark circles under her eyes from all her crying. She patted them with a wet wash cloth and then put on a little foundation and powder. The rest of her makeup went on smoothly and quickly. Patti didn't wear much, but it covered those dark circles very nicely.

From her jewelry drawer, she drew out the diamond necklace Mom had given her. She had never planned to keep it, but when she discovered it among her things, she didn't give it much thought. Betty gave it to her, didn't she? Patti put it on and then slowly headed for the door.

It was Ruby who saw her first. Just the other day, they had watched this little woman enter only to come running out about an hour later. That really got the ladies to talking—not that they ever were want for a subject on which to dwell.

"He has got to be the worst doctor in town, Reata," Ruby commented. "He can't get along with the poor child's mother for even an hour."

"No," responded the other woman. "He wasn't doing the running; she was. I imagine that means she couldn't put up with him for even an hour. I told you the women these days are worthless. They are only in it for themselves. Yep, they are."

"Yes, I suppose you're right." Then as the two were discussing the goings-on around the neighborhood, there was the mom, back again. This time, she was dressed up, very pretty, like the most beautiful actress in a Broadway musical.

"Do you see that diamond she has around her neck?" asked Ruby. "I'll bet she is milking the old man dry every month. Look at her prancing up to the door. She is probably going to take his last dollar. The poor little lassie. Do you think we had better call someone?"

"No," responded the other. "Let 'em fight it out. Survival

of the fittest, I always say. And she looks pretty fit to me, even if she is a half-pint."

Patti rang the doorbell a second time. Cal was still up. He opened the door softly and about fell backward when he saw the lovely picture that presented herself before him. Was he dreaming? He had tried to call her at least twenty times that day. He and Carissa even drove by her house, circling her neighborhood, but when he saw no evidence of life around the place, he and the little one returned home. At this hour of the night, Carissa was tucked safely in bed and sound asleep. He was about two minutes from retiring himself when this vision of loveliness graced his doorway and glided into the house.

She was a woman on a mission. She took his large hand in her small ones and headed for the large blue sofa in the living room.

"We need to talk, Cal." Patti was near tears. She knew they would burst any minute. At the couch she sat down and tugged at his arm, motioning for him to do the same. Once seated, Patti waited. Cal instinctively placed his arm around her and she snuggled close. Her strawberry blond curls felt soft on his neck. He found himself stroking her hair, it smelled sweet, like spring lilacs. At that very moment he knew she was his soulmate, that one-in-a-million girl that most men only hope to find. Only she could fill his empty heart. Then the flood of tears came. What do men do when women cry? It touched Calvin deeply. He felt so bad for her, he also wanted to cry. *But I must be strong,* he thought to himself.

"It's ok baby. You can cry on my shoulder anytime you want. I lov—" but Patti would not let him finish his statement. Instead, a small, soft hand reached up and with an equally small finger pressed against his mouth, preventing him from saying anything more for the moment.

"Please don't say anything until I tell you my story." She was silent for a few minutes and then continued, "At the age of seventeen, I fell hopelessly in love with the most handsome guy in school. He had perfection written on his very being. He was so handsome in every way that every single girl in our school wanted to be his girlfriend. He kept himself in super great shape. His hair was as blond as the summer wheat blowing in the wind. His sky-blue eyes were made from the heavens above, and I swear, no matter how dark or cloudy the day was, when Tad smiled, the sun always came out to greet him. When he asked me to the prom, I was on cloud nine. I mean, no girl was happier. Mother and I spent hours shopping for just the right dress, shoes, and all the accessories. When the night arrived and I was finally dressed and ready for my date, Mom and Dad told me they were so proud of me. Continuing on, they expressed how their beautiful daughter was very quickly changing from a little girl into a vibrant young woman. Even I was surprised at the transformation when I caught my reflection in the full-length mirror. Of course, I realized that was just the outside of me, but at the same time, I knew and could even feel many changes taking place inside. Finally, I was growing up. My date arrived on schedule that evening, and we went to the prom. We had five glorious hours during which we were the center of attention, just like Hollywood movie stars. We were elected and crowned prom king and queen. Immediately following the crowning ceremony, we danced to the song dedicated especially for the prom royalty. As we glided over the dance floor, I don't think my feet touched down once. Tad held me close in his strong arms throughout our time there together, and I began to feel whole ... you know, complete. The hands on the clock were getting closer to my curfew. Being the daughter of a clockmaker, I was always and ever aware of the time. Nearing midnight, I remembered clearly what my dad had made Tad promise: to have me home no later than one in the morning. And Dad clarified exactly what he meant.

"'Not even one minute later, Tad, or I will call the police! Mark my words!' Dad warned. After the prom, we got into Tad's car and begin to go, but where we were headed, I had no idea. Instead of taking me home, Tad drove away from our neighborhood and into the countryside. He must have set the whole thing up beforehand. He was able to grab can after can of beer while he drove. And the trash? Tad tossed the empty cans right out the window. I told him to quit. I tried demanding he turn the car around and take me home immediately, but he had his own transformation that night, and it was not human. No, not at all. I don't know what triggered this change, but drinking added fuel to the fire. He was this untamed, wild beast of a thing. Whoever it was driving the car was not at all like the guy I had fallen in love with at school. He kept driving and driving until he turned off the road into the driveway of an abandoned house. We were well hidden with overgrown bushes and trees all around. Any person yelling or screaming here would never be heard. The second he turned off the ignition, this wild beast came at me faster than a striking snake. I had no time to react or protect myself. He ripped my beautiful dress and forced me. When I cried for him to stop, he struck me. I cried again when his member penetrated me. He struck me again. Finally I gave in and let him have his way. He forced some of the rotten liquid down my throat. Said if anyone came, I had to be drunk too, for his own protection. Finally the beer took effect. There was a gray fog in my mind, protecting me from all of the ugliness. I believe the last straw came when I threw up all over him. He freaked out like a little boy. He looked at me with horror as if I was a monster out to kill him. He dragged me out of the car and threw me in the backseat. By then, I was thoroughly bruised, battered senseless, disoriented, and numb. Tad tore up the driveway, getting out of there. Wonder of wonders, he didn't kill me but drove me straight to my house. With one hand, he opened my door, and with his foot, he reached over the seat and kicked me out. Clearly he was not thinking straight. He must not have realized what he had done, or he would have killed me. Perhaps God had a hand in it. I am sure He did.

"Dad had been worried sick when one o'clock came and went with no sign of his daughter. Then two o'clock came. Still I was not home. Mom told me he was pacing the floor and cussing under his breath. When the lights showed in the driveway, he came running out of the house.

His face turned dark with rage and hatred though when he saw me crumpled and nearly naked on the grass. Dad was angry all right. I actually thought he was ready to kill Tad. By this time, however, his car was half a mile away, rounding a corner down the road.

"Dad had a twelve-gauge, double-barrel shotgun in the barn. He hid it there so no one would know about it, especially Mother. I knew about it though, and when I saw him go to the barn, I knew he was going for the gun. Marching straight to his pickup, he yelled over his shoulder that he was going to kill the … well, let's just pretend he said 'boy,' okay? I don't really know if Dad heard me wail a long, drawn-out noooooo! It didn't matter whether he heard me or not, his mind was set. He would blow that kid to bits. If he was even at home in bed, Dad was going to break down the door, grab him by his hair, and beat him senseless like he had beaten me. Then he would drag him out into the yard and pump several rounds into him as fast as he could reload. Dad left in the pickup, but he never made it to Tad's house. Filled with rage, he wasn't thinking straight until the red and blue lights behind him brought him back to reality.

"Dad quickly told the police how his daughter had been returned to his house from the prom. He detailed my condition down even to the shredded dress and almost unrecognizable face. He told who I had left with and that it was the same guy who had brought her back. For Dad's own protection, the police placed him in a cell and then immediately proceeded to Tad's place. They arrested him that same night for assault and battery, aggravated rape, and a DUI. He was placed in a cell right next to

Dad's. I can't even imagine what exchange in words or other things went between them through the bars. Tad fought the charges and let it go to trial; however, he wasn't counting on me testifying against him. I didn't want to, but I had to for closure to this nightmare. When it came time for the trial, I did testify, and it was the hardest thing I've ever done. But with my testimony, Tad left for a long stay in a not-so-cozy little room. He didn't see the light of day for several months. After that, my popularity at school dropped like a lead weight. All of my friends abandoned me like I had the plague or something.

"People throughout the community threatened us, shunned us, and when I say us, I mean my family. Our lives were turned upside down. We received threats in the mail, by phone, and in person. They told us that we were no longer welcomed in the community and suggested we move to the other side of the globe. There was another matter to consider, however. A most natural consequence followed that night's activity, and even though everyone wanted us to leave town because I blemished Tad's reputation, all three of us, Dad, Mom, and I, decided together that moving was not an option. You see, Cal, when I discovered I was pregnant, I really wanted to stay home. I wanted to continue living in my own house. Dad had his business there. By the time we came to that decision, I was six months pregnant, and I *did* stay home until the baby was born. I certainly didn't need any more stress like moving to a new place. I also had a tremendous decision to make about the new life inside me. With the help of Mother and Dad, together, we decided it was best for the baby to be put up for adoption just as soon as *he* was delivered. All the medical staff were telling me the baby was a boy, considering how he hung so low in my belly. I knew I could not handle raising Tad's son. And the other option was unthinkable. I would never be able to forgive myself if the alternative was urged upon me. I didn't believe the baby was a boy. In fact, I was so sure I was having a girl that I took up crocheting during the last two months of pregnancy and made her five little outfits. The day the adoption agency came to get her, I dressed her in the little pink one. It truly ripped out my heart to see her go. I needed to distance myself from that horrific nightmare."

Patti grew quiet for what seemed like a long time. She took this opportunity to cuddle close to Cal. His strong arms remained around her without wavering, so she found the courage to continue. "I wanted my first time with the father of our child to be something we both cherished forever. We would bring a new life into this world through a relationship based deeply in love. With all of my heart, I wanted my baby's conception to be a warm, loving, passionate memory. Tad took that away from me, but tonight you restored my heart and gave me so much more. You gave something far more precious to me than you can ever understand. I could not even imagine it in my wildest dreams. It is a blessing beyond measure, a miracle. Does any of this make sense to you, Cal? Patti was crying again, overcome with all the emotions from that troubled past coming to the surface. After a while, she found her voice and continued, "You see, Cal, when Carissa brought out those little clothes and asked me to dress her baby doll, it was at that exact moment I knew.

I knew she was my long-lost little girl. That little pink outfit I made when I learned to crochet was the very one I dressed Carissa in the last time I saw her. You and your wife adopted her, didn't you?"

Now it was Cal's turn to cry. He wept like a baby. The sobs came with deep groans and anguish from his tormented soul. He didn't even try to control them. Finally when the ache in his heart was freed, he spoke. "Yes, Patti, dear. My sweet love, yes. We did adopt her, and I'm so glad you turned out to be her mommy. I love you, Patti. I've loved you from the first moment I saw you hanging from the shelf in Safeway. You were like my little girl but all grown up. It nearly killed me when you said you were going off to bake a cake for that, that movie actor. I would have given anything to stop that plane because with it I felt my heart fly away. I'm so glad you came back though. So very, very glad. Would you consider helping me to raise your daughter? Please? Patti, please? Promise me you'll never, ever leave us. Never, Patti. Not now or anytime in the future. Now that I have found you, I never want you to go away."

Neither of them spoke for a little while. Then Cal opened his mouth to continue pleading his case, but Patti spoke first.

"I won't leave you, honey, if you don't want me to. It will make me the happiest mom in the world to be with you and Carissa. If you can stand to have me—accident-prone Patti Cake—around, if you don't mind us girls making a mess of things in the kitchen every now and then, I'd like nothing better than to raise my daughter with you as her daddy. I am ready to be her mommy now."

The two snuggled for a long while, enjoying the warmth and intimacy of one another. Entwined, Patti felt his powerful strength surrounding her, loving her, protecting her, making her completely whole again. If there were a heaven on earth, this was it. They remained in that restful pose for only a short time. Then, as though the two were of one mind, they arose together. There was only one thought now pulsing through their minds. They tiptoed quietly over to Carissa's room where she lay sleeping. One of her small arms was tucked underneath her curly black hair. The other was wrapped gently around her baby doll. The doll was still dressed in the little pink outfit Patti had made those long, lonely years ago. Patti and Cal bent down together at the same time and kissed the sweet little angel on her forehead. Carissa was reborn to them that night, more loved and more precious than ever before.

Patti whispered in the little ear of her newly found daughter, "I love you, Carissa. I've always loved you. There was a big hole in my heart after you left. Now it is full again. I am so happy. You may never know how happy I am. Everything will be okay from now on, sweetie. I promise. Your mommy has come home."

It was at that very moment both Patti and Cal realized the matchless miracle that had happened to bring them together. Back of it all, from His position high in the heavens, God had been looking out for them through all those long, lonely days and troubled nights. His will for their lives was being carried out. They knelt down together by the little bed and placing their hands under the curly head of their precious daughter, poured out heartfelt thanks to their Creator and Redeemer. He had come through for them. In the back of their minds, where that guiding voice speaks to all who will listen, came these wonderful words of assurance.

I know the plans I have for you, Patti. I know the plans I have for you, Calvin. I know the plans I have for you, Carissa. Those plans are not to harm or hurt you but to bring you peace and joy together in My love and give you a future filled with hope. Enter into My joy, enter into My rest. And low, I am with you always, even unto the end of the world.

RECIPES BY PATTI CAKE

Sauerkraut Cake

2/3 cup butter

2 1/4 cups flour

1 1/2 cups sugar

1 teaspoon baking powder

3 eggs

1 teaspoon baking soda

1 teaspoon vanilla

1/4 teaspoon salt

1/2 cup cocoa

1 cup water

1 cup or 1 small can of sauerkraut, rinsed, drained, and chopped

First cream the butter and sugar together until smooth. Beat in the eggs and vanilla. Sift in the dry ingredients alternately with the water to the mixture. Stir in the washed and well-drained sauerkraut. Turn the batter into a cake pan that has been sprayed with Pam or something similar. Bake at 350 degrees for 35 minutes or until cake separates from the edges of the pan and is done in the center. You can test when it is done by poking a toothpick in the middle. If it comes out clear without batter on it, it is most likely done.

The Astoria Red Cake

Mix together and set aside:
1 teaspoon vinegar with 1 teaspoon soda
1/2 cup shortening
1 1/2 cups sugar
2 eggs
1 cup buttermilk
1 teaspoon vanilla
2 ounces red food coloring
2 cups flour
1 teaspoon salt
2 tablespoons cocoa

Cream together the shortening and sugar. Add the eggs, vanilla, and food coloring. Alternate adding the buttermilk with the dry ingredients. These can be sifted together if you have a flour sifter. Beat the mixture for about 4 minutes. Fold in the vinegar and soda mixture. Do not beat. Bake in two, 8-inch layer pans, in an oven preheated to 350 degrees, for 30 minutes. You can bake in one large pan if you prefer. In a larger pan, you need to test the top of the cake to see that it is done. It usually takes longer to bake.

The Astoria's Creamy White Frosting

Cream together the following:

1/2 cup shortening

1/2 cup sugar

1 teaspoon vanilla

A pinch of salt

Cook until thick

2 level tablespoons flour

1/2 cup milk

Cool and add to creamed mixture. Mix on high speed until thick and the entire mixture is smooth and creamy. Spread over the cake, separating the layers if on a layer cake.

Heavenly White Bread

1 cup of warm water
1/2 cup of condensed milk
1 1/2 tablespoons dough enhancer
1/2 cup corn oil
1/2 cup sugar
1 teaspoon salt
2 teaspoons egg replacer
1 tablespoon yeast
3 tablespoons warm water with 1 teaspoon sugar
4 cups flour
1 cup oat flour
3 tablespoons gluten flour

Let the dry yeast rise in the warm sugar water for 10 minutes. Don't let the yeast come into contact with the salt or the oil until it is mixed in the flour. It tends to inhibit it from rising. Knead the dough, and add the yeast mixture later if necessary. After kneading it and adding the yeast, let it rise until doubled in size. Divide the dough in half, shape it into loaves, and let it rise in the pans until an inch above the rim; then bake in a preheated oven at 350 degrees. Bake the loaves about 30 minutes or until golden brown. The loaves should makes a hollow sound when thumped on the crust.

Tangerine Cream Cake

1 (8-ounce) package cream cheese
2 1/4 cups unsifted flour
1/2 cup shortening
3 teaspoons baking powder
1 1/4 cup sugar
1 teaspoon salt
3 eggs
1 cup milk
2 tablespoons grated tangerine peel
1 teaspoon tangerine extract*
6 drops yellow food coloring
2 drops of red food coloring
1/4 cup tangerine juice
1/3 cup sugar

Preheat oven to 350 degrees. Blend cream cheese and shortening until fluffy. Beat in 1 1/4 cups sugar; add eggs, one at a time, beating well after each. Add tangerine peel, flour, baking powder, salt, milk, and tangerine extract. Add food coloring; you may use more or less to give the pastel-orange color. Blend at low speed until smooth. Do not overblend. Fold batter into greased 10-inch pan; bake 45-50 minutes or until the edges of the cake separate from the pan. Combine tangerine juice and sugar. Pour over hot cake, allowing to run down the edges between the cake and pan. Cool 30 minutes. Remove from pan, finish cooling, and sprinkle with powdered sugar.

*If you can't find the tangerine extract, stop by a store that carries Altoids Tangerine Sours (candies). Take 8 candies, crush, and then dissolve in enough boiling water to form a thin syrup, 3-4 tablespoons.

Cat Litter Cake

Materials you will need.

1 small, brand new cat litter box.

1 brand new cat litter scoop.

1 box of German Chocolate cake mix.

1 box of white cake mix.

1 package of vanilla sandwich cookies.

1 bag of Tootsie Rolls.

1 package of vanilla pudding.

Some green food coloring.

Instructions.

Make the cake mixes according to the instructions on the back of the boxes. I bake a full sized white cake and divide the chocolate cake into 2 smaller pans since only half of the chocolate cake will be used. Bake them. Crumble the sandwich cookies in small batches inside a blender, scraping every so often. Set aside all but about 1/4 cup. To the 1/4 cup add a few drops of green food coloring and mix with a fork. After the cakes cool, crumble the large white one and half of the chocolate one into a large bowl. Mix with the half of the remaining white cookie crumbs and 3/4 of the chilled pudding. Save the remainder. Combine gently. Wash out the new, clean kitty litter box and line with a liner, if desired. Put the mixture into the litter box.

Unwrap 6 Tootsie Rolls. Microwave them until soft and pliable, (about 20 seconds). Bend them a little, giving them some unusual shape. Blunt the ends. Bury them in the mixture. Sprinkle half of the remaining cookie crumbs over the mix. Scatter the green cookie crumbs lightly over the top.

(This is to make this cake look like the green chlorophyll in that type of cat litter). Microwave 6 more Tootsie Rolls until nearly melted. Scrape one or two if desired on top of the cake and partially bury the rest. Sprinkle with all but 1/8 cup of the cookie crumbs. Place the litter box on newspaper and sprinkle the rest of the cookie crumbs around. Take some of the remaining pudding and pour a couple of dabs here and there on top of the mixture. Use your imagination to make it look realistic. Yield 24 servings.

CPSIA information can be obtained
at www.ICGtesting.com
Printed in the USA
LVOW11s0850050317
526179LV00001B/30/P